STUART GIBBS

spy camp

*Hodder
Children's
Books*

A division of Hachette Children's Books

A Catalogue record for this book is available from the British Library

ISBN 978 1 444 91025 4

Typeset in Adobe Garamond by Avon DataSet Ltd, Bidford-on-Avon, Warwickshire

Printed and bound in Great Britain by
CPI Group (UK) Ltd, Croydon, CR0 4YY

The paper and board used in this paperback by Hodder Children's Books
are natural recyclable products made from wood grown in sustainable
forests. The manufacturing processes conform to the environmental
regulations of the country of origin.

Hodder Children's Books
a division of Hachette Children's Books
338 Euston Road, London NW1 3BH
An Hachette UK company
www.hachette.co.uk

To Jeff Peachin, John Janke, Tracy Soforenko,
Jon Mattingly, Miriam Zibbell, David Simon,
Kent Davis and Kenly Ames, who made life
at 210 S. 42nd such a wonderful adventure

Contact

CIA Academy of Espionage

Washington DC

Armistead Dormitory

June 9

1500 hours

On the very last day of Spy School, my plans for a normal, uneventful summer were completely derailed by the delivery of two letters.

The first letter was waiting in my room when I returned from my final exam in Self-Preservation. I had already packed my belongings, hoping to make a quick exit from campus. The note was perched on top of the pile of suitcases.

Benjamin,
Come and see me at once.
The Principal

Up to that point, I'd been having a good day.

To start with, I felt positive about my exams. I'd been working hard at the academy and had improved in all my classes in the months since I'd arrived. I had sailed through my History of Espionage final, aced Codes and Cryptography and squeaked through Basic Firearms and Weaponry. (I hadn't scored any bull's-eyes, but unlike some of my fellow first years, I'd at least hit the targets and not accidentally wounded myself.) I'd been most concerned about Intro to Self-Preservation, which had always been my weakest class. That afternoon, however, I'd managed to last over an hour on the training grounds against a dozen 'enemy agents' armed with paintball guns, while most of my class had been smeared with royal blue before five minutes was up. I figured that had to be good for at least an A minus.

I was relieved to be done with school for the summer. Although I'd miss my friends from the Academy of Espionage, I was eager to head home, see my parents and have a decent home-cooked meal for the first time in five months. Plus, my thirteenth birthday was only a week away. I'd made plans to spend it with some old friends, without anyone trying to kill or maim me.

The note, however, suggested there was trouble ahead.

I picked it up gingerly, as though it were explosive. Frankly, I would have preferred finding a bomb in my room. I knew how to handle a bomb. The principal, on the other hand, was far more unpredictable.

I dropped the note in my paper shredder, then burned the remains. It seemed like overkill, but this was standard procedure for all written correspondence at the Academy of Espionage, even Post-It notes. Then I set off for the principal's office.

Outside, the sun was shining brightly, heralding a glorious summer. Fellow students finished with exams were happily playing Frisbee on the quadrangle and mowing down targets with semiautomatic weapons on the firing range. I entered the Nathan Hale Administration Building, climbed the stairs to the fifth floor, had my retina scanned by the sensors, entered the secure area and presented myself to the two guards flanking the principal's office door.

One frisked me for weapons. 'State your name, rank and business.'

'Benjamin Ripley, first year student. The principal asked to see me.'

The second guard picked up a secure phone and announced my presence. A few seconds later, the door clicked open.

When I entered, the principal was seated behind his desk, making a show of perusing some top secret documents. He might have looked dignified if his toupee hadn't been slightly askew. Or if I hadn't been aware that the principal was incompetent. It might seem surprising that the principal of the CIA's academy for future intelligence agents wasn't intelligent himself – but then, both the CIA and the academy are run by the government. 'Sit down, Ripley,' the principal told me.

I sat on the ancient couch across from his desk. It smelled like body odour and chloroform.

'My sources tell me you're planning to go home for the summer,' the principal said.

'Sources?' I asked. 'What sources?'

'Oh, the usual. I'm sure you're aware that we keep close tabs on our student body here. Listening devices, phone taps, that sort of thing.'

I hadn't been aware of this at all. 'You're tapping my phone?' I asked.

'It's standard procedure. We must keep our guard up at all times. As you know, we've had some trouble with double agents here at the academy.'

'Uh, yes. *I* was the one who caught the double agent,' I said. 'You don't actually think I'd work for the enemy after that?'

'They did offer you a job.'

'Which I turned down. Right before helping to defuse a bomb before it wiped out the head of every spy organization in the country.'

'Well, that's your side of things,' the principal said, unimpressed. 'Besides, in this business, one can never be too cautious.' He leafed through a thick report on his desk. It appeared to contain several transcripts of my private phone calls. 'According to this, you intend to spend the summer at the home of your parents and hang out at some place called FunLand with a Mike Brezinski?'

'That's correct,' I replied. 'Y'know, you could have just *asked* me what I was doing . . .'

'How did you plan on getting away with this?'

'Uh . . . Getting away with what?'

'Avoiding summer school.'

I suddenly felt queasy, which happened all too often at Spy School. 'The academy has a summer school?'

'Of course. Evil doesn't take holidays. Why should we?'

'No one ever told me there was summer school,' I said.

'Don't be ridiculous. Every new recruit is informed about mandatory summer education during the first assembly of the school year.'

'I wasn't at the first assembly of the school year,' I reminded the principal. 'You only recruited me in January.'

The principal stared at me blankly for a moment. It was his standard look when he realized that someone had screwed up royally – and it was probably him. I'd seen this expression quite a lot in my five months at Spy School. The principal ultimately recovered with his usual response to his screw-ups: blaming the person who'd been screwed. 'Well, you should have figured it out anyhow,' he told me. 'You're studying to be a spy, for Pete's sake. It's not like the school's existence is a secret.'

'The school's existence *is* a secret,' I countered.

'I've had enough of your lip!' the principal snapped. 'Would you like to begin summer school on probation?'

I shook my head, then realized something. 'All the other students have been packing up their things.

6

Aren't they attending summer school too?'

'Absolutely. Everyone at the academy is required to attend summer courses. They're just not taught *here*.'

'Then where are they taught?'

'At our wilderness education facility. It's located in the Shenandoah Mountains about two hours west of the city.'

'Wilderness education?' I repeated.

'Yes,' the principal said. 'During the summer months, we shift from classroom subjects to focus more on physical training and outdoor survival skills. After all, 99% of the world is outdoors. A good spy needs to know how to get along there.'

'So . . . it's kind of like Spy Camp.'

'It's not camp!' the principal snapped. 'It's an elite wilderness survival training facility. It merely happens to *look* like a camp. And as far as your family, friends or anyone else knows, you will be attending a camp. The Happy Trails Sleepaway Camp for Boys & Girls.' The principal rooted around in his desk drawer until he found a document, which he slid across the desk to me.

It was a single page with the address of the point in Washington where I would meet the official academy vehicle for transportation to the camp and a list of survival supplies to bring. At the bottom was the familiar directive to memorize the contents and then destroy it.

'When does it start?' I asked.

'In three days,' the principal replied. 'Go home and have a nice weekend with your family. But don't tell anyone about the true nature of this camp . . .'

'Or you'll have to kill me,' I finished. I knew the routine.

'Exactly. We'll see you on Monday at 1200 hours sharp.' The principal returned to his top secret documents, as though I had suddenly ceased to exist. Our meeting was over.

I let myself out of his office and headed back to my room.

My immediate reaction to the news that I had mandatory summer school was annoyance and frustration. I'd been working hard for the past five months and I missed my family and friends; I felt I deserved a few weeks off from my studies. But as I crossed campus, my mood began to change. While my first few weeks at Spy School had been difficult – I'd nearly been assassinated, kidnapped and blown-up – things had got much better after people stopped trying to kill me. I had come to enjoy school and made a lot of friends. In fact, for the first time in my life, I was regarded as sort of cool; preventing the destruction of your school and capturing the agent responsible does great things for your social life. Meanwhile, back home, my spy student identity was still a secret. Everyone thought I was attending some lame science school. I'd probably be even less popular than I had been before I'd left. So the idea of spending more time with my fellow spies-to-be wasn't too bad. And the fact that I'd be doing it outdoors, rather than cooped up inside dingy old classrooms, made it sound even better.

By the time I got back to my room, I was thinking a summer at Spy Camp might be kind of fun.

And then I found the second letter.

It was exactly where the first one had been, perched on top of my suitcases. Even though I'd locked the door to my room before going to see the principal.

Hey Ben!
Just wanted you to know we'll be coming for you soon.
Your pals at SPYDER

I sat on my bed, feeling as though the wind had been knocked out of me.

SPYDER was the evil organization that had planted

9

a mole in the school, sent an assassin to my room and tried to take out every leader in the intelligence community with a bomb. I hadn't heard a thing from them since helping defeat their nefarious plans.

Maybe this summer wasn't going to be so much fun after all.

Collaboration

Eisenhower Artillery Range
June 9
1600 hours

Although receiving a letter from the evil organization that once tried to kill you is generally a downer, in one strange way, I was also excited to get it.

It gave me an excuse to talk to Erica Hale.

Erica was easily the most competent and savvy spy-to-be at the academy, in addition to being the most beautiful girl I'd ever met. She came from a long line of spies, going all the way back to Nathan Hale himself, and she'd learned her trade from her ancestors. (However, her father Alexander Hale was proof that talent sometimes skips a generation.) Erica had been instrumental in helping me thwart SPYDER before, but while this had allowed us to be friends for a while afterwards – or at least, as close to friends as one could be with Erica – she had gone back to being her usual, distant self. I hadn't received so much as a glance in my direction from her all spring.

I hadn't been able to come up with a way to approach her. Erica wasn't exactly the type of person whose room you casually dropped by. For starters, her door was booby-trapped. But correspondence from the enemy was always an excellent conversation starter.

I found her out on the artillery range. That wasn't great sleuthing on my part; Erica spent more time working on self-preservation than she did sleeping. She was practising taking out terrorists with hostages from 300 metres away. With a crossbow.

The other students were giving her a wide berth. Somehow, Erica's standard cold vibe seemed frostier than usual, as though something was bothering her. Even Greg Hauser, the toughest kid at school, was keeping his distance. As I approached Erica, my fellow students looked at me like I was walking into a den of terrorists.

Erica barely glanced at me. She just slammed

another bolt into her crossbow and fired it. It nailed her target right between the eyes, splitting the previous bolt in two, Robin Hood style. 'How was your meeting with the principal?' she asked.

'How'd you find out about that?' I asked the question before I could think better of it. I already knew what her answer would be.

'I'm studying to be a spy,' she said. 'It's my job to find things out.'

'It would have been nice to have heard about Spy Camp before today.'

Erica shrugged. '*You're* studying to be a spy. It's your job to find things out too.' She loaded another bolt and took aim.

I held up the note from SPYDER for her. I'd placed it in a clear evidence bag to protect it. 'I found this in my room just now.'

Erica read the note through the plastic. She tried not to act surprised, but when she fired again, she missed her target's heart by a millimetre.

I couldn't help but smile. Catching Erica off-guard was like seeing a lunar eclipse: it didn't happen often and you had to savour the rare occasions when it did.

Erica quickly collapsed her crossbow and slipped it into its sheath. 'Let's go and talk somewhere quieter.'

She walked away without even waiting for me to respond.

I followed her off the range and into the nearby Chemical and Biological Warfare Building. As classes had finished for the summer, the building was empty. It still wasn't secure enough for Erica, however. She entered a code on a vending machine, which then swung free from the wall, revealing a hidden staircase. We followed it down to the secret underground levels beneath the school. Erica approached a door marked Restricted: Do Not Enter Without Authorization, then jimmied the lock and entered without authorization.

I reluctantly followed her inside. The restricted room was quiet as a morgue, which was fitting, because it *was* a morgue. Or at least, it looked like the ones I'd seen on TV. The walls were lined with giant refrigerated drawers. 'Are there bodies in those?' I asked.

'Probably.' Erica found sterile tweezers in a drawer and carefully lifted the note from SPYDER out of the evidence bag. 'Some of the fifth years take a forensic analysis class here, but it's most likely been shut down for the summer – and since morgues give most people the creeps, I figure it's safe to talk here.'

The morgue gave *me* the creeps, but I did my best

to hide it in front of Erica. 'Think this note's really from SPYDER?' I asked.

Erica laid the note on an autopsy table and examined it closely. 'Who else do you think it'd be from?'

'Someone playing a prank on me,' I suggested hopefully.

'What kind of person would think it was funny to send a fake note from an enemy organization?'

'Chip Schacter. Or one of his goons.' I didn't think Chip would have done it to be mean. Although he and I had started off on the wrong foot, we'd actually become friendlier after I'd revealed that Chip wasn't an enemy mole at Spy School. We weren't friends, exactly; I felt more like the mouse who'd pulled a thorn out of a lion's paw. Chip no longer bullied me, but sometimes it was worse to be on his good side than his bad side. Chip routinely insulted, teased and mocked his friends. And he had a penchant for lame practical jokes. 'Last week he froze my chemistry textbook in liquid nitrogen,' I told Erica. 'I didn't realize he'd done it until I dropped it in the mess hall and it shattered.'

Erica shook her head. 'It's not from a student. You and I are the only students who know SPYDER exists. In fact, most *real* agents don't know SPYDER exists.'

'There have been security leaks before.'

'True, but this information has been highly classified. You remember how hard Internal Affairs came down on us?'

I nodded. After Erica and I had defeated SPYDER's plot, there had been a massive internal investigation at the CIA. The top brass at the national spy agencies had been extremely annoyed to find out that they had all nearly been killed – and they wanted to figure out who to blame for the security failure. Erica and I had been grilled for hours on end. Our interrogators had been stunned to find out we'd had contact with SPYDER and then swore us to secrecy under penalty of expulsion from the academy. We were never to mention SPYDER, even to each other. Which probably meant we were violating a dozen security directives at the moment. But then, I don't think any of the interrogators had expected SPYDER to drop me a note.

'Well Internal Affairs came down that hard on everyone involved,' Erica went on. 'Knowledge of SPYDER is security level AA1.'

'Still, someone could have found out about it.'

'Anyone smart enough to do that would know not to be cavalier with that information. Only a moron would play a practical joke with highly classified data -- and this institution does not accept morons. It has a few delinquents, scoundrels and reprobates, but no morons.'

I nodded. 'So then, this note's really from SPYDER.'

'I didn't say that.'

'Then who else could it be from?'

'Another enemy organization who wants you to *think* it's from SPYDER.'

I looked at the note warily. It seemed so innocent, lying on the autopsy table. Just a piece of paper with seventeen words typed on it. And yet the idea that an enemy organization could have slipped it into my room triggered a deluge of unsettling questions. 'How do you think they even got it to me?' I asked. 'There's a ton of security on campus.'

'SPYDER has got past our security before,' Erica replied. 'As you may recall, they sent an assassin to your room once.'

'Yes, but the academy has stepped up security significantly since then.'

'That doesn't mean it's impermeable.'

'The assassin also infiltrated campus in the middle of the night. This happened during broad daylight. The whole campus was awake.'

'That's not necessarily a deterrent,' Erica cautioned. 'Infiltrating somewhere crowded is easier than somewhere that isn't. What looks more suspicious: someone wandering around campus on a warm summer afternoon – or someone creeping around campus in the middle of the night?'

'Good point.' I was annoyed I hadn't thought of that, but then, I wasn't due to take my first Enemy Infiltration class until next semester. 'Still, it wouldn't have been easy to get this to my room. There's guardhouses, armed patrols, security at the dorm entrance – and I had my door locked.'

'You're right,' Erica said. 'So we have to consider that the enemy used the easiest way to get past most of that.'

'Which is what?'

Erica gave me a hard stare. Apparently, the answer should have been obvious to me. It took me a few seconds to realize what it was.

'Oh no,' I said. 'They have someone on the inside?'

'It makes sense,' Erica said. 'If they could recruit one mole, why not two? And then, if you do catch one – as we did – you're so proud of yourself that you drop your guard, allowing number two to quietly wreak havoc.'

'But if that's the case, why would number two reveal himself—'

'Or *herself*,' Erica interrupted.

'—like this?' I finished. 'Leaving me a note isn't exactly being quiet.'

'True.' Erica pursed her lips. 'It's a strange thing to do, all right. But SPYDER's not run by idiots. They must have a very good reason for revealing themselves now. We just have to figure out what it is.'

'Unless, like you said, it's some other group wanting us to *think* it's SPYDER,' I suggested. 'Then they'd be using this to deflect our attention.'

'And yet, whoever they are would still need someone inside,' Erica said. 'That'd give them relatively easy access to the dorm, and frankly, it's not that hard to pick the lock on your room.'

'How do you know that?' I asked. 'Have you done it?'

'Like I'd ever want to break into your room. The standard dorm door lock here is a Pearson Alpha Deadbolt. It's a joke. I've been able to pick those since kindergarten.' With most people, I would have assumed this was an exaggeration, but not Erica. I could imagine her as a five-year-old making a high-tech raid on the family cookie jar.

'The mole would still have to pass the security cameras to get to my room,' I said.

'Yes, although as you know, those aren't tremendously difficult to elude. Still,

I'll jack the security system and check the camera feeds to see if anything suspicious shows up. Hmmm.' Erica seemed to notice something. She moved over a large magnifying lens and examined the note through it.

'Find a clue?' I asked.

'Maybe,' Erica replied. 'This note's practically sterile. It's not just that there aren't fingerprints; there's *nothing*. No dust, no dirt, no fibres. It looks as if it's been kept in a vacuum. Which kind of fits SPYDER's modus operandi. But there is *this*.' Erica used the tweezers to pluck something off the note. Or at least, she made the motion of plucking something off it. When she held the tweezers up to me, they appeared empty.

'I don't see anything,' I told her.

'Oh, come on.' Erica's voice was heavy with disappointment. 'It must be at least half a millimetre across.'

I peered through the magnifying lens. On the very tip of the tweezers was a dot so small, it looked like something a fly would have coughed up. 'What is that?'

'A clue to the identity of whoever wrote this.' Erica whipped out another evidence bag and dropped the tiny grain inside. 'It was embedded deeply in the paper, as though it was lying on a table and the paper got pressed down on top of it. That'd be far more likely to happen when the note was being prepared, rather than when you – or whoever delivered it – was just carrying it around. Looks like a piece of soil or a rock fragment. If I can figure out where it's from, that might be a lead.'

'Can you really determine that from something so small?' I asked.

'Well, not everyone can, but I'm not everyone. You made the right call, bringing this to me.' Erica gave me a quick, perfunctory pat on the shoulder and headed for the door.

'Wait!' I called, a bit more desperately than I'd intended. 'That's it? You're going?'

'Yes.' Erica held up the evidence bag with the grain of whatever-it-was. 'I have work to do.'

'But according to the note, SPYDER, or whoever sent it, is coming for me soon.'

'And you were hoping I'd protect you?'

'Well, yes.' It was embarrassing to admit – and yet, Erica had protected me from bad guys before. 'I'm not even sure what I should expect. Are they coming to kill me?'

'I'd doubt it,' Erica said.

'Capture me?'

'Far more likely.'

'Or maybe they're just coming to have a nice talk with me.'

'Don't get your hopes up.'

I frowned. I'd figured that last one was a long shot, but it was still disappointing to have Erica confirm it so definitively. 'So you really think it's a capture situation?'

'I can't guarantee it, but that's what seems the most logical. SPYDER offered you a job as a double agent before. They obviously see some potential in you and these aren't the kind of guys who generally take 'no' for an answer. My guess is, they're looking to up the stakes.'

'How?'

Erica shrugged. 'I'm sure we'll find out soon enough.' She abruptly turned for the door again.

I was thrown by this. Erica was treating me the way she treated . . . well, pretty much everyone. The way she'd treated me when we first met, before I'd proved myself to her. It wasn't as though I expected Erica to give me a hug goodbye, but I felt I deserved more than being abandoned in a morgue after learning I was in danger. Before I could stop myself, I asked, 'Erica, are you angry with me?'

Erica paused once more, then looked at me curiously, as if she didn't quite understand the question. Erica was probably the most brilliant person I'd ever met, but while she could comprehend a dozen languages, she seemed to find basic human emotions more difficult. 'You? No. I'm not angry with *you*.'

That begged another question, of course. Who *was* she angry with? But before I could ask, Erica cut me off.

'Don't worry about SPYDER, Ben. I'll keep an eye on you.' With that, she disappeared out of the door.

She'd left the note behind for me. I used the tweezers to place it back in its evidence bag. As I did, I noticed my hands were beginning to shake.

Despite Erica's reassurances, I *was* worried about SPYDER. The last time I'd faced them, they'd been one step ahead of me, Erica and the entire CIA until the very end. The organization was clever – and it was dangerous. There was always a method to their madness. So there must be a far more sinister purpose to their leaving the note than simply giving me a heads up they were going to drop by. Unfortunately, I had no idea what it could be.

I only hoped we could figure it out before it was too late.

Reassignment

Armistead Dormitory
June 9
1700 hours

Although I knew Erica wouldn't be happy about it, I decided to seek out some back-up. It wasn't that I didn't trust Erica; I trusted her more than anyone else. It's simply that when you get a potentially life-threatening message from an organization that has previously sent an assassin after you, it makes sense to inform someone other than a 14-year-old girl.

Like a 17-year-old girl.

Tina Cuevo was the resident advisor on my floor. She acted as the go-between for the students and the administration, because the administration generally wanted as little to do with the students as possible. And, unlike the much of the administration, Tina was approachable and competent. She'd been extremely helpful when I'd found the assassin in my room – and perhaps just as importantly, had been there for the entire hall when the toilets had backed up in the communal bathroom.

She was almost finished packing when I found her. It was a shock to see her room so bare. Tina's room had always been the most welcoming on the hall, full of homely touches like knitted blankets and throw pillows. She was the probably the only person on campus who put photographs in frames, rather than tacking them to the wall. But now, with everything stuffed into suitcases, the room looked as cold and boring as everyone else's.

Tina herself didn't look quite as warm as usual. Instead of her usual bright smile, I got one that looked forced. 'Hey Smokescreen,' she said. 'I was hoping I'd see you before I left. You're getting in just under the wire.'

I winced. With everything else that had happened that afternoon, I'd forgotten the last day of classes was also A-Day for the sixth year students: the day they got their field assignments. Everyone was assigned to an internship at a field office for the summer before reporting to the University of Espionage in the fall. It was something that every student eagerly awaited. From Tina's grumpy demeanour, I could tell the news wasn't good. 'Where are you going?' I asked.

She proffered her assignment papers to me. I took them, expecting to find she was shipping out to a war-torn third world country. Instead, I found . . .

'Vancouver? That's not so bad.'

'Oh come on,' Tina groused. 'It's in *Canada*.'

'I hear it's really beautiful,' I said helpfully. 'And it's supposed to have very good restaurants.'

'You know what it doesn't have?' Tina asked sullenly. 'Crime. It was ranked the second-safest city in the world last year. Its homicide rate is almost non-existent. What kind of field experience am I going to get there?'

'There's been an increase in smuggling exotic animals through the port there,' I suggested. 'Maybe you'll get to help investigate that.'

'I didn't join the CIA to bust panda-smugglers.' Tina flopped into her armchair. 'I joined to keep the world safe. Remember when the administration said they wouldn't hold any of that business with Murray against me?'

'Yes.' Tina had been heavily investigated after the whole SPYDER fiasco at school because Murray Hill, SPYDER's mole, had used her to get his information. Tina hadn't known, of course, but several members of administration had been unhappy she'd been duped.

'Well, they obviously held it against me.' Tina sighed. 'I wanted to go somewhere dangerous. Mogadishu. Bogota. Anywhere in Pakistan. And they're sending me to Vancouver. They think I'm a screw-up.'

'No,' I said. 'You're one of the best in your class.'

'Tell me about it. I have the highest GPA *and* I'm the only one qualified to fly a helicopter or do field surgery. But one lousy mole takes advantage of me and I'm a pariah. A mole who suckered the entire administration, I might add. But you don't see the principal taking the hit for this. Just me.'

'It could be worse,' I said, desperate to find something comforting to offer. 'They could be sending you to Geneva. Talk about a city that's safe. They haven't had a murder there in five years.'

'That's a lie,' Tina said, but she gave me a genuine smile this time. 'I appreciate the sentiment, though.' Her eyes flicked to the note in the evidence bag in my hand. 'Is that a goodbye note? You're so sweet . . .'

I winced again. 'Uh, actually . . . it was for me.' I held it up so Tina could read it through the plastic.

Her smile faded again. 'You have to be kidding me. I'm getting shipped off to the most boring place on the planet and you're getting sucked into more international intrigue? It's not fair!'

'I'm sorry,' I said. 'I didn't mean to drop this on you now . . .'

'You're only a first year!' Tina cried. 'And you're already getting death threats! Do you have any idea how lucky you are?'

'I was actually hoping it was more of a capture threat . . .' I began.

'I'm never going to get a death threat,' Tina muttered. 'Certainly not in Vancouver. You probably don't even know what the proper protocol for this is, do you?'

'Er, no. That's why I came to you.'

Tina sighed and took the note. 'OK, I'll get onto it. Might as well. It's not like I'll get to do anything this exciting in Canada. First thing to do is fill out a VG-68 Unsolicited Enemy Contact form. Then you'll have to get an evidence voucher and send this note to the central lab. Meanwhile, I'll inform the administration and see about establishing a covert security detail for you so we can catch their guys when they come for you again. Unfortunately, that's probably all I'll have time for. I'm shipping out tonight, so I'll pass the baton to your resident advisor for next year.'

'Who's that?' I asked.

'Here he is now. Speak of the devil.'

I followed Tina's gaze to the door of her room and jumped. The guy standing there looked like an upgraded version of Chip Schacter. He was taller, his jaw was squarer, his hair was blonder and even more muscles bulged under his tank top. He wore a big smile that was so bright it was almost blinding.

'This is Chip's older brother,' Tina said. 'Hank Schacter. Hank, this is Ben Ripley.'

Hank snapped his fingers and pointed at me. 'Smokescreen, right? I've read your file. And the transcripts from your interrogation. Good to finally put a face to the name.' He extended a hand that dwarfed mine.

I shook it. 'Chip never told me he had a brother.'

'That's because he doesn't like me. I've just spent a semester abroad, studying in London at the top secret school for British agents.'

Before I could express surprise that there was a top

secret school for MI6, Tina asked, 'How was it?'

'All right, I guess,' Hank replied. 'I picked up a few new forensic techniques, learned how to manage a car chase while driving on the other side of the road, drank a boatload of tea. It's good to be home, though. What's going on here?'

'Ben's just received a death threat,' Tina said.

Hank's jaw dropped. 'No kidding? Wow. I've only been on the job five seconds and I've already got a death threat to deal with?'

'It's really more of a capture threat,' I put in.

'Ben, give Hank the full update. I'm heading over to inform the administration.' Tina tousled my hair like a big sister might. 'In case I don't see you before I leave, be strong.' She hurried out of the door.

Hank shut and locked it behind her. When he turned back to me, his smile had vanished. Apparently, he'd only been acting nice in front of Tina, but now that she was gone, his true colours were showing. He looked at me in the same menacing way that Chip had when I'd first met him — only Hank was far more menacing than Chip. 'Let's get a couple things straight here, Smokescreen. Number one, I don't like you.'

'What?' I asked. 'Why not?'

'I understand you're friends with my brother.'

'Yes.'

'I hate my brother. Therefore, I hate my brother's friends. Therefore, I hate you.'

'Actually, Chip and I aren't *great* friends,' I said. 'In fact, he really didn't like me when we first met—'

'But there's another, more important reason I don't like you,' Hank told me. 'You're trouble. And when a student is trouble, his residential advisor ends up looking bad. Look what happened to poor Tina. She's getting a raw deal because of this SPYDER business.'

'That's not *my* fault,' I protested. 'Murray was already using Tina by the time I came along.'

'No matter how you slice it, you were involved. Which makes you trouble. I intend to run a tight ship here – and I don't want any trouble from my students. That would make me very angry, understand?' Hank put a hand on my shoulder and gave it a squeeze. He'd barely used any force, and yet it was incredibly painful. It felt as though his fingers had furrowed my scapula.

'I understand,' I managed to eke out.

'Glad to hear it,' Hank said. 'Now then, is this death threat thing going to be trouble for me?'

'I don't think so,' I said, hoping it was the truth. After all, Tina was alerting the administration and Erica had already begun her own investigation. If all went well, the whole issue should be taken care of well before the summer was over. Either SPYDER would be foiled – or I'd be dead.

'All right.' Hank steered me out of the door and into the hall, as though Tina's room was already his own. 'I'll see you on Monday.'

'Monday?' I asked. 'You'll be at Spy Camp too?'

'Of course,' Hank said. 'I'm not just your resident advisor. I'm also your camp counsellor.'

I winced. It looked like I'd be causing Hank Schacter some trouble.

Manifestation

FunLand Amusement Centre
Alexandria, Virginia
June 11
1400 hours

'Camp?' Mike Brezinski frowned at me through the fence of the batting cage. 'What on earth do you want to go there for? Camp stinks.'

'This one's supposed to be a lot of fun,' I lied.

The automatic pitching machine launched a ball at eighty miles an hour. Mike effortlessly swung his bat and cracked a home run. 'That's what they all say. And then you get there and find out they think "fun" means getting mauled by mosquitoes and pooping in an outhouse.'

We were at FunLand, a combination of batting cages, arcade games and miniature golf course, all designed with a completely inexplicable mediaeval theme. Normally, I wouldn't have ventured into such a public place knowing SPYDER was targeting me, but Tina had come through for me in a big way. The administration had assigned me a covert security detail. In fact, since SPYDER was involved, they'd gone a bit overboard. Only half of the bored parents waiting for their kids at FunLand were actually bored parents waiting for their kids; the rest were undercover CIA agents. Several of the kids were as well. The CIA had deployed every one of its shortest agents to protect me.

In my batting cage, I swung at a ball and whiffed. Apparently, all the hand-eye coordination exercises I'd been doing at Spy School didn't apply to baseball. 'It won't be that bad,' I said.

'Maybe not, but it won't be as much fun as staying here. I had an awesome summer planned for us.' Mike smacked another ball downtown. 'For starters, my brother thinks he can get us a job here.'

'How is work supposed to be more fun than camp?' I actually made contact with the next ball. Unfortunately it nearly took out a seven-year-old in a batting cage down the row.

'Because it's not really work,' Mike explained. 'We'd be the change guys in the arcade. Which means we'd basically get paid to hang around here and play video games all day.'

I doubted that plan would have worked for anybody – except Mike. Just about everything always worked out for Mike. He took easy classes so he could get As without ever opening a textbook. He was the star of any team he played on. And all the girls liked him. He was now dating Elizabeth Pasternak, the most beautiful girl at my old middle school.

Of course, I had done my share of cool things as well lately, but I couldn't tell Mike about a single one. If anyone would have been impressed by a death threat, it was Mike. But Spy School was top secret. Even my own parents thought I was attending St Smithen's Science Academy for Boys and Girls. Which meant that they, like Mike and everyone else, thought I was a nerd.

Shortly after I'd arrived at Spy School, however, Mike had come close to learning the truth about me. He'd sneaked onto the academy campus to spring me for a party, and been taken down by a horde of CIA agents who mistook him for a SPYDER operative. Afterwards, the CIA had tried to convince him that he'd merely stumbled upon a very overzealous neighbourhood watch, but he'd seen right through this and told me as much. I'd informed the Academy, and the CIA's Department of Misinformation had subsequently redoubled its efforts to mislead him. They'd actually pretended to recruit him to St Smithen's, plying him with glossy brochures and inviting him to the science fair, knowing full well that Mike would never attend a lame science school. (The science fair never happened, but the CIA was prepared to stage a full-blown fake one just in case Mike felt like dropping by.) Meanwhile, the Agency sent a team of 'lawyers' to Mike's house to 'admit' that Mike had stumbled upon a CIA 'exercise' – but they claimed they had nothing to do with St Smithen's and even pretended to fear a lawsuit from the school for conducting manoeuvres on its grounds without authorization. Mike, being Mike, asked what they'd be willing to give him to keep his mouth shut, and the CIA coughed up his future college tuition, membership for Mike's family at the Pasternak's country club – and a car, even though Mike wouldn't be allowed to drive for three more years. (Like I said, everything always worked out for Mike.) Ultimately, after expending a tremendous amount of time, energy and money, the Department of Misinformation declared that Mike was officially fooled, although every once in a while, I found myself wondering if Mike had seen through all this as well and simply kept his doubts to himself.

The pitching machines launched our final balls. I barely nicked mine. Mike almost knocked the hide off his, then stepped out of the cages with me. 'It's bad enough that you had to switch schools,' he groused. 'Now you'll be away all summer too?'

'I'm sorry,' I told him. 'I *thought* I was going to be here. My parents had already paid for camp by the time I found out.' Another lie: The CIA paid for the camp in full, but told everyone's parents that we'd won scholarships there.

'Your parents would let you stay here if you told them you wanted to,' Mike said. We turned in our batting gear and started up the walkway toward the fake medieval castle that housed the arcade. Two of the agents pretending to be bored parents waiting for their kids tailed us.

'I did tell my folks,' I told Mike. 'They said no.'

'Really? I thought they were all excited to throw your birthday party next week.'

'They said we could just do it at the end of the summer . . .'

'Oh, for Pete's sake, Ben, just be honest with me.'

I turned to Mike a little too quickly, wondering if he could possibly know the truth.

'Erica's going to be there, isn't she?' he asked.

'Yes,' I admitted, relieved.

'That's all you had to say,' Mike told me. '"My super-hot girlfriend's going to camp and I want to go with her." Totally understandable.'

Mike was under the mistaken impression that Erica and I were dating, as the one time he'd seen us together, we were sneaking back onto campus at one-thirty in the morning. The truth was that I'd just been abducted by SPYDER and Erica had saved me, but I couldn't tell Mike that – and he probably wouldn't have believed it anyhow. So for the time being, I let him believe what he wanted – not that it pained me to do this. It was the first time in my life Mike had ever been jealous of me.

'Hey, you don't start camp for another two days,' he said as we entered the arcade. 'Why don't we double date tomorrow? You and Erica and me and Elizabeth. We could all go to the movies or something.'

'I told my parents I'd spend tomorrow with them,' I said. 'I'll have the whole summer to see Erica.'

'So then, this is it?' Mike asked. 'I won't see you for the rest of the summer?'

'I'm not sure,' I said, and before Mike could argue, I added, 'so let's make the best of it. I bet I can kill more zombies than you.'

'No way,' Mike told me. 'Loser buys lunch.' He plugged a couple tokens into one of the dozen video games that allowed us to kill the undead and handed me a fake firearm.

The last time I'd played Mike in any shoot 'em up game, he'd destroyed me. Actually, any time I'd played Mike in *anything*, he'd destroyed me. (I could have smeared him in chess, of course, but guys like Mike didn't play chess.) However, today was different.

I'd spent a lot of time on attack simulators and the shooting range over the last few months. I'd been under the impression that I wasn't really that good – but I suddenly realized that was because I was comparing myself to other future spies. Next to Erica, for example, I was a basket case. But compared to your average kid, I had become impressive. Now I blew away zombies with impunity, splattering virtual green goo everywhere and sending severed body parts wheeling through the air. I barely missed. I was racking up points and extra men as fast as possible.

I was so pleased to be defeating Mike in something for once, I didn't notice a crowd had gathered around us. Apparently, word had got out that I was gunning for the high score and kids were coming from all over the arcade to watch. Mike practically stopped playing so he could watch me himself. 'Are you even studying at that science school?' he shouted over the sounds of zombie screams. 'Or are you just playing video games the whole time?'

Before I could answer, I noticed someone trying to get my attention. It was one of the undercover agents, a young woman posing as a soccer mom. She was shaking her head slightly, signalling me to ease off on the zombie-slaying. Apparently, in my rush to display my skills, I was threatening to blow my cover.

I almost backed down and let my avatar get eaten. But then it occurred to me that the CIA had robbed me of a summer off and put me in danger once again. The least they could do was let me be cool for an afternoon. So, instead of taking a dive, I snatched Mike's gun from him and started blasting away with both hands. I mowed down an entire army of the undead in seconds.

A roar went up from the crowd. Kids slapped me on the back and cheered as I racked up points.

I shot a cocky smirk to the CIA agent, who gave me an annoyed frown in response.

And then Murray Hill emerged from the crowd.

He was suddenly only a few inches away from me, flashing a big smile. 'Hey, Ben,' he said. 'How's it going?'

I didn't say anything in response. Murray's arrival was so startling and improbable – he was supposed to be imprisoned, after all – that for a few moments, I couldn't comprehend that it was really him. I just gawked at him in a way that made him laugh.

'Sorry,' Murray said. 'Don't blow your high score on my account. Fire away.' He gave me a friendly pat on the back, as though he'd forgotten that the last time we'd seen each other, he'd tried to shoot me.

The game no longer meant anything to me, however. And I wasn't about to turn my back on Murray Hill. I found myself wishing the guns in my hands were real. 'What are you doing here?' I snarled.

Murray took a step back, holding his hands up. 'I'm here on behalf of SPYDER. We said we'd be coming. We really need to talk to you.'

'About what?' I demanded.

Murray started to say something, but it was drowned out. The crowd around me had turned on Murray as well, annoyed at him for distracting me from a record-setting game. Lots of people were yelling at him to back off, or at me to focus, and the encroaching virtual zombie horde was roaring angrily as well.

Mike leaned in beside me, giving Murray a hard stare. 'This guy making trouble for you?' he asked.

On the video screen, the zombies pounced on my avatar. A huge groan went up from the crowd. Sensing trouble, the Soccer Mom CIA agent approached, her hand dipping into the handbag where her gun was concealed.

Murray glanced toward her, his smile fading. 'Maybe this isn't the best time to talk,' he told me. 'There's a little too much heat around here.' With that, he ducked back through the crowd and bolted for the exit on the far side of the arcade from Soccer Mom.

'I've got to go,' I told Mike, and then went after Murray. It was probably foolish to run *towards* the enemy, but as enemy agents went, Murray wasn't exactly imposing. Besides, if he'd wanted to hurt me, he could have done it while I was distracted by the video game. Unfortunately, a knot of teenagers got in my way, demanding to know why I'd just given up. By the time I broke free of them, Murray was already out of the door.

Soccer Mom fell in beside me as I raced past the Skee-Ball games. 'What's going on?' she asked.

'Murray Hill just approached me,' I said.

The sun was blinding as I emerged from the cave-like arcade – and the mini golf course was a labyrinth of places to hide: 96 holes of castles, dragons and fake waterfalls spewing water dyed neon blue. As I desperately scanned it for Murray, Soccer Mom emerged beside me.

'It *couldn't* be Murray Hill,' she said. 'He's incarcerated.'

I caught a glimpse of someone disappearing behind a cheesy representation of Stonehenge on the seventh hole. Murray wasn't exactly an athlete; he had the very distinct gait of someone with a constant stomach cramp. 'I'd check and make sure,' I told Soccer Mom, then took off again.

Soccer Mom stayed right on my tail. 'Stand down!' she ordered. 'If it really is Murray, we can handle him.'

I ignored her and kept going. I tore across the miniature golf course, dodging small children and poorly hit balls. I zigzagged through Stonehenge, knocking over a few fake druids, then cut around a large plastic object that was probably supposed to be a dragon, although it looked more like a dyspeptic stegosaurus.

Several holes away, Murray was closing in on the chain link fence at the back of FunLand. On the far side of it, a sedan with tinted windows idled, waiting for him. A large fake pond filled with neon blue water and Viking ships lay between us. I didn't have enough time to go around it . . .

But there was a chance I could go over it. To my left, a six-metre high plastic volcano rose above the rest of the park. It didn't really fit with the medieval theme; I think the builders of FunLand just thought it was cool. Every fifteen minutes, it would belch smoke and spit water dyed red; the water was supposed to look like molten lava, although it actually looked far more like blood. (For which reason every kid in town called the volcano Mount Haemorrhoid.) To power these anaemic displays, an electrical wire ran from the top of the volcano down to an old generator by the back fence.

I snatched a putter away from a nearby girl, who burst into tears.

'I'll give it back,' I told her, then scrambled up Mount Haemorrhoid. I swung the putter over the electrical wire, then grabbed onto both ends, creating a makeshift zip-line, and launched myself after Murray. I shot down the wires even faster than I'd expected, roaring right over the Vikings.

Murray was scrambling over the back fence, but he was taking his time, winded from his run. I bore down on him, closing the gap quickly.

And then the electrical wire snapped. It ripped free from the top of Mount Haemorrhoid and went slack, dropping me flat on my back in the middle of the sixteenth fairway. The live wire plopped into the fake lake and shot a bolt of electricity through it that instantly cooked all the resident koi fish. The old generator overloaded and blew out in an incredible display of sparks that started several other fires as well. The ridiculous structures that adorned the golf holes all turned out to be extremely flammable. Within seconds, the air was thick with smoke as mediaeval churches, castles and dragons flamed.

As this happened in the midst of peak family hours, it started a bit of a panic. Parents grabbed their children and stampeded for the exits. The CIA agents who were rushing to catch up with me were nearly trampled.

I sat up, groaning, and saw Murray clambering into the getaway car. Before he closed the door, however, he couldn't help but take a look back. He flashed me another smile and waved goodbye. 'We'll be in touch, Ben!' he called, and then the car peeled out, disappearing into a cloud of smoke.

Soccer Mom caught up with me. She'd wisely decided to go around the electrified lake, although she'd arrived too late to see the getaway car. She begrudgingly helped me to her feet, then waved to the flaming golf course. Nearby, King Arthur and the Knights of the Round Table were being roasted alive. 'This is why I told you to stand down,' Soccer Mom said testily.

'It was an emergency,' I said.

'It was a wild goose chase,' Soccer Mom snapped. 'I already called it in and got confirmation. Murray Hill is still under maximum security at the Apple Valley Reformation Camp for Delinquent Teens.'

'Then something's screwed up,' I said. 'I know Murray. It was him.'

'You took a pretty nasty fall just now,' Soccer Mom told me. 'Maybe you hit your head.'

There didn't seem to be any point in arguing any more. I had no explanation for how Murray could have been in juvenile hall *and* in FunLand simultaneously. 'I also got the number plate,' I said. 'Virginia VGG-228.'

Soccer Mom looked the tiniest bit impressed; after all, that was more than she'd got. 'You're sure?'

'I'm sure,' I replied. I have a gift for maths and I excel at remembering random sequences. I still know every phone number I've ever been given by heart.

Soccer Mom left my side to call the plate in.

Two seconds later, Mike emerged through the smoke from the blazing knights. He was looking at me curiously. 'What was all that about?' he asked. 'Who was that guy?'

I winced. In my haste to go after Murray, I'd forgotten about Mike. 'A kid from school,' I lied. 'He owes me money.'

'Must be an awful lot of money,' Mike said. 'You went after him like a crazy man.'

'He was also a jerk to Erica,' I added.

'Ah,' Mike said, although he still seemed suspicious. He stared at me a while longer, 'Well, buddy, looks like you made the right call.'

'How's that?' I asked.

Behind Mike, a flaming dragon toppled, crushing a small castle. 'No point in getting a job *here* this summer,' Mike said. 'This place is toast.'

Orientation

CIA Academy of Espionage, summer training
facility
Aka 'Happy Trails'
June 13
1100 hours

My first reaction upon seeing Spy Camp was that it didn't look nearly as bad as I'd expected.

This was because Spy School itself had set the bar awfully low. I'd expected the summer facility to be more of the same: unattractive, unappealing and outdated, but in the woods. Instead the camp turned out to be quite charming. My family had never been able to afford to send me to camp before, but Happy

Trails looked almost exactly as I'd imagined a normal camp would: rustic wooden buildings with screen windows and wide porches; a wide-open central lawn with a large communal fire pit; a crystal-blue lake with a dock and dozens of watercraft; and plenty of outdoor equipment like obstacle courses and climbing walls.

My parents weren't allowed to drop me off there. No one's were, as the camp's location was classified. (Our parents were told that the camp didn't like parents to bring their kids there as this created 'a constricting emotional bond that some campers may have difficulty overcoming.') Instead, my fellow students and I were taken by our parents to designated rendezvous sites in major cities, where we boarded the official covert academy vehicles – which turned out to be average, everyday school buses. I came on a bus with all the other kids from the DC area. The drive had been rough; I'd spent much of it feeling sad and homesick. Even though Spy School was close to where my parents lived, I hadn't been able to see them much during the school year and had been hoping to spend the summer with them.

Meanwhile, my mind was full of questions: How could Murray Hill have been at FunLand when he was also supposed to be incarcerated? What had he wanted to talk to me about that was so important? What was SPYDER up to this time – and how did I fit into their plans?

I also had to wonder about Erica. I hadn't heard a thing from her since our conversation in the morgue. Had she learned anything? If she was truly keeping an eye on me, as she'd promised, where had she been when Murray showed up at FunLand? Why hadn't I heard anything from her? Had something happened to her – or was she merely being her usual, cryptic self?

Despite all this, my spirits lifted on seeing the camp. The armed guards and the electrified fence around the perimeter made me feel safe – and the whole place had a different vibe to Spy School. Spy Camp actually looked like it'd be fun.

I hadn't paid much attention to our route, but I figured we were somewhere near the border of Virginia and West Virginia. We'd been on the road much less time than I'd expected – just a little over two hours. I had assumed the CIA's outdoor training facility would be as remote as possible – up in the northern reaches of Maine or Michigan, or deep in the Rockies. And yet, despite the short drive, we seemed surprisingly far from civilization. There was nothing but green forest and blue water for as far as I could see. I stepped off the bus and took a deep breath of fresh air.

'Smokescreen! You made it!'

Zoe Zibbell shoved through my fellow campers and threw her arms around me. Seeing her was a boost to my spirits as well. A fellow first year, Zoe had become my best friend at Spy School, mostly because she was under the delusion that I was an incredibly talented spy – albeit a spy who often feigned incompetence to make everyone else underestimate him. Any time I displayed my actual incompetence, Zoe inevitably assumed it was a ruse. Zoe was the one who had christened me Smokescreen – as well as doling out nicknames to virtually everyone else at the Academy. Zoe was big on nicknames. Like all the other campers, she was wearing cargo shorts and a green Happy Trails t-shirt.

'Hey,' I said. 'How long have you been here?'

'Over an hour already,' Zoe reported. 'Your bus was the last to get here. We'd better get you to your cabin before all the good bunks are taken.'

'Too late,' someone behind me said.

I knew, without even turning around, that it was Warren Reeves. Warren was another first year, a snide, weaselly kid who followed Zoe around as if he were a dog she had rescued. He was completely smitten with her – a fact that was obvious to everyone at Spy School except Zoe, who thought they were merely just good friends. Zoe had named Warren Chameleon because he was a master at camouflaging himself, although when she wasn't around, the rest of us called him Stalker. Warren was jealous of Zoe's adoration of me, so every time she tried to put me up on a pedestal, he rushed in to knock me off.

'We're in the same cabin?' I asked him, not bothering to hide my disappointment.

'That's right!' Zoe exclaimed obliviously. 'You're both Muskrats!'

'Muskrats?' I asked.

'Every cabin has its own name,' Zoe explained. 'I'm a Polliwog. I wish I could be a Muskrat, but there's no co-ed living at Happy Trails. In fact, the boys' and girls' cabins are on separate sides of camp.' She nodded toward the central lawn. Beyond the main buildings that surrounded it, cabins spread out into the woods on both sides.

Word had got out that our bus was late and everyone who'd ridden with me was grabbing their gear and hurrying to their respective cabins to claim the best bunks left. I hoisted my army surplus duffel bag out of the bus luggage compartment and slung it over my shoulder. 'Where's our cabin?' I asked Warren. 'Might as well check it out anyhow.'

Warren pointed in the general direction and was annoyed when Zoe decided to lead me there instead. 'Muskrat Manor, this way!' she chirped.

We headed off across the central lawn. Zoe acted as tour guide, pointing out everything of interest along the way. 'That's the mess hall,' she said, indicating a long, single-storey building with a wraparound porch. 'Though it also doubles as the martial arts training room on rainy days. Then you've got the infirmary and the armoury. The armoury's a little different to the one at Spy School. They have more of a "frontier" kind of focus here. There's still plenty of guns, of course, but they've also got bows and arrows and tomahawks.'

'So we can defend ourselves if we ever time travel back to the 1700s?' I asked.

Zoe laughed. 'I think they just want us to be prepared for anything.' She shifted her attention to three wooden buildings on the other side of the main lawn. 'That's the wilderness outfitter, where you get tents and rock-climbing gear and stuff, the staff offices and arts and crafts.'

'Arts and crafts?' I asked.

'With an espionage angle,' Zoe explained. 'Tomorrow, they're going to teach us how to whittle our own spears.' She pointed to a cabin not far beyond the main buildings. 'That's your place right there. They keep the first-years closer in because it's more dangerous out on the perimeter. Not that *you* need any protection, right?'

'Er, right,' I said. Evidently, the top secret news that I'd been targeted by SPYDER hadn't leaked yet. I wished I could share it with my friends, but the penalty for leaking information at Spy School was expulsion.

'It's actually a pretty good cabin,' Warren was saying. 'It's close to the mess, it's right on the lake and it's upwind from the latrines.'

A dirt path snaked between the staff offices and the wilderness outfitter, heading through the woods to all the cabins. A group of fifteen students about a year older than me was coming the other way along it. I'd never seen any of them before. 'Who are they?' I asked. 'New recruits?'

'No,' Zoe replied. 'Exchange students. They're from the MI6 academy in England. They don't have any facilities like this over there, so a troop of them comes over every summer.' Zoe waved them down as they approached. The leader was a fresh-faced, redheaded girl with exceptional posture and a regal bearing. It was easy to imagine her having high tea with the Queen. 'Claire Hutchins,' Zoe said by way of introduction. 'This is Ben Ripley, the guy I told you about.'

'Ah! Smokescreen!' Claire had a delightful upperclass accent. 'Your reputation precedes you. It's a pleasure.' She held out a pale, dainty hand.

'The pleasure's all mine,' I said, hoping that sounded formal enough. I reached for her hand.

Claire suddenly grabbed me by my wrist and spun. The next thing I knew, I'd flipped over her shoulder and was lying flat on my back on the ground.

'This is your big shot student?' Claire asked Zoe. Her posh accent was gone, replaced by a Cockney one so strong I could barely understand her. 'Drops his guard easily, doesn't he?' She turned to her fellow students with a smirk. 'Told you these Yanks were weak.' Her fellow students laughed in response.

'I wasn't being weak,' I groaned. 'I was trying to be friendly.'

'I was being friendly too,' Claire told me. 'If I'd wanted to be mean to you, I'd have ripped your bloody arm from its socket.' She laughed, then continued on her way across the lawn, the rest of the Brits in tow.

I sat up, rubbing my head. I'd dropped my duffel

bag when Claire attacked and it had burst open on the ground. Clothes and toiletries were now scattered in the dirt around me. I started to pick them up.

'Lousy, tea-sipping limeys,' Zoe grumbled, glaring after the Brits. 'Always trying to prove they're better than us.' She then turned to me, impressed. 'That was amazing, how you let Claire flip you over so easily. Totally tricked her into thinking you're a wuss. Man, the next time she tries anything on you, she'll be sorry.'

'Ben wasn't faking,' Warren muttered. 'She really did flip him over.'

'Don't be such a dork,' Zoe shot back. 'Smokescreen once took out an assassin with just a tennis racket. You think he'd let some crumpet-sucker get one over on him?'

Warren sighed heavily. 'It sure *looked* like she got one over on him.'

'That's the whole point,' Zoe said. 'If it looked fake, Claire would've known the truth: That Ben's a lean, mean, fighting machine. You might want to be a bit nicer to him. There's a good chance he might need to save your life some day.'

'I hope not,' Warren muttered, thinking it was too quiet for any of us to hear.

Just then, Chip Schacter stepped out of the outfitting

cabin with a jet-black rock-climbing rope coiled over his shoulder. 'You two lovebirds want to stop bickering?' he asked. 'I can barely hear myself think.'

Zoe and Warren shut up, embarrassed.

'We're not lovebirds,' Warren said sullenly.

'I didn't know you *could* think,' Zoe told Chip.

'You're lucky you're a girl,' Chip told her. 'If Warren had said that to me, you'd be digging him out of the latrine by now.'

Warren gulped. 'But I didn't say it,' he said quickly. 'I didn't even think it.'

'You just get here?' Chip asked me.

'A few minutes ago.' I crammed the last of my dusty belongings into my duffel. 'We're on our way to my cabin.'

'I'm going that way,' Chip said. 'Let me give you a hand.' He hoisted my 50-pound duffel bag off the ground like it was a feather and casually slung it over his shoulder.

Neither Zoe nor Warren was pleased Chip had crashed our party, but neither one of them had the nerve to tell him to get lost either. Instead, they fell in behind us as we carried on to the cabin.

'I saw you and the Brits,' Chip confided. 'Way to drop your guard.'

'I didn't know I was supposed to be *on* my guard,' I told him. 'Aren't we all supposed to be on the same side?'

'You can be such a Fleming sometimes,' Chip said with a sigh.

I rubbed my aching neck. A Fleming was Murray Hill's term, derived from Ian Fleming, the inventor of James Bond. It meant someone who showed up at Spy School expecting the world of espionage to be just like it was in the movies. Like me. I'd assumed that all British agents would be well-mannered and proper, forgetting that England was also the world's number one producer of soccer hooligans.

'Your brother's my camp counsellor,' I said, trying to change the subject.

'Ooh.' Chip winced. 'Sorry about that.'

'Why didn't you ever tell me about him?' I asked.

'Cause he's a dorkwad,' Chip replied. 'And he always has been. When we were kids, his favourite hobby was sending me to the emergency room. Let's figure out where his bunk is and put some fire ants in it.'

'Uh . . . I'd prefer not to start off by antagonizing him,' I said. We reached the cabin. Like all the others, it was raised two metres off the ground on wooden pilings. There was a set of wooden stairs to it which could be hoisted off the ground by a pulley system. 'What's this for?' I asked.

'To stop wildlife getting in at night,' Zoe explained, then added, 'And assassins.'

Given my previous experience with an assassin, who'd somehow managed to infiltrate my locked dorm room in the centre of a secure campus, I didn't think retractable stairs would be much of a deterrent – especially when there were several easily-climbable trees right next to the cabin. But I was willing to take any bit of protection I could get.

We climbed the steps up to the cabin. Another advantage of being a couple of metres up was that it caught the breeze off the lake. A nice wooden porch lined with deckchairs faced the water. Inside, the only furniture was two rows of four bunk beds and some footlockers. It looked like a rustic army barracks, and it was a bit cramped given that sixteen boys would be sharing it, but compared to the frigid, claustrophobic room I'd had at school, it was like a suite at the Ritz.

Warren was right, however. Fifteen of the bunks had already been claimed. The only one left was a bottom bunk in the middle of the room. 'Looks like you're sleeping under Nate Mackey,' Warren laughed. 'Stinks to be you.'

I frowned. Nate Mackey had recently developed a stress-induced bed-wetting problem. It probably would never have surfaced if he'd gone to a normal school, but at the academy, where a pop quiz in Self-Preservation meant a surprise ninja attack, there was an unusually high amount of stress. Nate's future as a field agent was doubtful, although the CIA always needed data analysts.

'Where's your bunk?' Chip asked Warren.

'Over there,' Warren said, proudly pointing to the top bunk with the best view of the lake.

'Switch with Ben,' Chip ordered.

'Why would I do that?' Warren asked.

'Because if you don't, I'll throw you in the lake.' Chip flexed a bicep the size of Warren's head. 'It's the least you could do for Ben, seeing as you almost shot him last year.'

Warren's smile faded. 'Bunk's all yours, Ben.'

I tossed my things on top of it. Being friendly with one of the toughest kids in school had its perks. Normally, I wouldn't have taken advantage of the situation like that, but knowing Warren, he'd probably engineered my getting the bunk under Nate Mackey in the first place.

As I started to unpack, I noticed another building

through the window, tucked back in the trees up the hill. It was significantly larger than any of the camper cabins. 'What's that?' I asked.

'Administration,' everyone said at once.

'You mean, for the principal?' I asked.

'The principal?' Chip laughed. 'He wouldn't be caught dead out here. The guy's terrified of nature. Last year a squirrel got into his office and he practically had a heart attack. Woodchuck runs the camp.'

'Who's Woodchuck?' I wanted to know.

The other three looked at me, surprised. 'You've never heard of "Woodchuck" Wallace?' Zoe asked.

'Uh, no,' I admitted. But before I could ask more about him, my mobile phone buzzed in my pocket. Generally, I might have ignored it, but it was vibrating in a way I didn't know it could, like it was desperately trying to get my attention. I pulled it out and, instead of a number on the caller ID, I got a flashing message: CODE RED. URGENT. ANSWER NOW. Again, it was news to me that my phone could even do this. 'Could you guys excuse me?' I asked, then stepped out onto the porch and answered the phone. 'Ben Ripley.'

'Ben, this is Agent Hamilton. We met at FunLand two days ago.'

I recognized the voice: Soccer Mom. 'Did you

track down Murray Hill yet?'

'No. We're having a little trouble with that number plate you gave us. Are you absolutely positive you gave us the right number?'

'Virginia DAG-228,' I said. 'I guarantee that was it. Why?'

There was a long pause before Agent Hamilton answered. It sounded as though she might be discussing the situation with someone else. Finally, she got back on the phone. 'I'm not at liberty to disclose that to you at this time.'

'Why not?'

'I'm not at liberty to disclose that either.'

'But I'm the one who got the number plate – while I was chasing a known member of SPYDER – which has threatened my safety. Exactly how much more involved do I need to be before someone can tell me what's going on?'

My protest seemed to get through to Agent Hamilton. 'Give me a few minutes,' she said.

Before she could get back to me, however, my phone was yanked from my hand.

I wheeled around to find a strange man looming over me. He was probably the healthiest-looking person I'd ever seen, tall and muscular without an ounce of fat on him. This was extremely evident to me, as he was wearing only a loincloth – and he'd apparently made that himself. It was some sort of animal skin – beaver, maybe – and there was a hunting knife with a six-inch blade tucked into it. The man had piercing green eyes and a closely-cropped beard. His skin was darkly tanned from the sun and he smelled like pine needles.

'You must be Agent Wallace,' I said.

'Call me Woodchuck,' he said. 'Everyone else does.' Then, with a mighty heave, he flung my mobile phone into the lake.

'Hey!' I cried. 'I needed that!'

'Nobody *needs* a mobile phone,' Woodchuck shot back. 'They're just shackles to civilization. All anyone really needs in this world is the bounty that nature provides. Jerky?' He held out a gnarled piece of dried meat. 'It's possum. I made it myself.'

'You don't understand . . .' I began.

'Oh, I do,' Woodchuck told me. 'Now, you might be a little annoyed to be disconnected over the next few days, but by the end of the week, you'll thank me for cutting that bond.'

'I was talking to CIA headquarters,' I said. 'I was getting an update on the enemy group that's been targeting me.'

Woodchuck blinked in surprise. 'Oh,' he said. 'You must be Ripley.'

I glanced back into the cabin to see if Zoe, Chip and Warren were eavesdropping. They weren't. Zoe was helping Warren move his things to his new bunk and Chip was short-sheeting his brother's bed. I looked back to Woodchuck. 'I assume you've been briefed on my situation?'

'Yes. And rest assured, you're just as safe here as you were back at school.'

'I wasn't really that safe at school,' I said. 'SPYDER could infiltrate the campus any time they wanted.'

'Oh? Well, I guess you'll be safer here then. This facility is extremely well-protected. Plus, you've got me looking out for you.' In less than a second, Woodchuck snapped the hunting knife from his loincloth and threw it. It embedded point-first in one of the wooden posts that supported the porch roof forty feet away.

'Not bad,' I said.

'Look closer,' Woodchuck told me.

I went to the end of the porch. As I got closer to the knife, I heard a faint angry buzzing. To my astonishment, the blade had pinned a mosquito to the post by its wings. 'Wow.'

'Of course, it only does so much good for *me* to look after you.' Woodchuck came up behind me and yanked the knife free. 'It'll be far more convenient for you to look out for yourself. That's what we're going to teach you here this summer. How to survive anything: drowning, landslide, bear attack . . .'

'How about bad guys coming after me with guns?'

'Once you've gone a week in the wilderness surviving on nothing but your wits and peat moss, bad guys with guns will be a piece of cake.'

'Is that peat moss thing part of the standard timetable out here?' I asked warily.

'Nope,' Woodchuck said. 'Most of these poor kids don't get the opportunity to learn a fraction of what I do about survival. But I've been given special orders to whip you into shape.'

'Lucky me,' I groaned. I certainly wanted to learn how to protect myself against SPYDER, but full-on survival training seemed a bit overzealous. Spending a week in the wilderness with Woodchuck didn't sound like much more fun than being captured by the bad guys.

Woodchuck patted me on the shoulder with a hand so calloused, it felt like a paw. 'Get yourself settled and get some rest. Your training starts first thing tomorrow.'

He tucked the knife back into his loincloth and then, rather than taking the stairs down from the porch, he simply leapt off the railing, grabbed a tree branch and swung down like a monkey.

'Wow,' Zoe said behind me. Her nose was pressed up against the screen door. 'Woodchuck Wallace is going to personally oversee your survival training! You're going to end up an even more impressive spy than you already are!'

Chip stood right behind her, looking a bit more suspicious. I wondered how much of my conversation they'd overheard. 'Why do *you* get such special treatment? Even the best seniors here are lucky to swing two days of survival training from Woodchuck.'

'It's not exactly a reward,' I said, trying to deflect the conversation. 'You guys are going to be sitting around the campfire toasting marshmallows and I'll be in a cave eating raw grasshoppers.'

'You don't get to toast many marshmallows as a spy,' Chip said. 'This *is* a reward. A lot of the professors at Spy School don't know squat, but Woodchuck's the real deal. So how about answering the question this time: Why's he going to focus on *you*?'

Before I could come up with a way to weasel out of answering, Warren suddenly stepped between them, looking even more distrustful of me. 'I've got a better question, Ripley. What's all this about?' He held up a thick bound document. It seemed to be fifty pages long, with a separate single page clipped to the top.

'Where'd you get that?' I asked.

'It was in my footlocker,' Warren said. 'The footlocker that was supposed to be *yours*. It was in this.' He held up a torn manila envelope on which FOR BEN RIPLEY: CLASSIFIED was written a dozen times.

'You opened my classified mail?' I asked.

'It seemed suspicious,' Warren said proudly. 'And my instincts were right. It's from Murray Hill.'

Zoe gasped in surprise.

'Let me see that!' Chip snatched the document from Warren. I tried to grab it from him, seeing as it was mine, but he turned away and I only managed to snag the top page off it.

Chip quickly flipped through the document, his face screwed up in confusion. 'What is this?' he asked. 'It's just a whole bunch of legal mumbo-jumbo.'

Zoe had scampered up onto one of the top bunks to read over Chip's shoulder. Now, her eyes went wide at what she saw. 'It's a contract,' she said. 'Murray's offering Ben a job.'

'No,' I said. There was no way to keep everything a

secret any more. 'Not Murray. The evil organization he works for.'

Then I held up the single page from the top of the contract so they could see it. It was a note from Murray.

```
Hey Ben!
Sorry we didn't get a chance to talk the
other day. I was hoping to give you a heads
up about this. I know all the legalese can
give you a headache just to look at, so
here's the gist:
SPYDER is working on a very big project
that requires the services of someone with
your special skills. We could really use
your help on this one, and we're prepared
to pay you well for it.
That said, while we want you to work with
us, we really don't want you working against
us. So here's the deal: Either you join us
- or we kill you. That's not an idle threat.
As you've no doubt figured out, we can get
into Spy Camp easily.
If you're in, sign the contract and leave
it in the hollow tree stump by the entry
gate and we'll extract you. If you're out,
well . . . it was nice knowing you.
You have 24 hours to decide.
```

Protection

Happy Trails
Mess Hall
June 13
1300 hours

I had no intentions of working for SPYDER, of course. Since the alternative was death, however, I did find myself somewhat reluctant to reject their offer.

Murray wasn't bluffing about the death thing. It was written into the contract, under the heading Termination Clause. Although SPYDER's lawyers even made this sound boring: 'If the party of the first part (Ripley) opts not to engage in business with the party of the second part (SPYDER), then SPYDER reserves the right to terminate the existence of Ripley in the manner in which they see fit.'

The rest of the contract was written in exactly the same mind-clouding way, filled with words like 'heretofore,' 'injunctive,' 'irrevocable' and 'obfuscatory'. After I'd violated a dozen security protocols and explained to Zoe, Chip and Warren exactly what SPYDER was, the four of us leafed through the contract, trying to make sense of the pages until our heads hurt. There was a great deal about compensation packages, confidentiality agreements, warranties and such – and a particularly unsettling list of penalties for breach of contract, such as: 'In the event that Ripley is determined to be merely pretending to provide services for SPYDER while, in actuality, continuing to act in the capacity of a federal agent, then SPYDER shall retaliate in a manner such as, but not limited to, the following: removal of Ripley's head by force from the rest of his body, extraction of Ripley's cerebellum via his nasal passages, excessive bludgeoning or defenestration.'

Despite all the verbiage, there was no mention of what SPYDER was working on or what they actually wanted me to do for them.

'We need to take this to Woodchuck,' Zoe said.

'Right now. You don't just need survival training. You need your own security force ASAP.'

'Good idea,' I said. In fact, my gut instinct was to go to Erica with the contract, but there was no way I could do that without the others knowing and Erica wanted to keep her involvement covert. Besides, I figured I could always find her later – although, once Erica got wind of the contract, there was a good chance she'd come find *me*.

We found Woodchuck in front of the administration building, weaving himself a sun hat out of sawgrass. He made no attempt to hide his surprise after I showed him the contract, and his eyes grew wider and wider as he leafed through it, until I thought they might fall out of his head. 'Whoa,' he said. 'This is serious.'

'I know,' I said. 'What should we do about it?'

'First of all, we beef up security around the camp,' Woodchuck replied. 'Especially around your cabin. I'll set up a few extras snares and such to keep out anyone from SPYDER. But beyond that, well . . . I have to admit, this is a bit out of my league.'

'Really?' I asked. 'But you're in charge here.'

'I teach survival skills,' Woodchuck replied. 'Not counter-terrorism. I'll do my best to ensure your safety, but I'll have to report this to my superiors to find out what to do next. In the meantime, you ought to be safe. SPYDER gave you 24 hours to think about this, so they probably won't try anything until then.' Woodchuck looked up at the sun to assess the time. 'Looks like it's just past one. Lunch is on in the mess hall. Go and eat. I ought to have a response from the CIA by the time you've finished.'

'All right,' I said.

Woodchuck started into the admin cabin, then thought of something and turned back to Zoe, Chip and Warren. 'I shouldn't have to tell you, but SPYDER's existence is highly-classified. No one else is to know. Ben shouldn't have even shared this information with the three of you.'

'I didn't,' I said. 'This was SPYDER's doing. They left the contract in the wrong footlocker.'

'Whatever the case, keep it quiet,' Woodchuck ordered. 'Not so much as a word to anyone.'

We all nodded agreement and headed for the mess hall. Despite Woodchuck's assurances that I'd be safe for the next 24 hours, I couldn't help feeling unsettled. Death threats have that effect on a person.

I wasn't the only one. My friends were twitchy as well. Any time there was so much as a rustle in the trees, they wheeled towards it, expecting an attack. It was a relief to get into the mess, where we were surrounded by familiar faces.

The mess was surprisingly similar to the one at Spy School. The students ate with the same groups of friends, the same hair-netted staff loaded up our plates, and the food appeared just as likely to send us to the hospital. The only difference was the décor: At Happy Trails the walls were covered with the mounted heads of animals. There was a black bear, a moose, two wolves, an entire herd of deer and a passel of assorted rodents. They had obviously been put up long ago – each animal had a thick coating of dust and every set of antlers was thickly-strung with spiderwebs – but their presence in a dining area was still disconcerting. They gazed down at everyone dolefully, as though upset that we were eating their descendants.

Erica was there, behaving exactly the same way she did during normal meals at spy school. She sat by herself, with her nose in a book, apparently unaware of anything going on around her. This was misleading, however. I'd never known anyone as in-tune with her surroundings as Erica. Even though she hadn't so much as glanced in my direction, I was sure she knew I was there. In fact, knowing Erica, she probably somehow knew more about the contract from SPYDER than I did.

There was no chance to approach her, though. Zoe and Warren didn't leave my side. And even Chip, who normally wouldn't have been caught dead eating with first year students, followed me to a table.

I knew what was going on. It was the first time any of them had been privy to an active investigation. It's hard to act normally when you're in circumstances that aren't normal at all. Despite our direct orders, it was only a matter of time before one of them cracked and began talking. I would have bet money on Warren, but Zoe turned out to be the first to go.

'I've been thinking,' she said. 'Ben said SPYDER put the contract in the wrong footlocker, but they didn't—'

'We're not supposed to be talking about SPYDER!' Warren hissed. 'We have direct orders!'

'Keep your hair on,' Chip said. 'We're not supposed to *tell* anyone about it. But everyone here already knows.'

'And this room is full of spies in training,' Warren said. 'Who knows who might be eavesdropping on us? I don't want to get booted out of school for violating a secrecy directive and revealing SPYDER's existence.'

'So we won't call it SPYDER,' Chip said. 'If we call it something else, we can't get in trouble for revealing it.'

'How about SPORK?' Zoe said, holding up her plastic utensil.

'Works for me,' Chip said.

Before Warren could protest, Zoe pressed on. 'Anyhow, SPORK didn't get the wrong locker. They got the right one; they just didn't predict that you guys would switch bunks. Which means that whoever delivered that contract for SPORK must have been keeping a close eye on Muskrat Cabin.'

Warren suddenly grew more skittish than usual. 'Maybe SPORK's man is *inside* Muskrat Cabin,' he whispered.

'Hey, you're in Muskrat Cabin,' Chip said. 'Maybe it's you.'

'What?' Warren gasped.

Chip leaned closer, pointing a finger at Warren. 'In fact, we never actually saw you take the contract out of the footlocker. Maybe you just *said* you'd found it.'

'I *did* find it!' Warren swivelled towards Zoe, desperate to prove his innocence to her. 'I swear! I'd never work for the enemy!'

Chip suddenly burst into laughter. 'Relax,

Chameleon. I'm just messing with you. As if SPORK would ever hire a whack-job like you.'

To Warren's annoyance, Zoe laughed as well.

'Ha-ha, very funny,' Warren steamed. 'An enemy organization has infiltrated our school, Smokescreen's life is being threatened and it's all just one big joke to you.'

'What's this about enemy organizations and Smokescreen?' Jawaharlal O'Shea slipped into the seat between Warren and me.

I winced. So much for keeping a lid on things. 'It's nothing. We were just imagining potential dangerous scenarios so we'd be prepared if they occurred.'

'My mistake,' Jawa said, although I was quite sure he didn't buy it. Jawa was one of the best future spies at school. He was partly Indian, Irish, Nicaraguan, Kenyan, Indonesian and Chinese, with perhaps a dozen other ethnicities thrown in. He was an exceptionally diligent student, working so hard in part to prove that he hadn't merely been accepted at Spy School to fill several minority quotas at once. Jawa was incredibly smart and a great athlete, the captain of both the school chess *and* fencing teams.

Nate Mackey slipped into the seat across from him. Although Nate and Jawa were good friends, they were polar opposites in capability. Nate was one of the worst students at school, almost as bad as Murray Hill had been – only Murray had been bad on purpose. Lousiness came naturally to Nate. The only reason he'd been accepted at Spy School was that he, like Erica, was a legacy. But while Erica came from a long line of spies renowned for their derring-do, Nate came from a short line of CIA accountants renowned for their cost-cutting.

'What kind of scenario were you imagining?' he asked.

'It's not important,' I said. 'We were only goofing around.'

'Hold on, Smokescreen,' Zoe said. 'Why not let Brainiac and Potatohead play too? At least Brainiac might have some ideas on the subject.'

'Which one of us is Brainiac?' Nate asked.

'I'll give you a hint,' Chip said. 'It's not you.'

'Let's hear it,' Jawa said.

'What if one of us were being targeted by an enemy organization?' Zoe asked. 'They want you to do something for them within 24 hours. And if you don't, they'll kill you.'

'What do they want you to do?' Jawa asked.

'It doesn't matter,' I said. 'We're really more

78

concerned with the "how do you not get killed" part.'

'You could always just do what the bad guys asked,' Nate said.

'Yes, if you're a wuss,' Chip said. 'But suppose you *didn't* want to sell out your country and do dirty work for the enemy?'

'Which of us are they targeting?' Jawa asked.

'What's it matter?' Zoe said.

'Because the scenario is different depending on who the target is,' Jawa replied.

'Let's say it's Smokescreen,' Chip suggested, trying to make this sound like a spur-of-the-moment decision.

Jawa grinned at me. 'Well if it's you, that's easy. First thing you do is go ask Erica for help.'

Everyone else immediately chimed agreement. Even Chip. 'That's right,' Zoe said. 'That's exactly what you should do.' Then, for Jawa and Nate's benefit, she added, '*If* this was really happening.'

I looked over at Erica, who still hadn't moved. 'Maybe,' I said.

'Oh come on!' Zoe cried. 'Ice Queen helped you out last time – and she certainly couldn't resist the chance to be the hero again. Besides, she likes you.'

This last statement made my pulse race, though I did my best not to show it. Zoe couldn't actually know anything about Erica, I told myself. She was just saying things to provoke a reaction from me. 'She does not,' I said.

'Well, she likes you more than anyone else here,' Jawa said. 'She actually put her arm around you once.'

'She put her arm around me once, too,' Nate said.

'That was in martial arts class and she was flipping you on your ass,' Chip said. 'Jawa's talking about touching someone *willingly*.'

Zoe turned back to me. 'If I were you, I'd definitely bring Ice Queen in. If your life is in danger, you can't just sit back and hope the administration here is going to protect you. They didn't exactly do a great job of that last time you were in trouble.'

'No,' I admitted. 'They didn't.'

'Zoe's right,' Warren chimed in. 'You have to protect yourself any way you can. My life hasn't been threatened, and *I'm* totally on edge. I can't imagine what you must be going through.' He clammed up as Zoe and I simultaneously booted him in the shins, reminding him that this scenario was only supposed to be imaginary. 'I mean, I'm on edge in *theory*,' he said quickly, glancing at Jawa and Nate.

Nate hadn't picked up on it. But Jawa had. 'What's going on here?' he asked.

Before Zoe, Warren, Chip or I could figure out how to respond, however, there was a gunshot behind me.

I leapt in surprise. So did Zoe and Chip. Warren screamed in terror and dove under the table.

Now I heard laughter behind me.

I spun around to find Claire Hutchins standing there with a popped paper bag and devilish grin. 'My, my,' she taunted, peeking under the table at Warren. 'You really *are* on edge.'

'That wasn't funny!' Zoe said.

'Not to *you*, perhaps,' Claire replied. 'But to everyone else, it was.' She waved a hand towards the rest of the mess hall. Her fellow MI6 students were laughing hysterically at us – and so were quite a lot of our fellow Americans.

'Let's see how funny you think it is when I punch your face in,' Zoe said, leaping out of her chair. She might have actually tried to do what she'd threatened, but Chip caught her and held her back.

Claire didn't even flinch. 'Oh, come on,' Claire said, watching Zoe with amusement. 'It's just a bit of fun. No harm done, right?' She headed back to her table, where several of her friends high-fived her.

'She is terrible,' Zoe said, staring bullets at Claire. 'I know we're supposed to be on the same side and all, but I've got half a mind to start the American Revolution over again.'

'Let it go,' Chip said. 'No point making a big scene.'

'You're only saying that because she's a girl,' Zoe griped. 'If one of those British guys had done that, you'd have already kicked his teeth down his throat.'

Warren emerged from under the table, steaming. 'I'll bet, if anyone here's working for SPYDER, it's one of them,' he muttered under his breath. 'We don't really know those guys at all, do we?'

I realized this was a good point, even though Warren was the one who had made it. I looked after Claire and the Brits . . .

And saw something strange through the screened windows of the mess hall. Someone wearing a tuxedo had just parachuted onto the main lawn. I didn't have a clear look at the person's face because the parachute instantly collapsed over him, but it wasn't hard to guess his identity. I could think of only one person who would make such a grand entrance – let alone jump out of a plane in formal wear: Alexander Hale.

It didn't take long for everyone else to notice his arrival as well. Within two seconds, everyone in the mess hall was crowded around the windows.

Well, almost everyone. I glanced over at Erica. Her

nose was still aimed at her book, although it seemed that her eyes had narrowed angrily.

Out on the lawn, the tuxedoed man emerged from beneath his parachute, revealing that it was, indeed, Alexander Hale. There was a gasp of excitement from almost everyone in the room. Even Chip, who usually prided himself on having cool reserve, seemed star struck. Meanwhile, Zoe was completely smitten. Her eyes, which were already huge, widened to the point where I thought they might fall out of her head.

Alexander abandoned his chute on the lawn and trotted up the steps to the mess hall. His tuxedo was somewhat ruffled, but his silver hair remained perfectly coiffed; he must have used an entire tube of sculpting gel on it. Alexander burst through the screen door as dramatically as possible, scanning the room until his steel blue eyes fell on me. 'Benjamin!' he cried. 'Just the man I'm here to see!'

Everyone's gaze shifted towards me. Even Claire and the MI6 gang had respect in their eyes. Most of my fellow students would have walked across fire to simply get a smile from the CIA's most revered spy. The fact that he'd parachuted into spy camp just to see me made me cool by proxy.

A few months before, I would have been thrilled by

the attention, but since then, I'd learned that Alexander Hale wasn't as great as he led everyone to believe he was. The man was a fraud, a middling spy at best whose glorious reputation was built on stealing the credit for other people's work and exaggerating his own exploits. For example, although Erica and I had defeated Murray Hill and saved Spy School from SPYDER the previous winter with only the slightest bit of help from Alexander, Alexander had filed a report in which he was the hero. Virtually everyone at the CIA bought it hook, line and sinker. Unaware of this, I'd told the truth during my debriefing, only to be met with scorn by people who thought *I* was the one trying to steal the credit from the great Alexander Hale.

It was upsetting to learn what Alexander had done, but Erica had advised me not to make a fuss. Alexander's reputation at the CIA was bulletproof. Any attempt to undermine it would only make me look bad. This was one bit of information that *hadn't* leaked to the student body. Only Erica and I knew the truth, which was why every wannabe spy in the mess hall now stared at Alexander like he was the president, a rock star and the Superbowl MVP all rolled into one.

Alexander swept across the room to my side. 'Thank goodness you're all right,' he said. 'I hear you've received a death threat from our old friends at you-know-where.'

I glanced at my fellow students, quite sure that Alexander shouldn't have been saying this in front of them. 'It was more like a contract for a job,' I said quietly.

'Really?' Alexander asked. 'Well, in the wrong hands, even paper can be deadly. Once, when I was in Bangladesh, my enemies tried to kill me by placing a powerful neurotoxin on a dinner menu. If I hadn't trained myself to smell neurotoxins, I'd be dead right now.'

Everyone within earshot suddenly looked very impressed, while I found myself wondering if Alexander Hale had ever actually been to Bangladesh.

'Maybe we should discuss this somewhere more private,' I said.

Alexander looked slightly embarrassed, but recovered quickly. 'I was just about to suggest that myself,' he said. 'Good to see you're as nimble of mind as I am.' He took me by the arm and steered me into the kitchen. The chefs looked up in surprise, and then awe, when they saw Alexander. One of them dropped what looked suspiciously like a skinned raccoon into a stewing pot.

'Could all of you make yourselves scarce for a few minutes?' Alexander asked. 'Agent Ripley and I have something of great importance to discuss.'

The chefs looked at me, wondering who on earth I was to merit a one-on-one with Alexander Hale, then obediently scurried out of the door.

Alexander began poking about the kitchen, checking the stove, the refrigerator, the pantry.

'What are you doing?' I asked.

'Checking for bugs.'

'Well, you've come to the right place. This is cockroach heaven.' Even as I said this, a horde of them was making off with a loaf of bread.

'No, I mean "bugs" as in listening devices . . .' Alexander trailed off as a realization came to him. 'Ah. You were joking, weren't you?'

'I was.'

Alexander forced a laugh. 'Nicely done. A good spy should never lose his sense of humour, even in times of great danger.' He came across the room, his search for listening devices already forgotten. 'Now then, Benjamin. How are you holding up given this current SPYDER business?'

I gave Alexander the hardest stare I could muster. This was the first time I'd seen him since learning that he'd undermined me. 'You parachuted in here just to ask me that?'

'No. My time is a bit more precious than that.' If Alexander felt the slightest bit guilty about what he'd done to me, he didn't show it. 'I'm here on direct orders from the highest level. I was told to come ASAP. Thus, my rather unorthodox attire.'

'What are you supposed to do?' I asked.

'I'm been assigned as lead agent on this investigation. My objectives are to uncover what SPYDER's nefarious plans are this time and to ensure your safety. Don't worry, though. I won't cramp your style. I'm a master of camouflage, you know. I once spent three days in a terrorist den disguised as a rock. You won't even know I'm here. And more importantly, neither will SPYDER.'

'If SPYDER's keeping an eye on the camp, then they already know you're here,' I said. 'You couldn't have picked a flashier way of showing up here than parachuting down in a tuxedo.'

Alexander swallowed. The tips of his ears turned red in embarrassment as he realized I was right, though he recovered quickly. 'Intimidation, my young friend. I *wanted* them to see me. Now, they know that if they want to get to you, they have to go through me. That'll make them think twice about coming after you.'

I doubted that was true. SPYDER seemed to know more about the CIA than the CIA did. Which meant they probably knew Alexander was as dangerous as a wet napkin.

'Furthermore, it wasn't like I had the time to change,' Alexander went on. 'I was called directly in from another assignment. There was no time to spare where your safety was concerned. Now then, where is this contract SPYDER left you? I'd like to examine it.'

'Woodchuck took it,' I said.

'What for?' Alexander asked.

'I suppose he wanted to examine it too.' It occurred to me that I wasn't actually sure what Woodchuck intended to do with the contract.

'Ah. Very good,' Alexander said. 'I should probably reconnoitre with Woodchuck and find out what he's learned. Then I can ditch my monkey suit and get into some more suitable attire for the surroundings. But don't worry, I won't be gone long.' He gave me a pat on the shoulder that was supposed to be reassuring.

'I'll be OK without you,' I said. And I meant it.

'That's the spirit!' Alexander started toward the door, then turned back. 'Just out of interest, any idea who SPYDER's man might be?'

'No,' I said. And even if I had, I knew better than

to share anything I'd deduced with Alexander again.

'Ah well, I'm sure we'll hound the fiend out soon enough. You have my word.' With that, Alexander slipped out of the door.

As I watched him try to figure out the way to Woodchuck's cabin, I realized I felt even worse than I had after receiving the death threat. My situation was now bad enough that the CIA had sent in a high-level operative to protect me. Unfortunately, they'd sent the worst one possible.

Physical Education

CIA summer training facility
June 14
0500 hours

'Get up, Muskrats! Now, now, now!'

Hank Schacter's yell would have been enough to shatter anyone's REM sleep, but just to make sure that he ruined everyone's morning, he was also banging a pair of metal dustbin lids together.

My cabin-mates responded in a variety of ways to the alarm. Some snapped to attention immediately, some leapt out of bed ready for an enemy attack, and others took a bit longer to figure out what was going on. Nate Mackey forgot he was in the top bunk, groggily rolled out of bed and began his day by belly-flopping onto the floor.

I fell into the 'ready-for-attack' group, but only because I'd spent most of the night wide awake. Even though SPYDER claimed I had 24 hours, it wasn't the most trustworthy organization; perhaps they'd given that time simply to get the CIA to drop its guard until then. If that was the case, I didn't expect Alexander Hale to be much help. Despite his assurance that he'd stay close, I hadn't seen him since dinnertime. I had gone to bed with a baseball bat under my sheets; it was one of the few weapons that I was completely qualified to use – and the only one I was sure I wouldn't accidentally impale myself on or shoot myself with while I slept.

After several hours of tensing in fear every time I heard so much as a cricket chirp, I'd finally managed to pass out from exhaustion around four-thirty a.m. So when Hank Schacter barged into the cabin a mere thirty minutes later, I was hardly at my best. I came to, ready for battle, but my bat got tangled in the bedsheets. By the time I'd extricated it, I realized I wasn't under attack – although I still gave serious consideration to using it on Hank anyhow.

'Let's move it, you maggots!' he shouted, clanging

his dustbin lids together. 'This isn't a resort! This is a training facility – and you lumps of lard are in need of some serious training! The last one of you to get dressed and get his rear out of the door does an extra fifty push-ups!'

It didn't take me long to suit up. I was already wearing my clothes. If the enemy showed up during the night, I wanted to be wearing more than just my boxer shorts. I darted for the door well ahead of most of my cabin-mates, many of whom were sleepily trying to figure out how to get their shirts on.

Hank lashed out a hand and snagged my arm as I tried to duck past him. 'I want fifty push-ups out of you.'

'But I'm not the last one out,' I protested.

'No one ever said life was fair,' Hank told me. 'Besides, you look like you could use some beefing up.' He shoved me outside, then addressed the cabin. 'I intend to win this year's Colour War, Muskrats. But to stand a chance at that, I obviously have to whip you losers into shape. So this morning we will be doing five miles over rough terrain. Anyone complains and I'll make it longer.'

I dropped to the porch and started doing push-ups. Jawa dropped in beside me.

92

'Why are *you* doing push-ups?' I asked him. 'Hank didn't tell you to.'

'A little extra upper-body strength never hurt anyone,' Jawa replied. The exertion wasn't even making him breathe hard. 'Besides, I want to win Colour War as bad as Hank does.'

'What do we compete in? Tug-of-war, dodgeball, that kind of stuff?'

Jawa looked at me askance. 'At other camps, maybe. But here, Colour War is an actual *war*. A full-on simulated battle. Whichever cabin wins gets straight As for the summer.'

'And the losers?'

'Humiliation. And extra homework next semester.'

The rest of the cabin filed out of the door past us, except poor Nate Mackey, who was still floundering about trying to get his trousers on.

'Fifty push-ups!' Hank barked at him, then wheeled on the rest of us. 'Everyone else does jumping jacks until he finishes them all!'

One of the Muskrats groaned.

Hank's eyes narrowed. 'Whoever did that just bought all of you an extra mile this morning.'

I heard another groan begin, though this quickly became the sound of the groaner getting punched in

93

the stomach by someone who didn't feel like adding on another mile.

Jawa finished his push-ups, leapt to his feet and began doing jumping jacks. Everyone else followed his lead.

As I made the shift from push-ups to jumping jacks, I took a moment to case the grounds outside the cabin. I didn't see any enemies lurking in the predawn light. Nor did I see Alexander. Either he really was good at camouflaging himself – or he was somewhere else entirely, probably sleeping. I would have bet all my money on the latter.

It took Nate Mackey three minutes to do fifty push-ups. When he was done, he was red-faced and wheezing. Several of my fellow Muskrats looked winded as well.

'Let's move out!' Hank ordered. He sprinted into the forest and we followed obediently. 'We'll start with the Challenge Trail around the woods, followed by Deadman's Route up Mount Roosevelt. I expect everyone to cover all six miles in less than forty minutes. Whoever takes more than that earns my unmitigated wrath for the rest of the day – and believe me, you do not want that.'

We skirted the lake, passing several other student cabins. Everyone in them was still sleeping peacefully.

'Just our luck,' Warren muttered. 'We get stuck with the drill sergeant.'

'Keep your mouth shut unless you want to do *seven* miles,' Jawa told him.

Everyone took that as good advice. We were silent as we ran.

I was actually a good runner, and I'd increased my stamina during my time at Spy School, but Hank was setting a hard pace and we were going over rugged ground. The land around our camp turned out to be much hillier than I'd realized; it was full of sharp wooded rises and cut with steep ravines. It would have been beautiful if I hadn't been on a forced run through it. After the first mile, I was starting to flag a bit and wondering how on earth I was going to cover another five – let alone scale a mountain. The Muskrats had already spread out along the trail in order of athletic ability, with Hank and Jawa in the lead, while Nate and Warren stumbled along at the rear. The line of us was stretching longer and longer as we went, so that every now and then, I found myself alone on a stretch of trail, without anyone visible ahead or behind through the thick trees.

I was just beginning to think this wasn't the safest place for me to be when the attack came.

A loop of cord that had been hidden in the dirt suddenly snapped tight around my right leg and yanked it out from under me. I hit the ground hard enough to knock the wind out of me and was dragged into the underbrush. Before I could scream for help, someone pounced on top of me and slapped a hand over my mouth.

My attacker was dressed in head-to-toe camouflage. She looked like a stretch of lawn that had come to life. I wouldn't have recognized her if it weren't for her ice blue eyes. Her usual lilac and gunpowder smell was overwhelmed by the scent of grass and soil.

Erica Hale.

She waited until Warren and Nate had staggered past and were well out of earshot, then took her hand away from my mouth.

'Y'know, when most people want to talk to someone else, they call them on the phone,' I said. 'Maybe drop by their room. They don't ambush them in the middle of the woods.'

'It's in both of our best interests if no one knows we're aligned on this matter.' Erica got off me, then helped me to my feet.

'I think you just enjoy ambushing me,' I told her.

It was hard to tell, given the green paint on her face,

but I think Erica might have smiled. It only lasted a fraction of a second. Then she was back to business as usual. 'If you were more attuned to your environment, I wouldn't be able to ambush you. You need to be much more alert with SPYDER on the prowl. I can't always be there to protect you.'

'Like the other day at FunLand?' I asked pointedly.

'There were a dozen CIA agents watching you. I felt they had things under control.'

'Well, they didn't. Murray Hill dropped by – and he got away.'

'So I heard.' Erica started into the forest, heading away from the running trail I'd been on.

'Where are we going?' I asked.

'We're taking a shortcut back to camp. Unless you were enjoying the scenic route.'

'Uh, no. This way is fine. As long as Hank doesn't notice I'm gone.'

'He won't.'

I plunged into the woods behind Erica. There wasn't any evident trail, but Erica seemed to know exactly where she was going. 'Do you believe that I saw Murray?' I asked.

'Why wouldn't I?'

'Because no one else does. They all claim he's locked

up at some juvenile rehabilitation facility.'

'Yes, that struck me as a bit odd as well.'

'Murray doesn't have a twin by any chance, does he?'

'No.'

'So it's possible that he escaped and no one has noticed?'

'I doubt it.'

'Then how can Murray be in two places at once?'

'I'm still working on that.' Erica led the way down a steep, rocky slope into a narrow ravine.

I carefully picked my way down after her. The rocks were slick with morning mist. 'Any ideas so far?' I asked.

'I'm still gathering data. Speaking of which, I found out why everyone was so freaked out about that number plate you got.'

'Why?'

'Because it belongs to the Director of the CIA.'

I froze on the rocky incline, stunned. 'The Director of the CIA is working with SPYDER?!'

Erica shot me an annoyed glance, disappointed by my limited powers of deduction.

'Oh,' I said, understanding. 'SPYDER stole it from him.'

'Yes.' There was a small stream at the bottom of the ravine, and Erica led us along it. 'The thing is, the director's identity is classified.'

'No it's not. He's on TV all the time!'

Erica shot me another annoyed look. 'The *real* director of the CIA,' she told me. 'The guy who actually runs it.'

'The other guy's just a decoy? No one told me that.'

'Most of the agents in the CIA don't know that. They don't know who the real director is – or where he lives. So it's quite disturbing when SPYDER swipes the number plate off his car.'

'Why would they do that?'

'To send a message to the CIA: They know *everything*. And they can get to anyone, anywhere.'

I felt a chill pass through me. 'So if I don't agree to work for them, they'll really be able to take me out?'

'Not if I can help it.'

'Do you have any idea what SPYDER needs me for?'

'No,' Erica admitted. 'But it must be something big. SPYDER's kept in the shadows for years – and now they suddenly start making public appearances just to get your attention? Every time they do that, it's a risk. And yet, SPYDER must think you're worth it.'

'But why me?' I asked. 'If they wanted the best agent at Spy School, why aren't they going after you?'

'There's two possibilities,' Erica replied. 'One: they think they can turn you. They know they can't get me. I'd rather die than work for them.'

'So would I.'

'Really? When they come for you today and point a dozen guns to your head and say "Work for us or we'll shoot you," you'll really have the guts to turn them down?'

'Of course,' I said, although while I really *wanted* to believe this was true, I was quite sure it wasn't. Death is a really good negotiating tactic.

Erica didn't look like she believed me either, but she let it slide. 'Possibility two: you have some latent talent that is extremely important to them.'

'Some talent that even I don't know about?'

'I guess. Some extension of your maths skills, probably. After all, SPYDER has made you an offer before.'

'And I shot them down.'

'So now they've upped the stakes in the biggest way possible. Think, Ben. What can you do that's so special?' Erica started up a steep rock face. It was almost perfectly smooth, but she bounded up it like a mountain goat.

It took me a bit longer to work my way up. By the time I got to the top, twenty metres above the creek, I'd had a good amount of time to think about why SPYDER believed I was so important – and I hadn't come up with anything. 'I have no idea what SPYDER thinks I can do for them,' I admitted.

'OK,' Erica said, seeming disappointed. 'Then let's focus on protecting you from them. What's the best way to do that?'

'Get to them before they get to me?'

'Exactly. And how do we do that? I thought for a moment. 'Well, the easiest way for them to be delivering things to me like the note and the contract would be to have another mole on the inside, right?'

'Yes. If not more than one mole.'

'So if we can figure out who it is, we're on the right path.'

Erica nodded. At the top of the slope was a windswept rocky stretch, mostly bald except for the occasional stunted tree. Erica and I were finally able to walk side by side for a while. 'Any idea who it might be?'

'I was going to ask *you* that.'

'You're closer to all this than I am.'

I considered that as we walked. 'Whoever put the

contract in the footlocker did it *after* all fifteen other bunks were claimed – but before I showed up with Chip, Zoe and Warren. Because whoever put the contract there *thought* they were putting it in my footlocker.'

Erica gave me one of her rare smiles. 'Exactly. That wasn't a lot of time.'

'I saw Claire Hutchins and the rest of her MI6 gang coming from the direction of my cabin right before I got there,' I said.

'Interesting,' Erica said. 'The CIA probably doesn't vet the MI6 students as tightly as its own because they expect MI6 to do it for them. Did you see anyone else near your cabin?'

'No,' I said.

'No one?' Erica asked pointedly.

'Well, no one but Zoe and Warren.'

'Also interesting,' Erica said.

'No,' I told her. 'There's no way Zoe's the mole. She's my friend.'

'So was Murray. And look how that turned out.'

'I didn't know Murray all that long. I've known Zoe for five months.'

'You can't trust anybody,' Erica said.

'*I* can,' I shot back. 'I trust Zoe.'

'How about Warren?'

I thought about Chip's joking accusation that we hadn't seen Warren actually find the contract inside the footlocker. Then I shook my head. 'I don't think Warren's exactly SPYDER material.'

'No one would have thought that about Murray, either,' Erica cautioned. 'It takes an awfully good double agent to convince you that they're a really bad agent.

'I suppose Warren could have delivered the contract,' I said.

'Of course, there are nearly three hundred other students who got here before your bus did,' Erica put in. 'Plus thirty faculty and assorted groundkeepers. Plenty of them probably had an opportunity as well.'

'Are there security cameras posted around the cabins?' I asked.

'Of course,' Erica replied.

'Have you checked to see if they recorded anyone entering my cabin?'

'What do you think?'

I frowned, knowing what the answer would be. 'You did . . . and they didn't show anything.'

'Exactly.'

'Someone jacked the cameras?' I asked. 'The same

way the assassin did when he came to get me?'

'No. These recorded just fine. They simply didn't record anyone going in or out of your cabin during that time.'

I stared at Erica, incredulous. 'How is that even possible?'

Erica shrugged. 'I don't know. But when we figure it out, we'll probably have a darn good idea who our mole is.'

The bald area ended abruptly at a tall cliff. It plummeted straight down into the woods twenty storeys below. I could see the camp in the distance: most of the buildings were hidden by the trees, but the oval of the central lawn was the only big gap in the forest.

'How are we supposed to get down?' I asked.

'With this.' Erica pulled a camouflaged tarp off a boulder nearby. One end of an ancient zip-line rig was bolted to the rock. The wire angled down into the forest, so thin it was almost impossible to see.

'You have to be kidding,' I said.

'Have you ever known me to kid?' Erica withdrew a small zip-line pulley from somewhere in the recesses of her camouflage gear. She whipped it over the wire and locked it in place. 'I only have one of these. We'll have to share.'

'I don't think that wire will hold both of us,' I said.

'It will,' Erica told me. 'It's either this or go back the way we came. Which means Hank will beat you back to camp by half an hour and discover you've gone AWOL. You want to earn his wrath?'

'I kind of got that for free,' I said.

'Stop being such a weed and get on the wire.'

There may be no bigger motivator to a twelve year old boy than not wanting to look like a weed in front of an attractive girl.

A harness was attached to the zip-line pulley. Erica quickly cinched it around us, so we were strapped face to face. If I hadn't been terrified of the drop, it might have been the most thrilling moment of my short life.

Erica checked the pulley to make sure it was properly situated on the wire – and then, without any warning at all, leapt off the cliff.

Her gravity took me with her. A second later, we were whizzing down the line.

To my surprise, it wasn't scary. It didn't even feel like falling. It was more like taking an elevator, albeit a cramped one where your nose was practically touching that of the only other passenger. The ride went on long enough that it seemed I ought to say something.

'How did you even know about this?' I asked.

'I've taken some time to familiarize myself with the terrain,' Erica replied. 'Just as I did at school.'

I shook my head, not buying it. The school was only a few buildings and a couple of miles of subterranean tunnels. The camp property, on the other hand, was massive. It would have taken years to explore it all. Plus Erica was a legacy. All her ancestors had been spies. 'Someone must have showed you around,' I said. 'Your father maybe?'

Erica's eyes hardened. 'No. Not my father.'

There was something in her voice that surprised me. Something like pain.

'Joshua Hallal?' I asked.

Erica turned away from me, which wasn't easy to do while we were strapped together.

I instantly felt bad for bringing it up. Joshua Hallal had been a top student at Spy School, the rare person Erica had respected – and SPYDER had killed him. His death the previous January had been the tip-off that SPYDER had a mole in the school in the first place. Which had triggered my recruitment.

This was the first time I'd ever mentioned Joshua to Erica, and she instantly iced up. Even though we were inches apart physically, she seemed a mile away emotionally. I'd heard rumours that Erica had been the one who found Joshua's remains – which would have been unsettling even if they hadn't been friends, as he'd been blown up by a bomb in his dorm room. I'd never been able to confirm this, though, because even at a gossip-happy place like Spy School, no one seemed comfortable talking about Joshua's death. I considered asking Erica about it now, but given her cold expression, I couldn't bring myself to do it. There was only one thing I could think of to say.

'I'm sorry,' I said.

'Why?' Erica asked frostily. 'You didn't kill him. Tuck in your legs. We're coming in for a landing.'

I'd been so distracted, I hadn't noticed the ground coming up. Our feet skimmed over the tops of the trees, and then we were dropping through the branches. I brought my knees up to my chest, as directed, and noticed that the wire ended very suddenly at a large rock below. We seemed to be heading for it very quickly. Below the point where the wire anchored in, there was a faint but large red splotch that looked like the bad result of a high-speed impact.

Before we slammed into the rock, however, Erica tugged on a latch and the harness came loose from the pulley. We dropped a couple of metres – and landed on what had looked like ground, but which was actually a canvas stretched taut over a pit to cushion our fall. It was like a trampoline built at ground level. We bounded off it once, then tumbled over each other until we came to a gentle stop.

Erica was on her feet in a second, undoing the harness that held us together and hurrying off to retrieve the pulley. 'We're a little behind time. We'll have to move quickly so Hank doesn't notice you're gone.' She snapped the pulley off, tucked it away, and took off into the woods.

I ran after her. 'So where are we left with this SPYDER business?' I asked. 'We only have around six hours until SPYDER's deadline is up. What am I supposed to do?'

'Keep your eyes and ears open,' Erica told me. 'Try to work out who might have planted that contract and how they got past the cameras. I'll try to figure things out on my end.'

Her statement jogged my memory. 'Did you ever find out what that speck on the first note from SPYDER was?'

'Yes. It was a fragment of bituminous coal.'

'That's it?' I asked, not bothering to hide my disappointment.

'What were you hoping for? A canister of microfilm

that detailed all SPYDER's plans?'

'I was hoping for something that would tell us something. Coal isn't exactly rare. It won't help us narrow anything down.'

'It still could,' Erica said. 'Every seam of coal is different. They all have different impurities in them, no matter how minuscule. If we can determine what all those are, we could pinpoint where the coal is from – and thus tell us where SPYDER wrote that note.'

'How long will that take?'

'A little while longer. It involves a lot of very expensive equipment that I'm not supposed to have access to.'

'So how are you going to access it?'

'I'm not. Luckily I have a friend who can do the work for me. But he can't just drop everything and slot this in first.'

Before I could ask Erica who her friend was, she pressed a finger to my lips, then yanked me down into the bushes.

A few seconds later, Hank Schacter ran past. The rough pace he'd set had winded him. He was huffing and puffing and coated with a sheen of sweat. Jawa wasn't far behind him. He looked almost serene, as though he'd found the six mile slog through the forest refreshing. The remaining Muskrats were spread out even farther behind him than before. It was a good thirty seconds until the next one came along, and the next was a minute after that.

'This looks like your spot,' Erica told me, and before I could protest, she shoved me through the bushes onto the trail.

When I turned back, she'd already melted into the forest. I knew it was pointless to go after her, so I followed the path instead.

Five minutes later, I emerged from the trees onto the main lawn.

Jawa was in a lotus pose, serenely meditating, while Hank and the two Muskrats who'd arrived before me were doing their best to keep from collapsing.

Hank fixed me with a hard stare. 'What are you trying to pull here?' he demanded.

'What do you mean?' I asked innocently.

'You don't look like you were working hard at all,' Hank said.

'Neither does Jawa,' I countered.

'Jawa's a freak of nature,' Hank growled. 'You're just a freak. No way did you run that whole six miles.'

'You're right,' I said. 'I only ran the first, then cut out, somehow found a shortcut through a wilderness area I've never seen before, and then jumped back onto the trail with only a few minutes to go.'

Hank frowned. The truth actually sounded harder to believe than the lie. 'Maybe, later today, you can prove to me how good a runner you are. Maybe we should do ten miles this afternoon and see how refreshed you feel then.'

I gulped. This hadn't worked out the way I'd hoped. Of course, SPYDER planned to either kidnap or kill me by lunchtime, so the chances were that I wouldn't have to do the run anyhow.

Just then, Woodchuck emerged from the woods carrying a string of freshly-speared brook trout. He was wearing a bearskin cloak and homemade moccasins along with his standard loincloth. 'I'm afraid there won't be time for another run today,' he said.

'Why not?' Hank demanded.

'Because Young Ripley here is leaving camp right after breakfast,' Woodchuck told him. Before Hank could protest he added, 'That's not my decision. It's an order straight from the top.'

Hank scowled, wondering why I merited such special attention, then stormed off to berate the Muskrats who'd arrived later than I had.

I was surprised to find myself feeling somewhat

relieved. So the CIA had a new plan: Get me out of Spy Camp before SPYDER arrived. I liked that much more than the previous plan: wait for SPYDER to arrive and pray Alexander Hale didn't screw things up.

'Where am I going?' I asked.

'Far from here,' Woodchuck replied. 'And into some *serious* wilderness.'

The feeling of relief instantly vanished. Since my life was on the line, I'd been hoping to hear that I was going someplace more like a maximum-security underground bunker with a hundred heavily-armed agents assigned to protect me. 'This isn't serious wilderness?' I asked.

'This?' Woodchuck laughed. 'This place is a spa compared to the real thing. But rest assured, there's nowhere safer. Your enemies will never find you out there. Not with me by your side.'

A thought occurred to me. 'Does Alexander Hale know about this plan?'

Woodchuck shrugged. 'He must – although I haven't seen him since last night. I suspect he's been ordered to focus on SPYDER while I keep you safe. We're leaving in an hour. Go get yourself a good breakfast. We're only going to eat what we can forage for the next few days.' With that, Woodchuck slung the fish over his shoulder and headed up to the mess, whistling happily.

I stared after him, wondering what I'd got myself into now.

Wilderness Survival

Shenandoah National Wilderness
June 14
1100 hours

Woodchuck and I weren't the only ones who set off from Spy Camp that morning. An entire busload of students rolled out of the gates. In part, this was to cover my evacuation: just in case SPYDER was tailing us, at some point Woodchuck and I planned to surreptitiously slip off the bus, which would then continue on with everyone on board serving as decoys. But in addition, Woodchuck had felt that my entire class was in desperate need of some wilderness training. In the single day that the first years had been at Spy

Camp, one student had been bitten by an opossum, one had been sick from drinking scummy water, and one had nearly blown up the latrine by striking a match dangerously close to the methane-rich trench. To top it off, poor Nate Mackey had made a pit stop in the woods during the morning's run and then wiped himself with poison ivy. He was currently in the infirmary, his bottom covered with pustules.

Woodchuck decided that, as long as he was dragging the first years out to the sticks, he might as well bring all the MI6 kids too. And then he needed all of our counsellors and a few older kids to wrangle everyone – so both Chip and Hank Schacter ended up along for the ride.

I was relieved to have some friends for the first part of the adventure. I sat with Zoe, which meant Warren had taken the seat directly behind us, where he could glower at me every time Zoe's back was turned. Chip sat next to him, taking up most of the seat and forcing Warren to squash himself up against the window. As we all had orders to keep quiet about the mission and were surrounded by future spies, everyone avoided the topic and talked about standard spy school things like what the best way to poison an enemy agent was and which professors we should avoid the next year. This was actually a relief. It was nice to be distracted from SPYDER for a while.

The scenery provided a diversion as well. I had thought that Spy Camp was located as far from civilization as one could get in the eastern United States, but it turned out I was wrong. Our bus was heading way off the grid. We began our journey on country roads, then shifted to one-lane tracks through the woods and finally ended up on bumpy, rutted trails that a bus had no business being on. Two and half hours after leaving camp, we were chugging up a narrow track carved into the edge of a steep mountain with a precipitous ravine dropping away below us.

Our fellow students were so focused on our surroundings – and busily praying that we wouldn't plummet to our deaths – that my friends finally felt it was safe to discuss what was really on their minds.

'Any idea what Woodchuck's plan is?' Zoe whispered to me. 'Once you get out into the wild and all?'

'Woodchuck says we're just going to lay low and stay way off the grid,' I replied. 'The deeper into the wilderness we are, the harder it'll be for SPYDER to find us.'

'And you're going total survivalist out there?' Chip asked.

'Apparently so,' I said grimly. I had spent a good hour in the mess hall that morning, stuffing myself full of waffles, bacon and sausage, fearing that I'd soon be eating insects. When I'd tried to bring a backpack of supplies on the bus, Woodchuck had stopped me. 'We need to move quickly and leave no trace. That means as few supplies as possible. No luxury items like matches or underwear.'

I'd never really thought of fire or underwear as luxury items; I'd considered them necessities. But I reluctantly left them behind. Except for the underwear I had on, of course.

'So the CIA's whole strategy for you to deal with SPYDER is to run away?' Chip asked.

'No,' I said. 'The agency is trying to figure out what SPYDER is up to. But the 24 hours SPYDER gave me is almost up. So instead of forcing me to choose between working for the enemy and death, they're removing me from the equation.' Even though I knew exactly what time it was, I nervously checked my watch to confirm it anyhow. It was almost exactly one day since I'd received the contract – and the ultimatum – from SPYDER.

'Why didn't the agency just let you accept their offer?' Zoe asked. 'You could have worked as a double-agent for *us*.'

'I'm not even a single agent yet,' I said. 'I don't think I'm quite ready to be a double-agent.' I *had* thought about doing what Chip suggested, but the thought of it was overwhelming and gave me stomach ache.

'Oh, I'm sure *you* could have handled it,' Zoe said.

Warren glowered at this. 'Does anyone have any idea where we are?' he asked grumpily, trying to change the subject.

I glanced out the window. If anything, the ravine seemed to have grown even steeper. 'I'm guessing West Virginia,' I said.

'West Virginia?' Claire Hutchins called from a few rows up. 'I thought that was all strip mines and inbred hillbillies.'

'You heard wrong,' Chip shot back. 'As you can see, there's plenty of wilderness here – and the locals are far less inbred than a bunch of cockneys.'

Claire was suddenly on her feet with her fellow students behind her. 'Mock me one more time and I'll rip off your head and cram it down your neck.'

Chip snapped to his feet as well. 'I'd like to see you try.'

'Hey!' Hank snapped. He charged down the aisle

from the front of the bus, grabbed Chip by the shoulder and slammed him into his seat. 'You're not going to survive three minutes out here if you can't be a team player.'

'What are you yelling at me for?' Chip asked, then pointed at Claire. '*She* started it.'

'It doesn't matter who started it,' Woodchuck announced. He stood in the aisle at the front of the bus, calmly peeling an apple with his bowie knife. 'Hank is right. The first key to survival is teamwork. Suppose this road were to collapse right now and our bus were to plummet into the ravine?'

'Is that a possibility?' Warren asked, terrified.

'Certainly,' Woodchuck said. 'These roads are in terrible shape. Now imagine: the bus plunges into the river. The wreckage is hideous. The carnage is terrible. But a few of you manage to escape. What is the first thing you do?'

'Call 911 and have the wilderness patrol come rescue us,' Jawa said.

Woodchuck frowned. 'Er, let's assume there are no phones. They've all been lost in the disaster. Now, there's just a few of you down there, stranded miles from civilization without any means of contact. What do you do to survive?'

'Eat the dead people!' Warren suggested, a bit too enthusiastically.

Everyone on the bus glared at him, disgusted.

'What?' he asked. 'We're going to need protein.'

'We start down the river,' Chip said. 'That will lead us to civilization.'

'You don't just head off into the wilderness!' Claire told him. 'That's dangerous.'

'Well what are we supposed to do?' Chip asked. 'Just stay in the bottom of the ravine and starve to death?'

'We wouldn't starve,' Warren said. 'There's plenty of fresh people . . .'

'Dude,' Zoe said. 'Drop the whole cannibal thing.'

'You don't leave the site of an accident,' Claire told Chip. 'When help comes, that's where they're going to look.'

'Who said help was coming?' Chip shot back.

'Staying at the site is standard procedure,' Claire said. 'It's straight out of the CIA rescue manual.'

'Well what moron wrote that manual?' Chip demanded.

'I did,' Woodchuck said.

Chip grimaced. He turned around to face Woodchuck. 'I didn't mean *you* were a moron,' he tried to explain. 'Just the manual . . .'

Woodchuck shrugged, unfazed. 'It's cool,' he said. 'We're all allowed a difference of opinion. You can think my manual's wrong. It's *not*, but you can think that it is. The point is, I'm not going to get angry at you. That gets us nowhere. It only wastes time and energy – and if this were a true survival situation, we would not have time or energy to waste. The first thing you do in a life-or-death situation is figure out how to work together.'

Jawa raised his hand. Woodchuck pointed to him and he asked, 'Why is it safer to stay with the wreck than to head to civilization?'

'Because you don't know what lies ahead,' Woodchuck replied. 'Yes, a river will often lead to a town, but who knows how treacherous that route will be? Suppose you take the river downstream, only to encounter an impassable obstacle – a waterfall, for example – and there's no way to get back upstream. Now, you're stuck. And when the search party comes looking for you – and a party *will* come – they'll find the wreckage, but they won't find you.'

Woodchuck finished peeling his apple, then sliced off a hunk and jammed it in his mouth. 'Survival is like a chess game,' he told us. 'You can't just think one step ahead. You have to think several steps ahead. You have to examine all the scenarios: if you go down the river, what's the chance of someone getting injured? If they get injured, how do you help them? Once you analyse everything, you choose the course with the least risk. In nearly 100 per cent of cases, staying at the crash site is the least risky option.'

'Told you,' Claire said under her breath.

Chip sat back down, frowning. He muttered something to me, but I didn't hear it.

I was too busy looking at the bus driver.

I hadn't paid much attention to the man when I got on. I'd been distracted by Woodchuck confiscating my extra underwear. And throughout the drive, I'd only been able to see the back of the man's head, and that was from a distance, as I was towards the rear of the bus. But now, while Woodchuck had been speaking, I'd been looking forwards. There was a mirror at the front of the bus, as on most buses, designed so that the driver could look back at all of us. So the mirror allowed me to see the driver's eyes – and I'd noticed they kept flicking toward me.

The driver was watching me.

I didn't get scared, however. Not quite yet. There

was something familiar about the eyes, as though I'd seen them before.

I kept my gaze locked on the mirror.

The eyes flicked up again, locking with mine.

They were ice blue. I only knew one man with eyes that colour: Alexander Hale.

He'd disguised himself. In truth, he'd done a pretty good job: he'd dyed his hair, affixed a fake moustache and maybe even added a bit of latex around his jowls to make himself look pudgier. But still, if I'd been paying better attention – which I should have been doing, given my situation – I would have noticed it was him.

Alexander returned his attention to the road ahead and steered us around a hairpin turn. A large trestle bridge that looked at least a century old came into view. It spanned the steep gorge only a hundred metres or so ahead.

'Oh no,' Zoe said. 'Tell me we're not going over that.'

'No need to worry,' Woodchuck said. 'It's perfectly safe.'

I scurried up the aisle to the front of the bus, slipping past Woodchuck to get to the driver's seat.

'Alexander?' I asked.

'No,' Alexander said with a wink. 'My name is Enrico Palaterri.'

'What are you doing here?'

'Getting you to your destination safely.' Alexander was playing up his role for the benefit of Woodchuck and anyone else within earshot. He was trying to do an Italian accent, although he actually sounded Irish. 'My mission is to ensure the safety of all academy students.'

'But you're not supposed to be protecting me any more!' I hissed. 'Woodchuck's been assigned to do that now. You're supposed to be figuring out what SPYDER's up to and neutralizing them.'

'I don't know what you're talking about. I'm only here to drive the bus,' Alexander said, then lowered his voice to whisper back. 'I made an executive decision. Woodchuck might be a great survivalist, but he's not a great spy. If SPYDER comes after you, you're going to need someone with my skills to protect you.'

'The whole idea was for you to stop them *before* they came after me,' I said.

'Ben, relax,' Alexander said. 'You're in good hands here. SPYDER isn't going to be any trouble at all.'

At which point, SPYDER attacked.

Evacuation

Shenandoah River Gorge
June 14
1130 hours

The first explosion detonated in the road directly in front of our bus. There was a blinding flash of light and then a concussion of air that shattered the windscreen and knocked me flat. The bus was thrown sideways like a matchbox car and slammed into the rock face. Dust and debris ballooned through the gap in the window, coating me, Alexander and everyone in the first three rows.

Someone screamed in terror next to me. I thought it was one of the girls, but when I sat up and wiped the

125

dust from my eyes, I found it was Nate Mackey.

He was on the floor in the foetal position, white as a sheet. 'We're going to die!' he screamed. 'We're going to die!'

I looked to Woodchuck for help. Unfortunately, he was slumped in his seat, unconscious. Perhaps he'd been clocked in the head by a piece of flying debris. Or maybe he'd simply fainted in fear. Whatever the case, he wasn't going to be any help.

A second explosion went off in the road behind the bus. From the back window, I saw part of the road crumble and plummet into the gorge, cutting off our escape route.

Nate screamed again. 'I don't want to die!' he wailed. 'I'm too young!'

The students on the bus were reacting in a dozen different ways, ranging from abject terror to cool aplomb. Warren was at the terrified end of the spectrum, hiding under his seat. Zoe was somewhere in the middle, trying to be calm, but obviously frightened. Most of the others handled themselves with dignity, if a bit of confusion. Chip and Jawa were popping out the emergency windows, trying to evacuate the bus. Hank had thrown himself on top of Claire to protect her, although Claire wasn't too pleased by his chivalry. 'Get off me, you twit!' she snapped. 'I'm not some helpless damsel-in-distress!'

Suddenly, a voice amplified by a megaphone rang out from above, loud enough to drown out everyone else. 'Benjamin Ripley, your twenty-four hours are officially up. Kindly surrender yourself – or we will blow you and your companions to smithereens.'

The bus immediately fell silent. Every pair of eyes focused on me.

Zoe shook her head, not wanting me to give myself up. Chip and Jawa seemed torn, unsure what I should do. Claire, meanwhile, gave me a heated stare. 'What are you still doing here?' she demanded. 'Get off the bus!'

I nodded and headed for the front door. There didn't seem to be anything else to do. 'OK!' I yelled. 'Hold your fire! I'm coming out!'

As I passed the driver's seat, however, Alexander suddenly lashed out and seized my arm. 'Follow me,' he whispered. 'The moment you step off this bus, we make a run for it.'

I froze on the bus steps. 'But if I do that, what's to stop SPYDER from blowing up my friends?'

'My orders are to protect *you*, not them.' With that, Alexander snapped out the gun he'd hidden under his bus driver's uniform and yanked me off the bus.

I tried to hold myself back, though Alexander was bigger and stronger than me and he was having a major adrenaline rush to boot. I was dragged along in his wake as he raced along the road, leaving the bus behind.

'Agent Ripley!' The voice on the megaphone echoed through the ravine. 'Stop, or we will shoot the bus!'

There was a chorus of panicked screams from my fellow students. Several shouted at me to stop.

Alexander kept pulling me onwards, however, his hand clamped around my wrist like a handcuff. 'They're just bluffing!' he said.

I glanced behind us. Now that we were outside the bus, I had a better sense of what was going on. SPYDER was attacking from above. There seemed to be only two men, perched on a ledge high above the road. They were readying a rocket launcher for another attack on the bus.

'They don't *look* like they're bluffing,' I said.

'Trust me,' he said. 'I've been in this situation plenty of times.'

I didn't know what to do. I normally wouldn't have trusted Alexander, but now, in the heat of battle, he certainly seemed sure of himself.

Directly ahead of us, the first explosion had cleaved

a massive divot out of the road so cleanly it looked as though a giant ice cream scoop had been used on it. There were only a few centimetres of flat ground left, a narrow ledge above a drop to the rocks below. It trembled under our feet as we ran across it, then buckled and gave way just as we made it to the far side. It sheared off the mountainside and tumbled down onto the rocks below.

Alexander and I had made it across safely, however. Now the road heading to the trestle was relatively wide and sturdy. I chanced another look behind us. The other students were piling out of the buses onto what remained of the road. As there was no cover and they were trapped, there was little choice but for them to raise their arms in surrender.

Up the mountainside, the two enemy agents had finished loading the grenade launcher and now aimed it down at the bus.

I dug my feet in, wrenching my arm away from Alexander. 'Wait!' I yelled. 'Don't shoot! Whatever you want me to do, I'll do!'

Unfortunately, the enemy agents were no longer paying attention to me. They were focused on my friends.

Before they could fire, however, a single shot rang

out from the bus. The SPYDER agents were too protected to be hit – but whoever had fired the shot wasn't aiming for them. The shooter was aiming for the grenade launcher itself. The shot was perfect. The launcher jostled out of the enemy's hands and bounced down the mountainside, clattering onto the roof of the bus.

There was only one person I knew who could make a shot like that.

A second later, Erica Hale bounded onto the roof and grabbed the grenade launcher. I had no idea how she'd got there; I hadn't seen her on board. She was dressed in camouflage survival gear with a bandolier of weapons lashed across her chest. She sprang from the roof, hit the ground running, and charged down the road toward Alexander and me.

The fact that a huge portion of the road was missing didn't slow her at all.

She whipped a small grappling hook off her bandolier and launched it in mid-stride. It snagged a tree jutting from the cliff above the gap in the road, trailing a wire behind it. Erica grasped the wire tightly and swung across the gap, landing perfectly on the other side.

It was all very impressive.

I expected Alexander would be beaming with pride at his daughter's exploits. Or at least thankful that she was safe. Instead, he regarded her as though he'd just caught her sneaking into the house after breaking curfew. 'What on earth do you think you're doing?' he demanded.

'What *you're* supposed to be doing,' Erica responded curtly. 'Taking down SPYDER.' With that, she swung the loaded grenade launcher around and aimed it uphill.

The two SPYDER agents had recovered from the loss of their launcher and pulled out their guns. Unfortunately for them, Erica had a much cleaner shot at them now than she'd had from the bus. The grenade burst from the launcher with a roar and screamed right into the bad guys' nest. The explosion sent them flying into the ravine.

Everyone back at the buses erupted in cheers.

Erica didn't even break a smile. She just slammed the launcher into Alexander's hands. 'Do something useful for once, Dad. Cover our escape.' Then she grabbed my hand and took off, dragging me towards the trestle.

It occurred to me that, although I'd known both Erica and Alexander for five months, this was the first time I'd ever seen them together. I was well aware that Erica had some issues with her father – she was the one who'd told me how inept he was in the first place – but the level of contempt she showed him surprised me. I thought back to our conversation in the morgue a few days before and how angry she'd been. Suddenly, it was all too clear who she'd been angry at – and things obviously hadn't improved since then.

Rather than do what Erica had requested, Alexander ran after us, lugging the grenade launcher under his arm. 'Erica! Wait…'

'What part of "Cover our escape" did you not understand?' his daughter demanded.

'You already took out the enemy,' Alexander explained.

Erica sighed in disgust. 'You think SPYDER sent only two agents to do this job?'

Before Alexander could answer the question, gunfire rattled from the mountainside above. There were, indeed, more agents. And now they were all shooting at us.

'Dad! Shoot them!' Erica yelled.

Alexander grimaced. 'I would, but . . . I don't know how to work a grenade launcher.'

'What?!' Erica's usual calm vanished. 'I thought

Grandpa taught you.'

'He *tried*,' Alexander admitted. 'I just didn't pay attention.'

'Is there *anything* you can't screw up?' Erica snapped.

We reached the trestle bridge. As we raced onto it, a line of bullets tore up the ground behind us.

'You watch your tone with me, young woman,' Alexander snapped. 'I was doing a perfectly good job here before you came along.'

'By leading the person you're protecting out onto an open road without any cover in direct line of enemy fire?'

Alexander swallowed, at a loss for words. 'Er . . .' he said. 'Well . . . I . . . uh . . . What exactly would you have done in that situation?'

'If I'd been in charge, I wouldn't have allowed us to get into that situation,' Erica replied.

We ran along the bridge. Far below us, the rocky cliffs gave way to churning river. More gunfire raked the ground. It was a long way to the far side.

'And what's *your* plan here?' Alexander demanded. 'There's even less cover out on the bridge than on the road.'

'We're not staying on the bridge for long,' Erica explained.

In that moment, I grasped what Erica had in mind. 'Oh no,' I said. 'Tell me we're not jumping . . .'

'OK,' Erica said. 'We're not jumping.'

Then she ran right off the side of the bridge, dragging me with her.

Water Safety

Shenandoah National Wilderness

June 14

1145 hours

Your perception of time can shift greatly, depending on what you're doing.

When you're having fun, a few hours can seem like mere seconds. And when you're plummeting off a bridge toward a raging river while enemy agents shoot at you, every second seems like an eternity.

Somehow, on the way down, I really did have time to look around and focus on things besides wondering if I was about to die. I glanced at the buses on the exploded road and saw that, while the enemy had been distracted by Erica, Alexander and I, the other students appeared to be escaping on foot. I looked up and saw that Alexander, apparently unsure what else to do, had leapt off the trestle and was plunging after us. I turned to Erica, who calmly met my gaze and said, 'Point your toes and keep your arms to your side so the impact doesn't break them.'

I did what she told me – and then we hit the water.

Thanks to Erica's advice, instead of smacking into the surface, we sliced through it and shot downwards. I'd expected to feel the pain of impact, but I didn't really. Instead, I felt the shock of the cold water and the terror that, after surviving the fall, I was now going to drown.

My feet touched the bottom of the river. I glanced upwards and saw the surface thirty feet above my head. My ears popped from the pressure of all the water around me.

Then the current yanked me downstream. I was tumbled like a sock in the washing machine, having no idea which way was up. I bounced off rocks and swirled through whirlpools. I was desperate for air, but every time I thought I was about to break the surface, the current would yank me back down again. After this had happened five times, I got sucked into an abyss.

Darkness surrounded me. The water pressure felt as though it would crush me flat. I could feel myself beginning to black out . . .

And then, by some miracle, the river spat me out. I burst into daylight, gasping for air. I found myself in a calm eddy of the rapids and was able to paddle to shore. I clambered out of the water and collapsed on the grass, hugging dry land.

A second later, Erica jogged out of the water. Rather than looking bedraggled and half-drowned, she appeared refreshed, as if she'd just had a dip in the pool. 'Wow!' she exclaimed. 'That was intense!'

'We nearly died ten times just now,' I groaned.

'But we didn't,' Erica told me. 'So we've got that going for us.'

I took in our position. We'd emerged on the opposite side of the river from where we'd been attacked by SPYDER, but there was no way to cross back; the water was too wide and treacherous. We were just past the mouth of the canyon. Upriver, the rock walls rose steeply on both sides, but here, at least, the banks were wide enough for a fringe of forest. The canyon was too steep and twisty for me to see the trestle we'd leapt from. I wondered how far we'd been washed downstream. A mile? Two? For all I knew, it could have been ten. I was about to ask Erica's opinion when a cry rang out.

'Help!' The voice was Alexander's, coming from close by.

I struggled to my feet. Erica was already moving toward the sound. She bounded over a few boulders and I followed.

Alexander was clinging to a rock by the shore while the current tried to drag him downstream.

Erica got to him much faster than I did. She sprang from shore onto the rock and knelt over her father, but as she reached out to help him, she seemed to think better of it and pulled back. 'Before I save you, I need you to promise me something,' she said.

Alexander's eyes went wide. 'Now? I'm in danger here!'

'Seems like the best time to get your attention,' Erica replied. 'Promise that, from here on out, I'm in charge of this operation. I get to make the decisions. You follow my orders, no questions asked.'

'Sure,' Alexander said. 'Whatever you want. Just help me!'

Erica frowned and fixed Alexander with a hard stare. 'I asked you to *promise*,' she told him.

Alexander actually wavered, as though making this

promise was worse than being swept downstream. Then the current surged and threatened to pull him off the rock. 'All right!' he cried desperately. 'I promise! You're in charge of the operation!'

I wondered what a promise from an ethically-challenged person such as Alexander was worth, but Erica seemed satisfied with it. 'That's better,' she said, extending her arm.

Alexander grabbed on. Since he was so much bigger than Erica, I had to help pull him out of the water.

He clambered onto the rock, no longer looking anything like the suave, debonair master spy he usually pretended to be. He was dishevelled and waterlogged. He'd lost the wig and latex jowls from his disguise in the river, while the fake moustache had somehow migrated to his forehead, where it now looked like a renegade eyebrow. In addition, he was visibly shaken from his near-death experience and peeved at Erica for how she'd treated him in front of me. 'I can't believe you'd risk your own father's life like that,' he snapped, wringing out his sleeves.

'You wouldn't have drowned,' Erica chided. 'You were a stone's throw from the calm section of the river.'

This actually made Alexander more upset. 'And you

let me suffer anyhow? I thought I raised you better than that.'

'You didn't raise me at all,' Erica said coldly. 'Mom did.'

Alexander huffed and stormed off the rocks onto land. 'Come along, Benjamin,' he said to me, pausing to shake a small fish out of his trousers. 'Let's find our way to safety.'

Before I could even respond, Erica lashed out an arm, preventing me from taking so much as a step toward Alexander. 'Have you already forgotten?' she asked her father. 'You're not giving the orders here. You promised I was in charge.'

'That agreement was legally non-binding!' Alexander protested. 'It was made under duress. Therefore, as the senior agent here, I order you to stand down . . .'

'You're unbelievable,' Erica said. 'It doesn't matter whether you're a senior agent – or whether the contract is legal or not. We're not listening to you.'

Alexander flushed red. 'Erica! I am your father! You are just a girl! Now, I know you've had some minor success in the spy game—'

'Success which *you* took the credit for!' Erica shouted.

'—but you are not a fully-fledged agent yet,'

Alexander finished. 'You are way out of your league here!'

Erica seethed; for once, her unflappable calm was gone. '*I'm* way out of my league here?' she yelled. 'I'm only in this situation because you messed everything up! SPYDER would have captured Ben by now if it wasn't for me!'

'That is patently untrue,' Alexander snapped. 'I was leading us to safety when you jumped off that bridge like a maniac.'

'SPYDER had an ambush waiting for us on the other side of the bridge,' Erica said. 'They would have killed you and taken Ben.'

Alexander gaped, at a loss for words. He closed his mouth, then opened it again. Then he desperately tried to regain his composure. 'I knew that,' he said.

'No you didn't,' Erica told him. 'What you don't know could fill a library. Come on, Ben. If you *really* want to get to safety, you know who to listen to.' With that, she hopped ashore and started toward the trees.

I looked toward Alexander, feeling slightly guilty for what I had to do. But the simple truth was, I wouldn't have trusted him to get me out of a cupboard. So I followed Erica.

This was probably the most devastating blow to

Alexander's ego yet. He'd *known* how his daughter felt about him, but it was a shock to see that I felt the same way. His eyes grew big and sad, like those of a puppy who's just been scolded for weeing on the rug. 'Et tu, Benjamin?' he asked. 'Et tu?'

I paused at the edge of the woods. 'You *did* take all the credit for capturing Murray Hill,' I said.

'That was for your own good!' Alexander protested. 'I didn't want SPYDER to know of your role in that for fear that they'd retaliate.'

I shook my head, not believing this for a second. 'SPYDER knows everything about everything,' I said. 'That's why we're here right now. The only people you really fooled were the top brass at the CIA.'

Alexander paused again, apparently surprised I'd put all this together. Then his look of betrayal was suddenly replaced by one of revulsion. 'Oh dear,' he said. 'I believe I have a leech in my underpants.'

With that, he quickly scurried behind a tree.

Erica took advantage of the distraction to pull me onward into the woods. Behind us, we heard Alexander give a shriek of terror. 'Good lord! It's huge!'

'Do you think this is the right thing to do?' I asked Erica as we trudged into the trees. 'Woodchuck just told everyone that it's not a good idea to split up . . .'

'We're not splitting up,' Erica said. 'My father will be back with us in five seconds.'

Sure enough, five seconds later, Alexander came crashing through the woods, fastening his belt and looking like he'd just witnessed something horrible. 'You should have seen this leech,' he gasped. 'It was the size of a cigar. I'll bet it siphoned a pint of blood out of me.'

Erica shot me a told-you-so look.

'Where were you on the bus?' I asked her. 'I didn't see you board.'

'I stowed away in the back,' she replied. 'With all the survival gear.'

'Did you know SPYDER was going to attack us?' I asked.

'No, but I had a hunch they might. It seemed like too good an opportunity for them to pass up.' Erica sighed. 'The brilliant minds at Spy School played right into SPYDER's hands. They responded to the threat of you being abducted by taking you off the protected campus and out into the middle of nowhere – where you could be more easily abducted. Plus, they assigned Bozo here to the mission.'

'I'm getting very tired of your tone, young woman,' Alexander snapped.

'Well, I'm getting very tired of you acting like this wasn't your fault,' Erica shot back.

'It's not my fault SPYDER ambushed the bus,' Alexander argued.

'It sort of is,' Erica replied. 'The moment anyone suggested taking Ben off-campus, you should have said "no". But you let it happen – and instead of investigating SPYDER like you were supposed to, you decided to tag along so you could play the hero. Then, when the attack finally came, you responded by abandoning an entire busload of students and nearly dragging Ben into an ambush. So now, thanks to you, we're miles from civilization, we're soaking wet, all of our weapons and communications equipment have been swept downriver – and SPYDER's agents are certainly still on the hunt for us.'

With that, Erica actually seemed to get through to her father. He lowered his eyes in shame and fell into an embarrassed silence.

On the other hand, Erica's assessment of the situation startled me into speaking up. 'We don't have any weapons?'

Erica shook her head. 'Not a one.'

'You don't have anything hidden away somewhere?' I asked. 'Maybe a vial of poison in your utility belt?'

'My utility belt got snagged on a rock in the rapids. I had to jettison it, or I would have drowned.' Erica seemed more upset about this than the fact that we were lost in the wilderness with enemy agents hunting us. 'Grandpa gave me that utility belt for my twelfth birthday. It had *everything* in it: my phone, food rations, Chinese throwing stars . . .'

'But at least you have a plan, don't you?' I asked hopefully. 'You always have a plan.'

'Of course I have a plan,' Erica said.

'What is it?'

'Try to get back to civilization without SPYDER capturing or killing any of us.'

I waited for more to come, but none did. 'Um . . . Could you possibly elaborate on that?'

Erica shrugged. 'That's all I've got so far. I haven't had much time to work things out, what with jumping off the bridge and nearly getting drowned and all.'

It was taking every bit of will I had not to freak out. The situation was as dire as any I'd ever been in.

The ground began to rise sharply ahead of us. The thick forest quickly gave way to a steep, rocky face. Erica continued towards it without another word.

'Wait,' I said, recalling the brief survival training I'd had on the bus. 'Why are we leaving the river? If anyone comes looking for us, won't they look there?'

'That'd be the best course of action in normal circumstances,' Erica said. 'Unfortunately, the people most likely to come looking for us are SPYDER.'

'Then shouldn't we at least be heading downstream?' I ventured. 'That'd be the fastest way to civilization.'

'True. But SPYDER knows that as well,' Erica explained. 'Their first reaction will be to cut off that escape route, so we're going to trick them by doubling back the way we came.'

'Hold on,' Alexander said. 'SPYDER's too crafty for this to work. They'll probably expect us to double back. So what we should really do is *double* double back and go downstream.'

'I thought we'd established that I'm in charge,' Erica said. 'And double doubling back is moronic. We're going this way.'

'No,' Alexander said firmly. 'As discussed, that decision to place you in charge was made under duress. I may have made some mistakes today, but I'm still an elite, highly-decorated professional spy who has won the Medal of Freedom four times for my work. Furthermore, I'm your father, so you'd best listen to me here. The organization we are up again is conniving, unconscionable and extremely dangerous. Heading deeper into the wilderness as part of some guessing game with them is a terrible mistake. So I'm not asking you, I'm *telling* you, we are turning around right now.'

With that, he wheeled around and started back into the woods, completely expecting us to follow.

'Dad!' Erica called. 'Wait! There's another reason we're headed this way!'

'Oh really?' Alexander asked. 'And what would that be?'

'The bears that are following us.'

'Don't be absurd,' Alexander snapped. 'There are no bears in this part of the country.'

A loud, angry growl echoed through the trees. A large bear emerged from the forest only a few metres away from Alexander. Then two more appeared behind it.

Alexander went as pale as a dead fish.

Erica sighed. 'Don't you *ever* get tired of being wrong?' she asked.

Large, Dangerous Beasts

Shenandoah National Wilderness
June 14
1210 hours

The bears were black bears. I'd read about them and seen them in zoos, but I'd never encountered one in the wild. I dimly remembered some National Geographic article claiming that black bears generally weren't aggressive or dangerous – unless you ran into a mother with cubs.

The three bears facing us were a mother with cubs. The cubs weren't cute little balls of fluff, however. Each was now a teenager (at least in bear years). Though none of them was as huge as a grizzly, they were all at least 150 kilos and armed with sharp teeth and long claws capable of doing serious damage. In addition, their guard was up, like we'd threatened them somehow. They sized us up warily, as if trying to determine whether or not they should attack us.

Alexander backed toward Erica and me, trying to remain calm. 'Don't worry,' he said, although his voice was quavering with fear, 'I know exactly what to do in this situation. On the count of three, everyone run as fast as you can.'

'You don't run from bears!' Erica hissed under her breath. 'We need to hold our ground and back away slowly.'

'Back away slowly?' Alexander echoed. 'We're not trying to escape turtles here. How is moving slowly better than moving quickly?'

'Because running will provoke their attack response,' Erica explained. 'And you can't run faster than a bear.'

'Of course I can,' Alexander sniffed. 'Where on earth did you hear that garbage?'

'The CIA agents' manual,' Erica replied.

Alexander couldn't quite hide his surprise. 'There's a section on *bears* in the CIA agents' manual?'

'There's a section on *everything* in the CIA agents' manual,' Erica told him. 'I'm not surprised you haven't read it, though. There are a lot of big words in it.'

The bears were getting closer, the mother in front of the cubs. She was growling angrily, although she slowed as she neared us.

'OK now,' Erica told us. 'Like I said, stay calm and back away nice and slow.'

'And what do we do if they come after us?' I whispered.

'First we try to fight them off – and if that doesn't work, we play dead.'

'Play dead?' Alexander asked. 'That can't be right.'

'Could you keep your voice down?' Erica asked. 'It's agitating the bears.'

'The bears are *already* agitated,' Alexander protested. 'And if we play dead, we're just going to look like a buffet to them. We need to run. *Now*. Before they get much closer.'

'Dad,' Erica pleaded. 'For once in your life, please listen to me . . .'

Before she could finish, the mother bear growled at us. Alexander cracked. 'Stay away from us!' he shouted and bolted away.

The bears instinctively took off after him.

'What a pinhead,' Erica muttered. Then she grabbed a rock off the ground and chased after them all.

I did the same as Erica, because my instinct was to follow her lead. It wasn't until a good three seconds later that it occurred to me that chasing after three angry bears was possibly even dumber than running away from them.

Erica was unfazed by any such thoughts. Not only did she pursue the bears, she actually tried to get their attention as well. 'Hey!' she shouted. 'Leave him alone!'

Meanwhile, Alexander was shouting at the bears. 'Sit!' he ordered them, as if hoping they were trained bears who had escaped from a circus. 'Stay! Bad bears! Bad bears!'

As Erica had warned, he couldn't outrun them. Soon, they were nipping at his heels. Unfortunately, Alexander forgot step one: Try to fight them off – and went right for step two: Play dead. He dropped to the ground so quickly that the mother bear actually tripped over him, like he was a human speed bump.

Her cubs were on him in a second. I hate to think what they might have done to him if Erica hadn't arrived and hit one of them behind the ear with her rock.

I threw mine as well, because I wanted to appear helpful in front of Erica. It glanced off the other's cub's thigh and hit Alexander in the shoulder.

'Owww!' he wailed, and then remembered he was supposed to be dead.

The bears wheeled toward Erica and me, as though surprised we'd been dumb enough to come after them.

Erica grabbed some more rocks off the ground and threw them. 'Get out of here!' she yelled. 'Or I'll make rugs out of all three of you!'

The bears didn't seem particularly bothered by the rocks, which bounced off their thick hides like baseballs thrown against a wall. They did, however, seem taken aback by Erica. They stared at her in confusion, apparently trying to decide whether she was a legitimate threat or a harmless lunatic.

I threw a few more rocks as well, though I let Erica do the shouting for the both of us.

'Go on!' she ordered them. 'Don't make me come after you!'

The mother bear stopped sniffing around Alexander and reared back on her hind legs, displaying her impressive muscles, claws and teeth. She gave a roar that rattled the trees.

At her feet, Alexander trembled so violently that it looked like he was experiencing his own personal earthquake.

Personally, I leapt a good distance backwards,

stumbled over a log and went down on my bottom.

But Erica stood her ground. She fixed the mother bear with a hard stare and roared right back at her. It wasn't quite as loud as the mother bear's roar, but it was more frightening. I hadn't known until that moment that the human body could make a noise like that.

The cubs scurried away, terrified, and cowered behind their mother.

Momma Bear cocked her head at Erica, curious, then seemed to bow in respect. She dropped back on all fours, turned away and shambled into the forest. Her children obediently followed.

I snapped to my feet before Erica could see that I'd fallen. 'That was amazing,' I said. 'Did you learn *that* from the CIA manual?'

'No,' Erica said. 'I came up with that myself. I figure bears can't be so different to humans. If you show fear, they get confidence. But if you act confident, they get scared.' With that, she approached her father, who was still lying on the ground, trying to look dead. 'They're gone, Dad. You don't have to play dead any more.'

Alexander kept his eyes closed and tried to speak without moving his lips. 'Are you sure? They might come back again.'

'I don't think they want anything more to do with Erica,' I offered.

Alexander sat up. The bears had slashed his clothes here and there, but he'd escaped the attack with only a few minor scratches and a good amount of bear drool in his hair. He looked to Erica, at once respectful of her and ashamed of himself. 'Thank you,' he said. 'If it hadn't been for you . . . Well, apparently you're right about me. I really am an utter screw-up.'

'Oh, that's not completely true,' Erica said. 'You were quite good at playing dead.'

'I was?' Alexander asked.

'Yes,' Erica replied. 'Though I suppose it wasn't much of a stretch. After all, your brain's been dead for years.'

Alexander sagged, even more ashamed than before. It was shocking to see how the man who had once represented all that was wonderful and glorious about espionage to me could now look so pitiful after a dressing down by his own daughter.

If this had been a heartfelt family movie, Erica and Alexander would have bonded over the near-death experience, with Erica suddenly realizing how sad she'd be if her father had died and Alexander learning a valuable lesson about honesty from his daughter.

Instead, Erica had used the event to finally drive home to her father how little she actually thought of him – and she seemed pleased by the result. A slight smirk formed on her lips as she started back up the rocky slope again.

I followed her. It was quite clear that she was the only one of the three of us who had the slightest idea how to survive in the wilderness.

Alexander had obviously grasped this as well. He took up the rear, picking his way up the hill behind us, although his mood was so sullen, I found myself worrying about him.

The climb was arduous – or, at least it was for Alexander and me. Erica moved up the rock face with startling ease. She almost seemed to be having fun. I moved faster than Alexander. This was partly because I was in better shape – I'd spent a lot of time in the gym over the past few months – and partly because he seemed too miserable to care.

When I finally got to the top, muscles aching, I found Erica lounging under the cover of a small tree, munching on some mushrooms she'd foraged. She offered a handful to me. 'Fungus?'

I'd been so preoccupied with trying not to die in various ways over the past hour, I'd forgotten all about eating. I'd never been a fan of mushrooms before, but now my stomach grumbled hungrily at the sight of them. 'Thanks,' I said, and wolfed them down. They were delicious. 'Are there any more?'

'Not here,' Erica said. 'But I'm sure we'll find more along the way.' She patted the ground next to her, indicating I ought to sit down and rest.

Before joining her, I peered back over the lip of the rock face. Alexander was still fifty metres below. 'Did you save any mushrooms for your father?' I asked.

'No. He's spent my whole life telling me how great he is at everything. I figure he can find his own.'

I sat in the small bit of shade beside Erica and was instantly aware that I reeked of sweat. She, on the other hand, smelled fantastic. Like she'd just been on a tour of a perfume factory. 'I think your father could use a bit of encouragement,' I said.

'Feel free to give it to him.'

'I meant from you.'

Erica fixed me with one of her patented icy stares.

'Why are you so angry with him?' I asked.

Erica flinched as though I'd just stuck my finger in a fresh wound. She turned away. 'I don't want to talk about it.'

I knew better than to keep prying. If Erica didn't

want to tell you something, she wasn't going to tell you. She had the best grades in the class in Intro to Withstanding Torture. So I changed the subject. 'Do you have any idea where we're going?'

'I have more than an idea. I know *exactly* where we're going.'

'Even without a Global Positioning System?'

'People managed to survive for a long time in the wilderness without GPS. They used these things called "maps".'

'Ha ha. There's a slight problem with us using maps right now.'

'What?'

'We don't have any.'

Erica turned back to me. 'Well, we don't have any physical maps. But we do have some mental ones.' She tapped her head. 'When I heard we were coming out here, I grabbed every map of the area I could find. Spy Camp has quite a cache of them.'

'You left them on the bus?' I asked.

Erica nodded. 'I didn't exactly have time to pack during the ambush. Luckily, I spent a good amount of time poring over them on the way here. So I have a pretty good idea of the terrain. From what I can tell, we're on the eastern ridge of Mount Sukoff. There ought to be an abandoned fire tower a mile and a half that way.' She pointed to the west.

I looked at her curiously. 'You can remember the map that accurately?'

'Why are you surprised? As I recall, you have an extremely good memory as well.'

'Only for numbers. This is different. Do you have a photographic memory?'

'I think the correct term is "perfect recall". And no, I don't. It's more like yours. I can't remember *everything* I see. Just certain things.'

'Like what?'

'Maps. Photos. Books.'

'You can remember entire *books*?'

Erica turned to me. 'You can't?'

'No!'

'Bummer. It makes studying for tests easier.'

I stared at Erica for a moment. It shouldn't have been any surprise that her memory was so strong. It explained how she knew so much and was so sure of herself all the time. And yet, I somehow hadn't put it together.

With a gasp, Alexander emerged over the lip of the cliff. He rolled onto the horizontal ground and lay there, panting like a dog on a hot day.

'It's about time you got here,' Erica said. 'C'mon. No time to dawdle. We still have a lot of ground to cover.' She snapped to her feet and started across the ridge.

Alexander groaned. 'Please. Just give me five minutes to rest.'

'We've already squandered enough time,' Erica told him. 'Every minute we waste is a minute SPYDER gets closer to us. If you want to lie there in the open with enemy snipers about, that's your decision, but we're moving on.'

At the mention of enemy snipers, Alexander jumped to his feet. Despite his exhaustion, he quickly caught up to us.

I was still pretty tired myself, but I fought through it and stuck close to Erica. For the most part, there was thick tree cover along the ridge – although there were also a number of open, exposed areas we had to hurry across. Luckily, we didn't see anyone from SPYDER along the way . . . and, more importantly, they didn't see us.

'How many of them do you think there are out here?' I asked Erica, after crossing one barren patch.

'I have no idea,' she admitted. 'The fact is, we know virtually nothing about SPYDER: how big an organization it is; how much money they have; how many men they can spare for an operation like this. Do they use their own men – or do they contract out? Who do they work for? Who runs it? How long has it been around? All giant question marks.'

'Doesn't the CIA have some sort of expert on SPYDER?'

Erica looked at me curiously. 'Yes. *You.*'

My step faltered. 'Me? How can *I* be the expert? I've only had one conversation with a SPYDER agent—'

'Which is one more conversation than anyone else at the CIA has had. Virtually everything the CIA knows about SPYDER is what Murray told you. Everything else is mere speculation. In fact, that conversation was the first direct evidence the CIA had that SPYDER even exists.'

I walked on a bit more, trying to fathom this. 'So . . . when the CIA says they're trying to protect me from SPYDER, they don't even know who that is?'

'No. So far, Murray Hill is the only SPYDER agent ever to have been captured – and you're the only person he spoke to. The CIA put its top interrogators on him. He didn't say a word.'

'That's not quite true,' Alexander said.

'OK, technically he said a word,' Erica admitted.

'He said plenty, in fact. He told the interrogators all sorts of things about SPYDER. But they turned out to be lies. Unfortunately, the CIA didn't realize that until it was too late. Murray had agents off on wild goose chases all over the world. The CIA had blown millions of dollars and who knows how many hours of manpower before they realized they'd been scammed.'

'So where does that leave us?' I asked.

'I'm not sure,' Erica said. 'In theory, this ought to be a bonanza for the CIA. They know SPYDER is active, so you'd think they'd send every man they have out here to engage them and try to capture at least one enemy agent. But SPYDER has already given the CIA one black eye today, so maybe they're holding back and trying to figure out what to do next before they get embarrassed again.'

'Then we might be on our own out here?' I asked.

'For the time being,' Erica said. 'Although, it's likely that the CIA doesn't *know* we're out here. They probably think we're either captured or dead. We need to make contact as soon as possible. Which is why we're heading *there*.'

We emerged from the trees to find an old fire tower sitting on top of a small rise close by. It was a small room perched four storeys up a steel framework, just high enough to see over the surrounding trees. It looked as though it hadn't been used in years. Most of the paint had flaked away and the steel was coated with rust.

'The forest service used to post men up here to keep an eye out for fires,' Erica explained, 'But they can do that with satellites now. They've probably forgotten this place even exists. Let's just hope they didn't bother to clean it out before they decommissioned it.' She hurried up the small rise towards the tower.

'Wait,' Alexander said. He seemed almost embarrassed to speak to his daughter now. 'If you know about this place, what's to say that SPYDER doesn't as well? They might be waiting up there to ambush us right now.'

Erica didn't slow for a second. 'There's over a dozen of these old things out here. I doubt even SPYDER would go through the trouble to set up ambushes in them all.'

'But suppose they *did* . . .' Alexander began.

'That's a risk I'm willing to take,' Erica said. 'We need to establish contact with the CIA.'

'Perhaps not,' Alexander said. 'They've activated Klondike.'

Erica stopped at the bottom of the fire tower stairs.

It was one of the rare occasions when I'd ever seen her express surprise. 'When?'

'A few days ago.'

'Why didn't anyone tell me?'

'Because you're a *teenager*,' Alexander said. 'Only agents with top security clearance were supposed to know.'

Erica frowned angrily. Then she started up the stairs anyhow.

I stayed on the ground. 'What's Klondike?' I asked.

'A very bad idea,' Erica replied.

I looked to Alexander for more, but he didn't offer it. 'Erica!' he yelled. 'Please come back down here!'

Erica ignored him, continuing upwards. The stairs ended underneath the small room. There was a trapdoor above which was padlocked shut, but the hasp was rusted and it only took Erica two karate kicks to break it. The trapdoor dropped open and, despite her father's continued protests, Erica climbed up into the small room. A second later, she called down, 'You can stop worrying! There's no one here!'

Alexander and I climbed the stairs quickly.

The crow's nest at the top of the tower was five metres square with windows on all sides, affording views for twenty miles in every direction. It hadn't been cleaned out. Everything had simply been left behind when it was abandoned. But though no humans had been there in years, plenty of other things had. Two of the window panes had fallen out, allowing access to any forest creature that could squeeze through the gap. The rafters were filled with bird's nests and most of the logbooks had been eaten by rodents. The floor was covered with years' worth of animal dung. A quick assessment of it indicated everything from bats to bobcats had used the lookout tower as a toilet.

Still, the two things we needed were in working condition.

The first was the water supply. There was a cistern on the roof to catch rainwater, which ran down a pipe into a small tap with a water filter attached. None of us had had anything to drink in hours and we were parched. We each guzzled about a gallon.

There was also a ham radio. It was ancient and it looked ready to disintegrate, but when Erica turned the crank on the side it came to life. Erica quickly set the dials to the CIA's frequency. Alexander grabbed the receiver before she could.

'Mayday,' he said. 'This is Agent 2364, Codename Silver Fox, calling for emergency back-up . . .'

'Hello Agent Hale!' The voice that answered was

electronically garbled so that we couldn't even tell if it belonged to a man or a woman. 'We've been hoping to hear from you!'

Alexander sighed with relief. 'It's good to hear your voice as well,' he said.

'What's your location?' the voice asked.

Alexander started to answer, but Erica snatched the receiver from him. Her face was etched with concern. 'What's your security clearance code?' she asked.

There was a pause, and then the voice at the other end laughed. 'Ah. This must be the famous Erica Hale. I knew we couldn't trick *you* with such a simple ruse.'

'Wait,' Alexander said. 'You're not the CIA?'

'No,' the voice replied cheerfully. 'I'm with SPYDER. Is Ben Ripley there with you too?'

'No,' Erica replied. 'We got separated from Ben in the river. We think he got washed farther downstream.'

'Well you'd better track him down,' the SPYDER agent replied. 'We need you to bring him to us.'

'And why would I want to do that?' Erica asked.

'Because we've captured a few of his friends,' the agent said. 'And we'll kill them if you don't.'

Negotiation

Shenandoah Wilderness Fire Tower 14
June 14
1430 hours

A disturbed silence settled over the room. Alexander and I were too shocked to say anything. Erica, however, seemed lost in thought, as if she were quickly trying to figure out what her next move should be.

'Are you still there?' the voice asked. There was a taunting quality to it, as though the speaker was having a great time. It reminded me of Murray Hill, and I wondered if it could possibly be him. 'Hello? Erica? Hello?'

The words jolted Erica back to action. There was

now a look of confidence in her eye, which I hoped meant she had a plan. 'I'm here,' she said. 'But I'm wondering if you're telling me the truth.'

'You think I'm lying about the hostages?' the voice asked.

'You guys aren't exactly known for your honesty,' Erica replied.

'Touché,' said the SPYDER agent. 'How's this for proof?'

There was some scuffling as the handset was passed to someone else. 'Erica? Is that you?' a voice asked.

Zoe.

She sounded so frightened, I wanted to shout out to her, to tell her everything was going to be all right. But revealing myself would have ruined whatever Erica's plan was.

'Yes, it's me,' Erica replied. 'How are they treating you?'

'All right, I guess,' Zoe said. 'They haven't tortured us or anything.'

'Who else is there with you?' Erica asked.

'Warren, Jawa, Chip, Claire and Hank.'

'Are they all right?'

'Yes. Well, Warren's been crying a lot, but other than that, I guess we're OK.'

'What about everyone else who was on the bus?'

'I don't know,' Zoe said. 'I guess they're all still back in the wilderness. SPYDER only took us.'

Erica took her thumb off the radio switch so she could speak to us in private. 'Makes sense,' she said. 'No need to trouble yourself with forty hostages when six will do. The others ought to be OK. Woodchuck can get them to safety.'

'Assuming he's not in league with SPYDER,' I said.

Erica nodded, conceding that might be the case. Then she got back on the radio. 'Zoe, how many SPYDER agents are there?'

'I don't know. They have us blindfolded. Although I've recognized at least four different voices . . .'

Zoe was suddenly silenced. It sounded as though someone had clamped a hand over her mouth. Then the garbled voice got back on again. 'OK, that's enough of that. You heard the girl. So you know I'm telling the truth. Now here's how things are going to play out: at the intersection of Virginia State Road 522 and 37, there is a farm with a large red barn. We will be at that barn with your friends in exactly six hours. If you are not there with Ben Ripley at that time, we will kill the first hostage . . .'

'Whoa,' Erica said. 'Six hours? Let's be reasonable here.'

'I'm trying to be,' the voice said.

'Six hours isn't anywhere close to reasonable,' Erica said. 'First of all, I don't know where Ben is. He could have washed halfway to Washington DC for all I know.'

There was a map table on one side of the crow's nest. Back in the day, the lookout posted at the tower would have used it to pinpoint fires. It had one drawer, which turned out to be full of maps and ancient rodent pellets. I started searching through the maps quickly, trying to find one of Virginia that hadn't been eaten.

'Don't jerk me around,' the SPYDER agent said. 'Ben's standing right beside you, isn't he?'

'He's not,' Erica said. 'But even if he *was*, I'm nowhere near civilization, thanks to you. I have no food, no water and no method of transportation except for my own two feet. It's a miracle I even found this radio. Now, I'd be happy to radio the CIA to have someone come pick me up, but I'm guessing you don't want that.'

There was a pause at the other end. When the voice got back on, it sounded considerably less taunting than it had before. 'You're right. We don't. In fact, if you contact the CIA – or any other law-enforcement agency . . .'

'You'll kill a hostage,' Erica said dryly. 'I know the drill. Now, I'll concede to that, but without any help, I've got a lot of work cut out for me. Six hours just isn't going to fly. I'm going to need six days.'

'Six days?' the voice asked. 'Unacceptable. We'll give you eighteen hours.'

'Oh come on,' Erica said. 'Where do you think I am, the Ritz? I'm in the wilderness here. It's not like there's a herd of deer with a rental car agency nearby. I'll need at least a day and a half to track down Ben and another 24 hours to get back to civilization.'

'Hold on,' the agent said.

Whilst we were waiting, I found a map of Virginia that was still in decent shape and spread it out on the table. Alexander and I quickly scanned it, trying to find the location the SPYDER agent had mentioned. Alexander found it first. He triumphantly thumped his finger down at the junction of state roads 522 and 37. It was just north of a town called Winchester, which looked to be a good hundred miles away from us.

The agent got back on the radio. 'The best I can do is two days.'

'That's ridiculous,' Erica said. 'I need three.'

'You have two and that's our final offer. And only you, your father and Ben better show up. Contact anyone else – the CIA, the FBI, the army, the police – and we'll know.'

'Two days from this very moment?' Erica asked.

'Yes,' said the voice. 'Let's say two thirty in the afternoon on June 16.'

'Do I have any leeway at all? I don't want you whacking my friends because I'm five minutes late.'

The voice sighed. 'OK. Two-thirty give or take fifteen minutes. How's that?'

'Still pretty lousy,' Erica said flatly. 'Seeing as once we swap Ben for the others, you're going to kill him, aren't you?'

'Er . . .' The SPYDER agent hedged a moment before answering. Erica seemed to have caught him off guard with such a direct question. 'Well . . . that's really up to Ben. He's still welcome to accept the very generous offer we made him. To be honest, though, we're getting a little tired of waiting for him to make up his mind.'

'Could you accept me in his stead?' Erica asked. 'I'm a much better spy than he is. Frankly, that kid has the fighting skills of a guinea pig.'

Alexander looked at Erica, unable to hide his shock

at what she was saying. Erica shook her head, letting him know she wasn't actually serious about this.

'True,' the SPYDER agent replied. 'And I must say, that's a very tempting offer. But the fact is, Ben has some very special abilities you don't. Abilities that he might not even be aware he has.'

'Like what?' Erica asked.

The SPYDER agent laughed. 'Nice try, Hale. But I'm not that easy. Now go find Ben. We'll see you in two days.'

With that, the radio went dead.

Erica looked at me curiously. 'I don't suppose you've figured out what these incredibly amazing special abilities you have are yet?'

'No,' I admitted, feeling as though I was letting her down. I racked my brain, trying to think of any incredible thing I'd ever done. Yes, I could do complicated multiplication and division in my head, but as Erica had pointed out, anyone with a calculator could get the same answers. As far as I knew, I couldn't instinctively crack codes or hack computers or disarm ninjas. 'What I don't understand is, how could SPYDER know I have this ability when I don't even know I have it?'

'Murray Hill,' Alexander said. 'He was obviously

studying you closely while he was working as a mole.'

Erica looked at her father, intrigued.

He flashed her a proud smile. 'See? Your old man might not be as big a fool as you think.'

'Even a broken watch is right twice a day,' Erica said, and Alexander's spirits immediately deflated again.

Erica snatched the map off the table and hurried out of the trap door. 'Come on,' she said. 'We need to get moving.'

Alexander and I hustled down the steps behind her. 'How hard is it going to be for us to make it to the hostage swap in two days?' I asked.

'Oh, not hard at all,' Erica said. 'It's not really that far. I was just bluffing. We could easily be there in a day if we had to.'

'Then why did you ask for two?' Alexander asked.

'Because we're not going there right away,' Erica said, in the tone that one might have used to explain things to a two-year-old. 'We have one other place to visit before that.'

'And that's why we're in such a hurry?' I asked.

'No,' Erica said. 'Right now, we're evacuating the fire tower before SPYDER attacks it.'

Alexander gave a gasp of surprise and picked up his

pace. 'You think that's possible?'

'Anything's possible with SPYDER.' Erica reached the ground first and led the way towards the safety of the forest. 'Getting a pinpoint location on a ham radio isn't as easy as doing it for a mobile phone, but it can be done. Or at least, they could figure there weren't many ham radios in the vicinity and deduce that we're at one of them.'

'But they *knew* we were going to use a radio, didn't they?' I said. 'They intercepted our call to the CIA the moment we made it.'

'I don't think they knew that we'd use a radio for sure,' Erica explained. 'I think that, as usual, SPYDER was simply prepared for any eventuality. They must have been monitoring every method of communication. I'll bet that, if we'd used a mobile phone to call, they would have intercepted that too. Or a pay phone. Or an email.'

'How long do you think we have until they get here?' Alexander asked.

'That depends on what they're sending after us,' Erica replied. 'If it's an assault team, it might be half an hour. If it's a helicopter, it might be a minute or two . . .'

There was a sudden roar in the distance. Through the trees, I spotted something racing across the sky towards us, a trail of black smoke in its wake. It covered the miles between us in seconds, screamed overhead and slammed into the crow's nest.

The lookout tower exploded.

'. . . though it appears they have missiles,' Erica continued. 'We should run.'

She took off like a shot. Alexander and I followed. We'd barely gone a step before the concussion of the blast hit us, nearly knocking us off our feet. A surge of oven-hot air braised my backside, then flaming debris began to rain down and chunks of twisted, red-hot metal slammed into the ground around us.

A dead tree buckled by the blast splintered with a lightning crack as we ran past.

'Look out!' I yelled.

We dove for cover as the tree toppled. The trunk crashed to earth right where I'd been a second before.

And then it was all over. Or at least, the big pyrotechnics were. All the large debris had landed, although thousands of flaming bits of paper still fluttered down from the sky. The lookout tower was reduced to four decapitated support beams, charred black and warped, looking like a really bad piece of modern art. Although my ears were still ringing from the blast, the aftermath was surprisingly quiet.

Erica and Alexander emerged from around the fallen tree, unharmed – although Alexander had dove into a bush and was spitting out leaves.

Something Erica had said right before we'd evacuated finally sank in. 'Did you say we have one other place to visit before you trade me for the hostages?'

'Yes.'

'Where?'

'Isn't it obvious?' Erica asked. 'We have to find out if Murray Hill is really in jail or not.'

Before I could ask her to explain exactly why we needed to do that, however, the woods caught fire.

13

Transportation

Wardensville West Virginia and vicinity

June 13

1500 hours

The woods around us were a tinderbox waiting for a match. It only took one flaming bit of paper to land in just the right spot and we were surrounded by flames.

However, there is one good thing about a forest fire: It gets the attention of every search and rescue squad for a hundred miles.

Luckily, the woods that went up were a relatively small patch surrounded by a great deal of open space. We were able to get out of the flames with only a small bit of singeing and then camped out on a bald peak a good distance away. The first patrol helicopter soon appeared on the horizon.

'Why is it so important to investigate Murray now?' I asked, waving my arms wildly to get its attention. 'Shouldn't rescuing the others be our priority?'

'No, taking SPYDER down is the priority. We have to figure out what they're up to: why do they need you so badly? And what's going on with Murray Hill?' Erica unzipped a flap on her camouflage. There was a large patch of silver material sewn into the other side, which she used to reflect the sun at the helicopter. It was much more effective than my arm waving. The helicopter quickly spotted it and banked towards us.

'Murray might just be the key to all of this,' Erica went on. 'And if we can learn what SPYDER's plans are, then maybe we won't have to exchange you for your friends after all.'

'Sounds good,' I said. I hadn't been too keen on the whole being-traded-to-SPYDER thing.

'One more thing,' Erica warned us as the copter lowered towards us. 'Don't tell anyone anything about what's going on here.'

'I'm not sure that's the best policy,' Alexander said. 'If this Murray Hill thing doesn't pan out, we're going to need a great deal of help to rescue your friends . . .'

'First of all, they're not my friends, they're my schoolmates,' Erica snapped. 'And second, you're an idiot. SPYDER told us to come alone or they'd kill everyone else. The moment we breathe so much as a word about what's happening to one person, we'll lose control of the situation. They'll call the police, who'll call the sheriff, who'll call the FBI, and before you know it, there'll be a thousand people swarming the countryside. SPYDER has ears and eyes everywhere. We mess with their orders and they'll know.'

'If we can contact the right people at the CIA, SPYDER won't hear a peep,' Alexander countered.

'As far as we know, SPYDER is monitoring all communication with the CIA right now,' Erica told him. 'They picked us up on a ham radio, for Pete's sake! That's prehistoric communication. There's no way we can contact the agency without SPYDER knowing.'

'Looks like we'll have to agree to disagree then,' Alexander replied.

Erica couldn't argue the point any further because the helicopter was so close it was deafening. It landed close by, its rotors kicking up a spray of grit and gravel that sandblasted our skin. We jumped in and it whisked us away.

Inside the copter cabin, the roar of the rotors was like having a jackhammer in each ear. We all clapped on headphones to mute the noise, but we still had to shout to communicate.

'You folks OK?!' the pilot yelled over the roar of the rotors.

'Yes!' we yelled back.

'You're awful far from civilization!' the pilot said. 'What were y'all doing way out here?!'

'Hiking!' Erica replied, before Alexander could say anything else.

'Y'all know what started that fire?!' the pilot asked.

'No—' Erica began, but then Alexander slapped a hand over her mouth.

'It was an enemy missile!' he said. 'I work for the CIA and the enemies of democracy are swarming these hills. I need to use your radio to contact headquarters immediately— Oof!'

He fell silent as Erica jabbed him in the solar plexus with an elbow, knocking the wind out of him.

'Unfortunately, my father was struck on the head by a piece of burning debris,' Erica told the pilot. 'He's been talking crazy ever since. He's not in the CIA. He's an orthodontist.'

As this sounded like a far more likely story than enemies of democracy blowing up random lookout towers with missiles, the pilot chose to believe it. 'Don't worry!' he assured Erica. 'We'll get your Daddy medical help as soon as we land!'

Although it had taken us eight hours to reach the lookout tower between the buses, the swimming and the hiking, we were only ten minutes from civilization by air. The helicopter landed by a reservoir where the forest fire combat effort was already well underway. Tanker planes were scooping up water and whisking it away to bombard the fire. Other rescue personnel were also on the scene: smokejumpers, park rangers and an assortment of law enforcement officials ranging from sheriff's deputies to local police. The pilot had radioed in Erica's request for medical attention and there was already an ambulance with two paramedics standing by. They raced to Alexander's side as he clambered off the helicopter.

'How's your head, sir?' one asked, checking Alexander's vital signs.

'My head is fine,' Alexander told them. 'It's the safety of our country that's in jeopardy. I need to borrow your phone to call the CIA immediately.'

'He's been saying things like this ever since that

debris hit him,' Erica said, and then pretended to break down in tears.

'Don't worry, sweetheart,' the second paramedic said. 'He'll be all right. He doesn't seem to have a concussion. Sometimes, a traumatic experience like this can cause temporary delusions in people.'

Then, each paramedic seized one of Alexander's arms and hustled him towards the ambulance.

'I am not delusional!' Alexander roared. 'I am a highly-decorated CIA agent!'

'Of course you are,' the first paramedic said soothingly. 'I'm sure you've saved the world several times.'

'Don't placate me!' Alexander snapped. 'I can prove I'm an agent!'

'Really?' Erica asked. 'Do you have some sort of official ID?'

'You know I do,' Alexander replied, and then flushed as he realized something. 'Only, it washed down the river. But if we call the CIA they can verify who I am.'

The paramedics shared a sceptical look, then bundled Alexander into the back of the ambulance and strapped him to a stretcher.

'Mind if we ride back there with him?' Erica asked,

putting on her best daughter-in-distress face.

'Sure,' the second paramedic said. 'Just be sure not to touch anything.'

'I wouldn't think of it,' said Erica.

We hopped into the back of the ambulance and the paramedics locked us inside. Alexander kept yelling at them as they climbed into the front seats, imploring them to call the CIA. While everyone was distracted, Erica quickly opened one of the cabinets in the back of the ambulance, located a vial of sedative, filled a syringe with it and lightly jabbed it into Alexander's backside.

'Yow!' he yelled, and wheeled on Erica. 'Did you just stick me with something?'

'It was a mosquito,' Erica said, and then slapped her neck, as though she'd just caught a bug biting her as well. 'Ouch. One just got me too.'

Alexander wobbled. The sedative was acting quickly. 'You *did* give me something,' he said, slurring his words. 'How dare you, Erica? I'm your . . . your . . . fathhhhppbble.' He fell asleep before he could even finish the thought.

'Is everything OK back there?' the first paramedic called back.

'Yes,' Erica replied. 'My father just fell asleep. I think all the stress of this has been too much for him.'

'Don't panic,' the paramedic said. 'We'll be at the hospital soon.'

The town was small and, with its sirens wailing, the ambulance had us at the medical clinic in less than ten minutes. The paramedics hoisted Alexander's stretcher out of the ambulance and parked it in the hall by the emergency room. They asked Erica a few questions about her father's insurance, all of which she claimed not to know the answers to. She then gave them a false name and social security number for her father. They handed her some paperwork, left us with a nurse, and took off.

The clinic was surprisingly busy for the size of the town. 'It's the beginning of summer vacation,' the nurse told us. 'Kids are arriving for camp. City folk are coming out to their summer cabins. Everyone's injuring themselves in imaginative ways. We've got sprains, burns, broken bones, sunburn, poison ivy, dehydration, two near-drownings and one guy who got attacked by a rabid chipmunk. Your father there is merely delusional, so it might be a while until we can see him.' With that, she ran off to take care of a man who had somehow managed to impale himself on his own fishhook.

Erica cased the hallway. Everyone was so busy

tending to their own injuries or trying to get the attention of a nurse that no one was paying any attention to us. 'Grab my Dad's feet,' she told me. 'We're getting out of here.'

Before I could even begin to protest, she had unstrapped Alexander from the stretcher and hooked her arms under his. I grabbed his feet and we lugged him down the hall. 'What exactly is your plan here?' I asked.

'I don't really have one at the moment,' Erica admitted. 'I was really hoping I wouldn't have to sedate Dad, but sometimes the man just won't listen to reason.'

One of the clinic's wheelchairs sat, unused, around the next corner. We plonked Alexander into it and Erica quickly steered him towards the exit. 'As far as I can tell, we're in Wardensville, West Virginia,' she said.

'How do you know?'

Erica handed me some of the paperwork she'd been given. At the top, it said, 'Viceroy Medical Clinic. Wardensville, West Virginia.' Erica led me out of the automatic glass doors and into the parking lot. 'Right now, we need some transportation. Stand guard for me.' Erica parked the wheelchair behind a rickety old car that seemed to be held together with duct tape. Within three seconds she had jimmied the driver's door open and ducked under the steering wheel.

I cased the parking lot to make sure no one was watching. No one was. The only other people were all racing into A&E. 'You're stealing this car?' I whispered.

'Borrowing it,' Erica corrected. 'Temporarily. I know it's not exactly the staunch moral thing to do, but like Alexander said, our country's safety is in jeopardy.' The engine roared to life as Erica hotwired it. 'OK, get Dad in the car.'

'Erica, are you sure this is the right thing to do?'

'Absolutely. Now stop questioning me. I swiped plenty of sedative from that ambulance. If I have to, I'm willing to knock you out too.'

I popped open the rear door, toppled Alexander into the back seat and then hopped into the front with Erica. There was no point asking her if she could drive. Erica had once taken out three SPYDER agents while steering a moving van. She had the pedal down before I was even buckled in.

'Remember where Murray's incarcerated?' she asked.

'The Apple Valley Reformation Camp for Delinquent Teens.'

'Right. That's located near a town called Vaughn, Virginia. Is there a map in this car?'

I popped open the glove compartment. There was a map, along with some spare change and a half eaten candy bar. I was actually hungry enough to consider eating the candy. I didn't, though this had less to do with my self-control than my fear of looking like a pig in front of Erica. I consulted the map and found Vaughn. 'Looks like it's about an hour or two away.'

Erica took the map and memorized the route in a few seconds. Then she cautiously drove through town, taking care not to exceed the speed limit. Alexander snored in the backseat.

'Any idea how long he'll be out?' I asked.

'Long enough to get to Vaughn, I think.'

'Do you think SPYDER knows we survived the missile attack?'

'Definitely. There's no question they do.'

'Why do you say that?'

'Because they weren't trying to kill us.'

'They launched a missile at us!'

'The velocity of a missile like the one they used is approximately half a mile per second – whereas the range is about thirty miles. And yet, that one didn't hit the tower until over a minute after I'd ended the radio call . . .'

'Meaning they knew where we were long before they launched it,' I concluded.

'Exactly. They gave us time to escape.'

'Then why launch the missile at all?' I asked.

'To let us know they mean business,' Erica said. 'It's a warning: they can take us out whenever they want, no matter where we are, so we'd better not try anything tricky and just do what they say.'

We reached the city limit of Wardensville. The main road turned into a state highway and Erica hit the gas.

I asked, 'If SPYDER knows we're still alive, do you think they know where we are right now?'

Erica stared through the windshield thoughtfully for a few seconds before answering. 'I doubt it – although I don't want to take anything for granted where that organization is concerned. Still, they can't have men *everywhere*. They might know we got on that helicopter, but the chances are they didn't have anyone on the ground when it landed. We've kept moving pretty quickly – and no one seems to be following us right now.'

I reflexively checked the rear-view mirror to make

sure. The road we were on was long and empty. There was no one behind us.

Even so, I couldn't relax. Having an evil enemy organization threaten to kill you has that effect. I kept wondering what the point of it all was. Why could SPYDER possibly need me so badly that they were willing to go through all this trouble? What could I possibly do for them? What on earth were they up to? I started to ask Erica another question, but she cut me off.

'I'm trying to work all this out, Ben. I just need some time to think. The moment I come up with something, I'll let you know.'

I nodded and returned my attention to the open road ahead, trying to figure everything out myself. In truth, I didn't just want to figure out why SPYDER wanted me; I wanted to figure it out before Erica did. I wanted to impress her. For the past few hours, she'd been the hero and I'd been the damsel in distress, constantly needing rescuing. It would be nice to remind her I wasn't merely dead weight.

Sadly, I couldn't come up with anything. Worse, Erica couldn't either – or if she did, she didn't show it. She didn't say a word for the rest of the drive.

We reached Vaughn in an hour and forty minutes.

It turned out to be a bucolic farming community nestled in a valley between two forested mountain ridges. There was only one place to stay in town, a small motel that looked like it had just reopened for the summer. 'Keep an eye on my father,' Erica told me. 'I'll get us a room.'

'How?' I asked. 'We don't have any money.'

'No,' she replied. '*You* don't have any money. I do.' She pulled out a wad of cash.

'Where'd you get that?' I asked.

'Our paramedics,' she replied.

'You pickpocketed them?'

'I had to, Ben. This is a crisis.' Erica gave me a smile and ducked into the motel office.

Two minutes later, she was back with a room key and a roll of duct tape. 'The manager let me have it,' she said. 'I told him we needed to tape the bumper back on.'

'What's it really for?' I asked.

'Isn't it obvious?' she replied. 'Security.'

Interrogation

Vaughn, Virginia
June 14
1800 hours

Lots of spies will tell you that there is no single item as useful and effective as duct tape. It can be used to splint broken bones, repair weapons, pick up evidence, patch clothing, staunch bleeding, attach explosives, seal electrical wiring, waterproof tents, remove warts and yes, even tape ducts. Professor Crandall, my Self-Preservation teacher, had said that if you wrapped enough around your body, you could make yourself bulletproof. (It was much bulkier than Kevlar, but considerably easier to find in the event that people were trying to kill you.)

We used it to bind Alexander Hale to a chair in our motel room. I had some qualms about this, but Erica was insistent. 'I need to go out to do some reconnaissance and I don't want Alexander going anywhere without my permission,' she explained. 'He'll only cause more trouble.'

So we sat him in the chair, taped each of his ankles to one chair leg, and then wound the rest of the duct tape around his torso and the back of the chair so that his arms were pinioned at his sides. He slept soundly through it all.

'Stand watch over him,' Erica ordered me. 'I'll be back later.' With that, she started for the door.

'Wait!' I said. 'Where are you going?'

Erica paused. 'Where do you think?'

'The Apple Valley Reformation Camp for Delinquent Teens.'

'Good guess.'

'Can't I come? Your father's not going anywhere.'

'No, but he could still be a problem. He could shout for help. Or thrash around, trying to get free and end up hurting himself. Plus, he'll probably be hungry and thirsty when he gets up and someone will need to feed him.'

'Well, shouldn't you do that? You're his daughter after all. And it was your idea to sedate him and tape him up, not mine.' The truth was, I really didn't want to be around when Alexander came to and found himself prisoner. 'I could go do the reconnaissance and you could stay here with your father, get some rest and, uh . . . work out any issues that you two might have.'

Erica's eyes narrowed. 'Do you have any idea how to infiltrate a penal institution with level four security?'

'Not exactly,' I admitted.

'That's why *I'm* doing the recon. Don't worry, I won't do anything fun without you. I shouldn't be too long.' Erica slapped some crumpled bills into my hand. 'This ought to be enough to cover a pizza and some drinks. My father's probably going to do everything he can to convince you to cut him free. No matter how charming he is, don't let him go.'

'What if he has to go to the bathroom?' I asked.

'According to Alexander, once when he was on a mission in Djakarta, he refrained from going to the bathroom for three days straight, so he ought to be able to handle another few hours. Don't wait up for me.'

Before I could utter another word of protest, Erica

was out of the door.

I considered my surroundings. Our motel room wasn't exactly a flea pit, but it was awfully close. Apparently, people didn't really come to Vaughn on vacation. Instead, they stopped there because it was on the way to someplace else and they were too exhausted to drive any further. There were two beds, both of which had ancient mattresses that bowed in the centre, as though rhinos had slept on them. There was a small wooden dresser in which two of the three drawers were jammed. (This was of little concern, however, as we didn't have any spare clothes to put in them.) And on top of a spindly little table, there was a small TV that pre-dated the invention of the remote control.

The bathroom was barely big enough to turn around in. There was a chipped toilet with a 'Sanitized for your protection' band on it that was obviously a lie. The shower didn't look much better, but as I was filthy and still a bit damp and had nothing else to do to occupy myself, I used it. For about four minutes, it was actually nice and therapeutic. And then the hot water shut off abruptly and I was doused with an icy stream that felt like it had been piped directly from the North Pole. I leapt from the shower and discovered, to my dismay, that the motel staff had neglected to place any towels in our room.

I used the bedcovers to dry off. Then I called the front desk and discovered there was no pizza delivery place in town. There were, however, vending machines by the entrance, and I could get change at reception. So dinner turned out to be a random assortment of chips, nuts and crackers, many of which had resided in the vending machine well past their expiry dates.

I had nothing to read and no phone to amuse myself with. The motel claimed to have cable TV, but while this may have been true, the TV in our room couldn't actually display it. Every channel showed only static.

So I decided I might as well go to bed. It wasn't that late, but the day had been exhausting and tomorrow promised to be more of the same. I nestled into the crater in the centre of one of the sagging mattresses and fell asleep instantly.

Quite some time later, I was awakened to the sound of Alexander groaning.

'Ohhhh. My head.'

I slowly came to and discovered it was nearly 4 a.m. To my surprise, Erica wasn't in her bed.

Alexander wasn't fully awake yet. He was merely

coming out of the sedation haze. 'My head is killing me. What happened?'

'You uh . . . got knocked out.' I felt that was technically true, so it wasn't exactly lying to him.

Alexander opened his eyes, although this seemed to be a considerable effort for him. He looked around the room with confusion. 'Where am I?'

'A motel in Vaughn, Virginia.'

'Is that near Washington?'

'No. It's not near anything, really.'

Alexander yawned. He tried to cover his mouth with his hand, and it was only now that he realized his arm was taped to his torso. He was suddenly wide awake, although he actually seemed even more confused than he had when he was groggy. 'What the . . . ? What's happening? Why am I tied up? Benjamin! Are you a double agent with SPYDER?'

'No,' I said.

'That's just the sort of thing I'd expect someone from SPYDER to say,' Alexander sneered. He struggled wildly against the duct tape. It held firm. 'Cut me loose at once! Or I'll have the entire brunt of the US armed forces brought down upon this motel!'

'Alexander, I know that's not true. And I'm not a double agent. I'm on your side.'

'Then why have you taped me to a chair?'

'It was your daughter's idea. She felt you'd cause less trouble this way.'

Alexander stopped struggling. All the fight went out of him in an instant. The anger in his eyes was quickly replaced by sadness and shame. 'She did? Really?'

'Really.'

'Why?'

I tried to think of a way to explain everything delicately, but couldn't. The best I could do was: 'I think you know why.'

Alexander's sadness deepened a bit more. 'Where is Erica right now?'

'Out doing some reconnaissance at Apple Valley.'

Alexander looked at me blankly.

'It's where Murray Hill is being held. In theory.'

'How long has she been gone?'

'Quite a long time, actually.'

'She might be in trouble. You should cut me loose so we can go look for her.'

'I don't think she's in trouble,' I said, although secretly, I wasn't so sure. Erica had been gone a lot longer than she'd said she'd be.

'Well, cut me loose anyhow,' Alexander said. 'Please. I assure you I won't cause any trouble.'

'I'm sorry. I can't. Erica told me not to.'

'I have to go to the bathroom.'

'I heard you once held it for three days in Djakarta.'

Alexander swallowed. 'Er, yes. Well, that was a little different. You see, for a few weeks before that, I'd been on a special training routine to get my kidneys to retain water—'

'Before you go on, you should know that Erica told me everything about you.'

Alexander looked as though I'd punched him. It took him a while to figure out what to say next. 'What do you mean?'

'She says you're a fraud.'

'And you actually believe that?'

'Yes.'

'Why?'

'For starters, you stole the credit for capturing Murray from me.'

'That's not true. I did what we call a "double-blind." It only *looked* like the CIA believed what I said to fool the enemy . . .'

'Alexander, if you keep lying to me, I'm going to put this tape over your mouth.'

'Did my daughter tell you to threaten that?'

'No, I came up with that on my own just now. For

once in your life, could you please be honest?' My own anger at Alexander surprised me. It had probably been simmering deep within me ever since he'd first taken the credit for nabbing Murray. Now, on the heels of Alexander putting my life in jeopardy, it came boiling out.

Alexander mulled over his options. 'If I am honest, will you set me free?'

'No. Erica would kill me.'

Alexander nodded, conceding the point. 'My daughter does have her ways.'

'Why is she so angry at you?' I asked.

'Well, the relationship between teenage girls and their fathers can be very difficult. I suppose I wasn't around much when she was a little girl, so she might harbour some animosity towards me . . .'

'That's why she's generally annoyed with you,' I said. 'But right now, she's at a whole different level. She *hates* you right now. Why?'

'I don't know what you're talking about,' Alexander said, although he couldn't look at me as he said it.

'I'm pretty sure you do,' I told him. 'Please. I need to know. Agents from SPYDER are out there somewhere trying to get me. The CIA has sent you to protect me and Erica's trying to do the same thing. It'd be nice if the two of you could work together.'

Alexander frowned. His desire to do the right thing seemed to be battling his general tendency to make himself look good at all costs. Finally, he broke. He stared at the floor and said, 'A few weeks ago, I sort of lost a briefcase full of important classified documents.'

'How? Did the enemy steal it?'

'Er, no. I think I left it in the bathroom at a McDonald's. These documents were quite important and I, well . . . it wouldn't have looked good if I'd simply admitted the truth. So I . . . um . . . I kind of blamed their loss on Erica.'

I winced for Erica's sake. 'What did you say?'

Alexander met my eyes. He didn't look anything like his normal self. Rather than debonair, he looked pathetic. And his usual glib tone had been reduced to meek stuttering. 'I, er, I . . . I told the top brass that she'd broken into my briefcase to see what was inside and then, um . . . that she'd spilled a glass of milk on everything and ruined them.'

I hadn't thought it was possible that I could be angrier with Alexander. But now I felt myself grow enraged on Erica's behalf. It took a tremendous effort for me to remain calm. 'And what did the top brass do?'

'They put a black mark on Erica's school records.'

'Which means what?'

'Her chances of going into the field after graduation are, er . . . seriously diminished.'

I was clenching my fists so tightly I could feel the knuckles go white. 'So first, you took all the credit for capturing Murray Hill when really, Erica and I had done the lion's share—'

'Well, I did give you two a special commendation in the appendix of my report.'

'— And then, rather than take the blame for your screw-up, you sabotaged your own daughter's future.'

'I didn't realize they were going to ding her!' Alexander whined. 'I thought they'd just let it slide.'

'You thought no such thing.' The voice startled Alexander and I, as it was coming from inside the room. We wheeled around to find Erica standing in the corner in the darkness. Somehow, she was on the far side of the room from the door. We hadn't even heard her come in. 'You knew exactly what they would do to me, but in your panic to protect your own reputation, you sacrificed me anyway. Your own flesh and blood.'

'How'd you get in here without us seeing you?' I asked.

'I've been here for hours,' Erica replied. 'I was sleeping on the floor until you guys woke me up.'

'Why were you sleeping on the floor?' I asked.

'Because that bed stinks,' Erica replied.

'Sweetheart,' Alexander pleaded to her. 'I told you I was sorry . . .'

'And I told you not to call me "Sweetheart." Or "Kitten." Or anything else cute and familial. If you're going to put your career before me, you don't get to act like my father.'

'It was a simple mistake,' Alexander wheedled. 'I'm working on cleaning it up. It's my number one priority.'

'Obviously that's a lie,' Erica shot back. 'Because if it *was* your number one priority, you'd have already admitted the truth about what happened and the black mark would be on *your* record, and instead of sending *you* out here, the CIA might have sent someone competent. But now we're both stuck with you and there's nothing we can do about it.' With that, she whipped out the knife she always kept strapped to her ankle and came at Alexander.

Alexander shrieked in fear, thinking she was about to go psycho on him, but instead, she jammed it into the tape holding his torso to the chair.

'You're cutting me free?' Alexander asked.

'Unfortunately, we need you,' Erica admitted.

'Ah,' Alexander said. 'See? I'm not as incompetent as you say.'

'No, you are,' Erica told him. 'We don't need you for any spy skills. We need you because you're old. The detention centre won't let us in unless we're accompanied by an adult.'

'Oh.' Alexander looked so dejected I almost felt sorry for him.

Erica paused halfway through slicing the tape. 'There are a few stipulations to your release, however. Otherwise, we can leave you here and find someone else to help us. One: you admit that I am in charge. You only do what I tell you to. You don't speak unless I tell you to.'

Alexander returned his gaze to the floor, ashamed at what he'd been reduced to. 'All right. What else?'

Erica tilted her father's chin up so that he could look her in the eye. 'When all this is over, you call the head of the CIA and admit what you did to me.'

Alexander took far longer to give in on this. Apparently he was much happier to be treated as a subordinate by his daughter than he was to admit the truth about what he'd done. 'Fine,' he said finally. 'I'll do it.'

'OK then,' Erica said. 'Let's get to the bottom of this Murray Hill business.'

Reformation

Apple Valley Reformation Camp for Delinquent
Teens
June 15
0800 hours

Before I visited Apple Valley, the only penitentiary I'd ever been to was Alcatraz. I imagined Apple Valley would look somewhat the same: lots of iron gates and concrete. I expected to see the inmates chained together by the ankles, breaking rocks with sledgehammers while the guards broke their spirits. It didn't look like that at all. In fact, it looked far nicer than Spy School.

It was set in a beautiful green valley at the end of a long, forested road. A cluster of cute white buildings sat in the centre of some well-tended gardens. Boys and girls in t-shirts and shorts ran about, completely unshackled. They played soccer, touch rugby and croquet. And in the distance, I was quite sure I could make out tennis courts and a polo field.

The only thing that even made it look remotely like a detention facility was the fence around it, and this was merely a plain old chain link one without any barbed wire at the top. It didn't even appear to be electrified. On the road in, there was a barrier and a guardhouse, but instead of an armed guard, there was only a cheerful college girl who seemed to be working a summer job. She set down the *Vogue* magazine she was reading as we drove up.

'Hello!' she chirped. 'How're y'all doing today?'

'We're fine, thanks,' Alexander replied. So as to not draw any attention, Erica had begrudgingly allowed him to drive. 'How are you?'

'I'm doing awesome, thanks.' The girl gave Alexander a blushing, somewhat smitten smile. 'What can I do for you today?'

'The name's Alexander Hale. CIA agent number 13625. I'm here to see one of your inmates. A Murray Hill.'

'Murray!' the girl beamed. 'Oh, he's such a sweetie.

He made me the nicest paperweight in his pottery class the other day. I'll let the office know you're coming.' The girl reached for a red button on her console, but then hesitated at the sight of Erica and myself in the backseat. For the first time, it occurred to her that our presence might be a bit odd. 'Um, are you delivering these children here for incarceration?'

'No, these are *my* children,' Alexander replied. 'Today's Take Your Kids To Work Day at the CIA.' Before the girl could question this, he flashed her a smile that made her go weak at the knees. Alexander might not have been the most competent spy, but when it came to flirting, he was extremely talented.

'Oh, that's adorable!' the girl cooed. 'OK, go on through. Have fun, kids!' She pressed the red button and the flimsy gate opened.

Alexander drove onto the property. We crossed the wide, open lawn towards the main building complex, passing a large group of prisoners playing ultimate Frisbee.

'I thought you said this place had level four security,' I muttered to Erica.

'No I didn't,' she replied. 'I only asked if you knew how to infiltrate a penal institution with level four security. Thanks to my reconnaissance last night, however, I learned that this place actually has a security level of minus three.'

'How can they keep a criminal as bad as Murray Hill *here*?' I asked. 'This isn't punishment. It's like sending him to a spa for five years.'

'Murray is only fourteen,' Erica said with a shrug. 'There aren't a lot of maximum security options for kids. So they just lumped him in here. Most of these inmates probably haven't done anything worse than shoplifting. However, I suspect Murray may be under a bit more scrutiny than most of the others.'

Alexander parked in the visitor's lot and we walked up to the main entrance, which was surrounded by burbling fountains and an edible garden. As we reached the front doors, a cheerful woman exited. She wore a bright pink pantsuit with matching high heels and was so chipper, I half expected to see an animated bluebird land on her shoulder. 'Hello there Agent Hale!' she said. 'Hello kids! I'm Brandi Russell! Thanks for coming here to see us at Apple Valley! I understand you're here to see Murray.'

'That's right,' Alexander said. 'I'm from the CIA and—'

'Oh, I know exactly who you are,' Brandi told him.

'You do?' Alexander asked.

'We're not hicks here,' Brandi said with a laugh. 'We've got a computer, for goodness' sake. I looked you up while you were coming up the drive, just to make sure you were on the level. It's an honour to have such an important agent visit us.'

Alexander smiled at the flattery. Now that he had someone to play to, he was back to being his old self, charming and debonair. 'Well, it's an honour to visit this fine establishment. And a pleasure to meet a woman as devoted to helping wayward children as you are. Unfortunately, we won't be here long. I just have a few questions to ask Mr Hill.'

'Certainly,' Brandi said. 'I've already arranged for him to be brought to our visitors' centre. I think you're going to be very impressed with his progress. He's been doing extremely well here. Not an ounce of trouble. But then, Murray was never all that difficult. In fact, it's hard to believe that boy did all the things he's been accused of doing. Would either of you kids like a lollipop?' She proffered some for Erica and me.

Erica glared at Brandi as though she'd just been offered rat poison on a stick, although I accepted mine. We'd skipped breakfast that morning.

Brandi led us inside. The buildings of the facility were open and spacious, full of windows and light. We passed down a glass corridor, flanked by Zen gardens on both sides. In one, a dozen students were doing yoga. In the other, another dozen were meditating.

'For a reformation facility, there doesn't seem to be a lot of reformation going on,' I said.

'Oh there is, I assure you!' Brandi chirped. 'In fact, you're seeing some right now. Here at Apple Valley we strongly believe in "Reformation through Contemplation". The best way to make a child a productive member of society isn't with the lash. It's with love.' Brandi beamed happily at the thought of this, and for a moment I thought she might burst into song.

'I don't see Murray in any of these classes,' Erica said.

'Well, no. Murray's a bit of a special case,' Brandi told her. 'He does participate in meditation and yoga, as well as some of our other classes – he's shown quite an aptitude for sculpting, by the way – but due to the nature of his alleged crimes, we do have to keep him on a tighter rein than most of our other guests here.'

I was pleased to hear this last bit. It had been driving me crazy to think that, after all he'd done, Murray was living the high life while I was suffering through Spy School.

'What does that "tighter rein" entail?' Erica asked.

'My, my, aren't you children just full of questions?' Brandi said. 'Well, for starters, Murray lives in our high security wing, he is under constant video surveillance and he only has permission to use the pool on weekends.'

'So you haven't noticed him missing any time recently?' I asked.

Brandi looked at me askance, then laughed. 'What a curious question. I guess you're hoping to be a great agent like your father here.'

'Oh yes,' Alexander said, giving my hair a paternal tousle. 'The nut doesn't fall far from the tree, I'm afraid. But Benjamin here does ask a good question. Has Murray gone missing at all since he's been here?'

'Heavens no!' Brandi gasped dramatically. 'He hasn't left these premises since he was brought here five months ago. Except for our annual field trip to Six Flags, of course. Other than that, he hasn't even gone close to the perimeter fence. I tell you, the boy has practically been a saint.'

'Saint Murray?' Erica muttered under her breath. 'That'll be the day.'

We stopped next to a door with a keypad entry. 'Here we are!' Brandi announced. 'The visitors' room!

Just wait until you see Murray. You'll barely recognize him!'

She entered the code and flung the door open.

Once again, the room was nothing like I'd imagined. Based on the many prison movies I'd seen, I had expected a room with a partition of thick clear plastic in the middle, and that we'd sit on opposite sides and talk through handsets. Instead, the visitors' room looked like a rich kid's rec room. There were lots of comfy chairs, shelves full of games and books, foozball, air hockey and a pool table. The only thing that seemed out of place was the guard. For once, however, someone actually seemed to know what a person who worked in a prison should look like. The guard wore a khaki uniform and a belt loaded with weapons. He stood ramrod straight, keeping a watchful eye over his charge: a fourteen-year-old boy who sat on one of the couches, reading a magazine.

'There he is!' Brandi squealed, pointing to the boy. 'Our Murray!'

She was right. I didn't recognize him.

Because it wasn't Murray Hill.

They both had brown, curly hair, but that was where the similarity ended.

'Uh, that's not Murray,' I said.

Brandi and Alexander looked at me curiously. 'It's not?' Alexander asked.

'You don't know?' Erica asked tartly. 'That's funny. I thought you captured him.'

Alexander grew pink around the ears. 'Well, I've captured so many people in my time,' he said for Brandi's sake. 'It's hard to keep track.' He wheeled on me and whispered. 'Are you sure it's not Murray?'

'Definitely,' I said. 'For starters, he's about three inches shorter. Also, he has different coloured eyes, his face is rounder, his ears are bigger, he has a mole on his neck and frankly, given the kid's blank expression, I'd say his IQ is around fifty points lower.'

Through all of this, the boy-who-wasn't-Murray sat on the couch, smiling brightly at us, as if he found our confusion amusing.

Brandi, meanwhile, appeared to be on the verge of a nervous breakdown. Her eyes darted back and forth rapidly between Murray and us. Sweat broke out on her brow. I'd seen the principal of Spy School behave this way enough times to recognize it: It was the standard reaction of a government employee who'd just realized that a serious mistake had been made, and who was desperately looking for a way to pin the blame on someone else. 'As far as I know, that is Murray

Hill,' she said, pointing at the boy. 'That's what the government agents who brought him here told me.'

'But you never checked to make sure?' Erica asked.

'How would I do that?' Brandi demanded.

'Run his fingerprints,' Erica suggested. 'Or maybe look up a photo of Murray Hill in the CIA database. Like you said, you're not hicks. You've got a computer here.'

Brandi grew even more flustered. She violently flapped her hand in front of her face to cool herself off. 'Why should it even occur to anyone to do such a thing? The CIA dropped him off here. They told me he was Murray Hill. Am I supposed to question the CIA?'

'Yes,' Erica said flatly. 'They've been known to royally botch things up on occasion. Did you even check to see if the agents had official ID when they dropped this kid off? Because no one here checked ours just now.'

'This is ludicrous!' Brandi gasped, completely avoiding the question. 'If that boy isn't Murray Hill, why didn't he ever say anything? Why didn't he complain? Are you actually suggesting he willingly took the place of a prisoner and never made a peep about it?'

I looked back to the boy-who-wasn't-Murray. He was laughing hysterically now.

'He doesn't seem to be suffering here,' I said.

Erica stormed across the room and looked not-Murray in the eye. 'What did SPYDER offer you to take Murray's place?'

'I don't know who SPYDER is,' not-Murray replied.

'Don't play dumb with us,' Alexander threatened.

'I don't think he's playing,' Erica told him. 'I think he really is dumb.' Then she asked the boy, 'Did someone *offer* you something to come here?'

The boy giggled. 'A hundred thousand dollars.'

'That's it?' I asked, unable to control myself. 'Murray's sentence was five years! You allowed yourself to be incarcerated for only twenty-thousand dollars a year?'

The boy shrugged. 'Still seems like a lot of money to me. And this place is a heck of a lot nicer than the juvenile hall where they found me.'

Alexander grabbed Erica and I by the arms and yanked us into a huddle away from not-Murray and Brandi. 'I'm a little confused here,' he admitted. 'What, exactly, is going on?'

'It seems our friends at SPYDER outwitted the CIA yet again,' Erica sighed. 'Once they found out that

Murray had been assigned to this lame facility, they found a dupe at some juvey hall, sprang him and swapped him out for Murray.'

'But how?' Alexander asked.

'The easiest way would be to corrupt the agents who were supposed to deliver Murray here,' Erica explained. 'Maybe those guys were moles for SPYDER. Or maybe SPYDER just paid them off. Whatever the case, Apple Valley's been babysitting the wrong guy for five months while Murray Hill's been free as a bird.'

I glanced back towards not-Murray. The kid was still laughing, which struck me as odd. I could see how revealing that you'd hoodwinked the CIA for five months might be funny, but it didn't seem *that* funny. It was like the boy knew there was more to the joke somehow . . .

A thought came to me that turned my stomach.

I wheeled back towards Erica. 'Murray Hill *wanted* me to see him before. He wanted us to know he was out. Therefore, he must have wanted us to figure out how he'd done it. And since SPYDER is generally always one step ahead of us . . .'

Erica's eyes went wide. 'They probably know we're here.'

With that, she spun on her heel and raced towards

the door we'd come in through. I was right behind her.

However, Alexander wasn't quite so quick. He stayed where he was, his face screwed up in concentration, as though he was still trying to make sense of everything.

'Come on, Dad!' Erica screamed. 'We've got to get out of here. Now!'

She yanked open the door.

At the far end of the hallway, down by the Zen gardens, six heavily armed men were racing toward us.

We were too late. SPYDER was already here.

Confrontation

Apple Valley Reformation Centre for Delinquent
Teens
June 15
0830 hours

I'd never seen so many enemy agents at once before. In fact, I'd never confronted more than one SPYDER agent at a time. The thing that surprised me most about them was what they were wearing.

I'd obviously seen too many spy movies. Spies in the movies are always wearing suits – and well-tailored suits at that. But suits aren't really that effective for physical activity, especially the shoes, which are almost impossible to run in.

These guys were dressed for action. They wore shorts, t-shirts and sneakers. Half of them had baseball caps. If it hadn't been for their weapons, they'd have looked like the coaching staff for a little league baseball team.

With the weapons, however, they looked really scary. When they saw us, they picked up their pace and charged down the hall.

Erica ducked back into the visitors' room, slammed the door shut and threw the dead bolt. 'Help me get something in front of this!' she ordered.

Alexander and I got behind a couch and shoved it across the room to block the doors. There was a terrible screeching sound as it scraped along the floor.

Brandi let out a terrible screech herself. 'Careful with the floor!' she cried. 'That's imported teak! We just had it stained!'

In her addled state, she did not seem to be grasping what was truly important at the moment.

'Get a hold of yourself, woman!' Alexander told her. 'There's been a security breach!'

Meanwhile, not-Murray was laughing even harder than before. 'Surprise!' he yelled.

There was another door behind him, the only other way out of the room. The armed guard, who seemed to have far more sense than Brandi – as well as considerably less commitment to his job – was already running for it. Erica, Alexander and I followed close behind him. Brandi brought up the rear, as she could only take mincing steps in her high-heeled shoes. 'None of this is my fault!' she declared defensively. 'I am not in charge of security at this facility!'

Behind us, the SPYDER agents slammed into the other door. The couch we'd placed in front of it held it closed, but skidded a few inches across the floor. It obviously wouldn't hold them long.

I raced out the other door right on Erica's heels. We found ourselves in another window-lined hallway, this one looking out onto a perfectly manicured lawn where teenage inmates did t'ai-chi. Beyond them, we could see the mountains that formed the end of the valley. They weren't high, but they were still quite steep. SPYDER had chosen a great place to ambush us. The valley was a natural dead end and they were blocking the only road out.

The guard headed down the hall to the right. Erica started after him, then stopped so abruptly that I almost slammed into her.

'What's wrong?' I asked.

Erica didn't answer. She was staring out of the window.

No, not *out* of the window, I realized. She was staring at something taped to the window.

It was a white envelope with a red arrow on it pointing to the left. Under it was a message written in red wax crayon: 'E – Go this way. – K.'

Erica snapped the envelope off the glass and went left. Obviously, she trusted whoever had left it. I stayed with her. So did Alexander. Brandi scurried after us. 'I expect full reimbursement from the CIA for any damages sustained in this attack!' she yelled.

From back in the visitors' room, I could still hear not-Murray laughing. And then, I heard the sound of the far door being knocked off its hinges, followed by that of the six SPYDER agents taking up the chase.

We reached another fork in the hallway. There was another red arrow drawn on the wall, pointing right this time.

So we went right. The route took us down another hall, past the pottery studio and the squash courts.

Erica tore open the envelope as we ran. There was a letter inside. She yanked it out and read it. This didn't take long, as it was only a few sentences, though whatever it said made Erica smile.

'Who's that from?' I asked.

'A friend,' she replied. Then she pulled something else from the envelope. It was a small, thin plastic packet with some liquid inside.

Brandi had fallen far behind us. There was no way we could wait for her. And besides, SPYDER wasn't after her anyhow. Our enemies rounded the corner into the hallway and overtook her quickly, barely giving her a glance.

'Please do not fire your weapons in this building!' she told them. 'We just had the walls painted!'

'Why are they ambushing us now?' Alexander gasped. 'We've got a hostage situation scheduled for tomorrow!'

'The element of surprise,' Erica told him. 'Why wait until tomorrow if they can capture Ben today?'

Another red arrow pointed us through a doorway marked Stairs. Inside the stairwell, another arrow pointed downwards.

As we headed down, Erica bit the end off the plastic packet and squirted its contents onto the steps behind us. The liquid that came out shimmered in the light, though once on the ground, it was transparent and thus almost impossible to see.

'It's VG-7,' she explained, as we reached the

basement level. A red arrow here directed us through a set of double doors. 'It's a liquid-polymer grease. The Navy designed it to lubricate aircraft engines . . .'

From behind us came the startled yelp of the two lead SPYDER agents slipping on the grease, followed by the sound of them tumbling painfully down the stairs.

'. . . although it's also very effective for taking out your enemies,' Erica continued with a grin.

The basement was the polar opposite of the floor above. While everything above had been sunny, clean and light, below was a dreary, tangled maze of dripping pipes and groaning machinery. There were only a few sporadic fluorescent lights to break up the darkness, and half of those were on the blink, winking on and off. The cement floor was slick with puddles of standing water and random valves that occasionally coughed out bursts of steam.

In short, it was a very unappealing place to head into, but there was yet another red arrow on the floor, pointing us forwards, so we headed into it.

Behind us, the remaining four SPYDER agents reached the bottom of the stairs and split up, fanning out into the labyrinth. Two stayed behind us while the others looked for a way to circle around and head us off at the pass.

There were more red arrows scrawled on random pieces of machinery. We obediently followed the path they indicated, heading deeper and deeper into the maze. We veered through the pipes, sloshed through the puddles, rounded a chugging hot water heater . . .

Erica suddenly stopped.

This time, I *did* run into her. And Alexander ran into me.

'Why...?' I began.

But Erica simply put a finger to her lips and pointed down.

There, whoever had left all the arrows for us had scrawled 'Stop here' in red on the floor.

I glanced around, worried. We seemed to be at the junction of several tunnels, although it was hard to tell, as the fluorescent light above us was flickering so badly it created a strobe effect. With all the steam venting around us and the pulsing lights, it was like being in the world's spookiest dance club. Whoever had led us down there couldn't have come up with a more unnerving place to sit tight while enemy agents bore down on us. I desperately wanted to ask Erica more about this person. Who they were, why she trusted them so much and what exactly she thought their plan was . . . Only I didn't want to make a noise and alert the enemy to our position.

Not that they weren't aware of our position anyhow. They were just as capable of following the red arrows as we were. But still, it didn't seem worth giving them any more help. I watched helplessly as two flashlight beams cut through the gloom behind us, letting us know that SPYDER was just around the corner. Agents one and two. Then two more beams appeared ahead of us. Agents three and four. We were now boxed in.

I looked around for anything I could use as a weapon. There were lots of heavy iron things, but they were all connected to one another.

Erica grabbed my arm and pulled me back into a small gap between two chugging pieces of machinery. Alexander tucked himself into another gap nearby. While these took us out of the open, they weren't very good hiding places. Our enemies wouldn't take long to find us, especially with 'Stop here' helpfully written on the floor nearby.

The space Erica and I were in was extremely tight. We were pressed against each other, face to face. It was a position I would have been delighted to find myself in with Erica in some romantic spot, like a moonlit meadow, or a fancy restaurant, but not in a dismal room full of clanking machinery with four armed enemy agents on our tail. Now, if anything, being face to face with Erica made me even more nervous. In addition to being terrified, I now had to try to not appear terrified at all, for fear of looking lame. I did my best to look calm and collected, even though I felt like curling into a ball and whimpering. Plus, I really hoped that my breath didn't stink.

We watched the flashlight beams grow brighter as the enemy agents closed in from both sides. We heard their footsteps grow louder and louder. And then, they all came together right in front of us. They were less than a foot away, although I still couldn't make out their features. Their faces were almost completely cast in shadow.

They all noticed the 'stop here' on the floor at the same time. I caught a quick glimpse of one's eyes. He seemed surprised by the words, and then his gaze hardened. Then the men began to search the immediate area, swinging their flashlight beams through the murk.

I held my breath, praying that our little niche in the machinery would cloak us in the darkness.

It didn't. It took approximately half a second for the SPYDER agents to spot us.

Their flashlight beams fell on us. I saw the closest

agent's lips curl into a cruel smile.

And then, someone dropped on them from the ceiling.

The attacker had been waiting up in a nest of pipes in the darkness. He or she – I couldn't tell which, as they were cloaked in black from head to toe like a ninja – swung down like an Olympic gymnast and kicked two enemy agents in the back at once, sending them flying face-first into the machinery. Their heads clanged off the iron and they collapsed to the floor. Before the other two agents even knew what was happening, our saviour had attacked them as well.

It was hard to tell exactly what was going on, as the light was terrible and the ninja was moving so fast. Even though I was only metres away, everything was a blur. I heard the SPYDER agents grunt in pain as blows caught them by surprise and saw them crash to the floor as their feet were suddenly swept out from under them. The agents tried to fight back, but our saviour seemed to be everywhere at once, doubling one bad guy over with a kick to the solar-plexus, flipping another onto his back, then cracking the other pair's heads together. Within thirty seconds, all four were sprawled on the floor, two unconscious, two incapacitated by pain.

The ninja turned towards us and tugged off his black mask.

To my astonishment, he was at least seventy years old.

Although he'd moved with the speed of a much younger man, his hair was white and his face was creased with lines. He had a neat moustache, an ancient scar across his left temple and blue eyes that twinkled with amusement, as though he was having a blast. 'Don't worry,' he said. 'You're all safe now.'

Erica pried herself out of our hiding place. She wasn't surprised by the man's age at all. Instead, she was thrilled to see him, flashing the biggest smile I'd ever seen on her face.

'Hi Grandpa,' she said.

Reunion

Apple Valley Reformation Camp and vicinity
June 15
0900 hours

'Grandpa, this is Ben Ripley,' Erica said, pulling me forwards to meet our saviour. 'Ben, this is my grandfather, Cyrus Hale.'

'Also known as Agent Klondike,' Alexander added.

Cyrus's eyes flicked over to Alexander and hardened for a moment. He wasn't nearly as pleased to see his son as he was to see his granddaughter. Then his gaze shifted back to me.

'It's a pleasure to meet you,' I said. 'Thanks for helping us out.'

Cyrus looked me up and down, no longer smiling. 'You'd better be worth all the trouble we've gone through for you,' he said.

Then he turned his attention to one of the two SPYDER agents who was still conscious. He rolled the bad guy onto his back and knelt on his ribs, adding a little extra pain to all that he'd doled out so far. Then he grabbed the guy by his t-shirt and pulled him up, so the two of them were eye to eye. 'What do you want with this kid?' Cyrus demanded.

The SPYDER agent only laughed in response. 'There are a lot more of us coming, Old Man. I'm not saying squat to you.'

Anger flashed in Cyrus's eyes. His grip tightened on the man's shirt. But then Erica placed a calming hand on her grandfather's shoulder. 'He's not bluffing,' she said. 'Listen.'

Cyrus cocked his head, then adjusted the hearing aid that was lodged in his right ear.

In the distance, somewhere in the Apple Valley complex, we could hear more footsteps coming.

'Dangnabbit,' Cyrus grumbled. He let the SPYDER agent's head drop back to the cement in the most painful way possible. 'Follow me,' he told us, then ducked into the maze of machinery.

'There's no point in running!' the SPYDER agent called after us tauntingly. 'This valley's a dead end. We've got you cornered.'

'We'll see about that!' Cyrus yelled back. He led us quickly through the basement, moving with startling speed for a grandfather. Despite having just beaten four grown men to a pulp, he wasn't even winded.

As opposed to Alexander, who was now bringing up the rear, audibly gasping for breath. 'I don't suppose we could slow things down a notch?' he wheezed. 'I've got a stitch in my side.'

'Sounds like someone ought to be spending a little less time snowing his superiors and a little more time at the gym,' Cyrus groused.

'I'm in perfectly good shape, Dad!' Alexander retorted. 'This is just a residual injury from my last mission. A terrorist in Afghanistan tried to waylay me with a monkey wrench . . .'

'Don't talk rubbish,' Cyrus snapped. 'I'm your father, Alexander, not some knucklehead CIA director. I know when you're lying.'

Alexander clammed up after that, looking wounded, and didn't say another word for a while. No one did. As we were trying to elude the enemy, making as little noise as possible seemed like a good course of action.

Cyrus led us out of the basement through a distant, dingy stairwell that I'd bet most of the employees at Happy Valley didn't even know about. It came up in a maintenance room for the swimming pool. The pool was quite far from the main building complex – and therefore our enemies – as well as being closer to the surrounding forest than any other building on the premises. Cyrus cracked the door open and peered through to survey the area.

Over his shoulder, I could see across the large lawn to the main road in the distance. There were now three minivans blocking it. SPYDER for sure. Each van could seat seven adults, which meant there might be twenty-one agents combing Happy Valley for us, although only three were visible. They stood by the vans, keeping a lookout for us, although they were all focused on the main building, away from the pool. I couldn't see anyone else.

Neither could Cyrus. 'Coast looks clear,' he whispered. 'Erica, take this, just in case.' With that, he slapped a snub-nosed semiautomatic into her hand.

'Why don't *I* get a gun?' Alexander whined.

'The last time I gave you a gun, you accidentally shot me in the leg,' Cyrus replied.

'I was eight years old!' Alexander protested. 'And it

was a BB gun . . .'

'Exactly. I'll be darned if I'm going to give you something you could actually hurt me with.' Before Alexander could say another word, Cyrus put a finger to his lips, then bolted from the maintenance room towards the woods.

We followed him, keeping low to the ground to stay out of sight. It was a nerve-wracking run, as we had to cross a wide expanse of lawn. Although Cyrus had carefully chosen the route that was least visible from the other buildings, we were still badly exposed and out in the open. I kept waiting to hear the SPYDER agents sound the alarm – or simply open fire on us. But we made it to the cover of the trees without incident. The enemy agents didn't spot us. SPYDER might have predicted nearly everything we'd done so far, but it hadn't predicted Cyrus Hale.

Cyrus led the way through the forest without hesitation, as though he'd already memorized the escape route.

'It won't be long before they realize we've found a way off the property,' Alexander said. 'Do you have a getaway car close by?'

'Not exactly,' Cyrus replied. 'It's about an hour's hike.'

'An hour?' Alexander moaned.

'It was the best I could do on short notice,' Cyrus snapped. 'You really put yourself in the firing line here, Alex. You couldn't have picked a better place to be ambushed by the enemy.'

'It wasn't *my* idea,' Alexander said defensively. 'It was Erica's!'

'Laying the blame on your daughter again, are you?' Cyrus asked pointedly.

Alexander winced.

'She's just a teenager,' Cyrus continued, and then, before Erica could say anything, he added, 'A very talented and capable teenager, but a teenager nonetheless. As her father, you're supposed to be looking out for her! Instead, you let her walk straight into a trap. If I hadn't been keeping an eye on you, your goose would be cooked right now.'

'How long were you tailing us, Grandpa?' Erica asked.

'Ever since you got off the helicopter,' Cyrus replied. 'I followed you on your little reconnaissance mission last night, so I had a good idea what you were up to. Gave me some time to plan an emergency escape route.'

'If you were so concerned about us, why didn't you

just stop us *before* we went to Apple Valley?' I asked.

Cyrus shot me an icy stare. 'You're questioning me? You, a first year at the academy. Do you have any idea who I am?'

'I'm sorry,' I said. 'I didn't mean any offence . . .'

'I'm Cyrus Hale, for crying out loud! I've been serving this country since your mommy and daddy were still in diapers. I faced down the Russkies in the Cold War. I personally ended the Bay of Pigs fiasco. If it wasn't for me, this planet would have gone thermonuclear ten times over . . .'

Cyrus looked fit to rage on for another few minutes, but then Erica said, 'Actually, Grandpa, it wasn't a bad question.'

Cyrus immediately stopped ranting and softened. 'Ah, I suppose you're right, Cupcake. In the first place, I had direct orders not to engage you unless it was absolutely necessary. Second, I figured you might actually learn some important information on your mission, even if you weren't taking the appropriate caution to protect yourselves.'

'You mean, you let us sacrifice ourselves?' Alexander asked.

'Sacrificing you would mean letting you get captured,' Cyrus growled. 'Obviously, I did no such thing. I've been up since three a.m. planning this escape route. And have I heard so much as a thank you? No. All I've had is lip.'

'Thank you for rescuing us,' I said.

Cyrus swung back towards me, then nodded appreciatively. 'That's more like it,' he said.

'We *did* get some useful information, didn't we?' Erica asked.

'You did, Princess,' Cyrus agreed. 'You determined that SPYDER infiltrated the system to make sure that this Murray Hill character was never sent to Apple Valley. Which means that SPYDER is far more entrenched in the CIA than anyone has realized. We've been thinking they have one or two double agents at most. But now I suspect they have far more than that.' He suddenly came to a stop in a small clearing, his eyes darting from tree to tree.

'What's wrong?' Alexander asked.

'Nothing,' Cyrus said. 'I'm just trying to remember the way to the car.'

'You mean we're lost?' Alexander cried.

'No, we're not lost! I'm just getting my bearings, that's all.' Cyrus pointed through a gap between two oak trees. 'The car's this way.'

We started moving through the woods again.

'Dad,' Alexander said, 'You wouldn't have to try to memorize a path through the woods like this if you'd just get a smartphone . . .'

'Bah!' Cyrus said, sounding exactly like my grandfather when I tried to show him how to use the computer. 'Smartphones! You kids today rely way too much on technology. Back in my day, we didn't need smartphones to fight the Russkies. All we needed were guts, brains and semiautomatic weapons.'

'They're indispensable for the modern secret agent,' Alexander argued. 'If you had one, you could be using the global positioning system to find the car . . .'

'You don't have to tell me about the global positioning system,' Cyrus said. 'I know plenty about GPS. Take it from me, it's not as accurate as everybody thinks.'

'Now Grandpa, don't be such a dinosaur,' Erica said. 'Dad's actually right about this.'

'There's a first time for everything,' Cyrus muttered.

'There are a lot of useful smartphone apps for spies,' Erica went on. 'For instance, there's a great one for fingerprinting. We could have taken the prints of one of those SPYDER agents you took out and transmitted them to the CIA already.'

Cyrus shook his head. 'It wouldn't have done us

any good, Sweetie-Pie. I can guarantee you, those men's prints aren't in the system.'

'Why do you say that?' I asked.

'Because the CIA doesn't have the prints for every single person in the world on file,' Cyrus explained. 'Only known criminals. And SPYDER's too smart an organization to hire known criminals. Plus, if we had a smartphone right now, they'd be tracking our position with it. It'd be doing us far more harm than good.'

Erica smiled at Cyrus, impressed. 'Good point, Grandpa. As usual.'

The ground had begun to rise sharply. The forest thinned and we found ourselves scrambling over stone, sometimes scaling steep sections that required a few rock-climbing moves. We fell silent and focused on our ascent.

After a while, I realized Cyrus was staring at me. He was scrutinizing every move I made and didn't look pleased by any of them. I got the sense that he and Erica were very similar; cool customers whose respect I'd have to work for. 'Is something wrong?' I asked.

'I'm just trying to figure out what's so all-fired important about you,' Cyrus said.

'What do you mean?' Alexander asked.

Cyrus rolled his eyes as though this was the world's

dumbest question. 'I mean that SPYDER has been content to lay low for years now. So low that, until a couple months ago, we didn't even know they existed for sure. During that time, they've wormed their way into the CIA. They've corrupted our agents and hacked our computers. And after going through all that trouble, what do they do? They come after this kid. A first year student who's still wet behind the ears. Why?' Cyrus narrowed his eyes at me. 'What's so darned special about you?'

'I don't know,' I admitted.

Cyrus snorted in disgust.

We reached a gap in the trees that allowed us to see back down into the valley. Cyrus signalled for all of us to stop, then pulled out a pair of binoculars and cased the reformation camp. 'Looks like they've figured out we've given them the slip,' he chuckled. 'They're running around like a bunch of chickens with their heads cut off. Probably won't be long before they figure out we've taken to the woods.'

'Think they'll come after us?' Alexander asked.

'I doubt it.' Cyrus stuck the binoculars back in his utility belt and started up the slope again. 'We've got too big a head start on them. Besides, they know we've got to meet them again anyhow.'

'They still have our friends,' I said. In all the excitement, I'd almost forgotten.

'Exactly,' Cyrus agreed. 'We still need to spring those kids. Plan A might not have worked out for SPYDER, but they still have Plan B. All they have to do is sit back and wait for us.'

'So what are we supposed to do?' I asked.

'What can we do?' Erica echoed. 'We have to go and get them.'

'Even though that's exactly what SPYDER wants?' I said.

'Yes, but that doesn't mean we have to play by SPYDER's rules,' Erica said. She and her grandfather shared a knowing smile.

'That's my girl,' said Cyrus proudly. 'I taught her everything she knows.'

'What do you mean?' I asked Erica.

'This time, we're going to get the jump on *them*,' she replied.

Simulation

Winchester, Virginia
June 15
1300 hours

It took us another hour to walk to Cyrus Hale's getaway car, which was parked on an old logging road up in the forest. It took another few hours to drive to Winchester, as Cyrus took a very roundabout route. 'SPYDER will be watching the main highways,' he explained. We grabbed lunch at a Burger King drive-through on the way and arrived in Winchester twenty-four hours before we'd told SPYDER we could get there – which had been Erica's plan all along.

'You never meet the enemy on their terms,' she

explained as we sped into town. 'You merely *agree* to their terms and then catch them off guard.'

'Exactly what I'd have done in this situation,' Cyrus said with a chuckle. 'Where are you supposed to make the exchange?'

'An old barn just north of the city, at the intersection of highways 37 and 522,' Erica replied. 'But that's not actually where they're holding the hostages.'

'How do you know that?' I asked.

'Because I scoped the place out last night,' Erica told me.

'I thought you were doing recon on Apple Valley last night,' I said.

'I *was*,' Erica said. 'And then I came here and did some recon, too. That's why I was gone so long. The best way to catch your enemy with their pants down is to show up way before they're expecting you.'

Cyrus chuckled again. 'Nicely done, Cupcake. So, what'd you find out?'

'SPYDER was already at the barn,' Erica said. 'Preparing a trap for us, I suspect. I followed some of their guys back to a different farm on the western side of the city. I *think* the other kids are being held in the main house there. SPYDER had an awful lot of security set up around it. But I didn't have the time to investigate fully.'

'Well, let's do it now,' Cyrus said. 'Where to, Erica?'

Erica gave him the address of the new location, which was on the outskirts of town. I had expected to find a rustic, peaceful setting, but as we got closer, we found mayhem instead. The roads were filled with bumper-to-bumper traffic. In every field we passed, hundreds of people were gathered. Half were dressed in standard tourist-garb – t-shirts, shorts and baseball caps, with cameras strung around their necks – while the others were dressed far more unusually. They appeared to be in the wrong century. The women wore hoop skirts and carried parasols, while most of the men were in military uniforms, either blue or grey.

'What on earth is going on here?' Alexander asked.

'It's a Civil War battle re-enactment,' I groaned.

'The Battle of Second Winchester, to be specific,' Erica said. 'It was one of the major battles of the Civil War. The celebrations start today and go on all weekend.'

'Very clever of SPYDER,' Cyrus said, not bothering to hide his admiration.

'Why do you say that?' I asked.

'Look around you,' Cyrus said. 'Total chaos. A

243

thousand distractions for SPYDER to take advantage of. A hundred crowds for them to blend into . . .'

'But then, it's easier for us to blend in too,' Erica said.

Cyrus grinned at his granddaughter. 'Yes,' he said. 'I suppose it is.'

He pulled into a field that had been turned into a temporary parking lot. A teenage boy in a commemorative 'The South Will Rise Again' t-shirt stopped us. 'It's ten bucks to park,' he said. 'Are y'all Yankees, Confederates or impartial observers?'

'Yankees, of course,' Cyrus said, and forked over the money. 'Is there a sutler nearby?'

'North end of the field,' the kid replied. 'They'll fix you up real good.'

We parked and emerged into a surreal combination of modern and Civil War times. Men in authentic civil war uniforms were waiting in line for state-of-the-art portable toilets. A pick-up truck rumbled past towing an actual cannon on a trailer. Out in the fields, soldiers were drilling the same way they would have in 1862, but they were surrounded by hordes of tourists eating take-away food and snapping photos with their smartphones. A regiment of cavalry practised manoeuvres in front of a brand new suburban community while a field hospital, filled with men pretending that they'd been hurt in battle, might have looked genuine if there hadn't been an ice-cream stall behind it.

'Where's the farmhouse in question?' Cyrus asked.

Erica pointed across the battlefield. On the far side, beyond a line of cannon, there was a two-storey farmhouse straight out of a storybook. It had a white picket fence, a wraparound porch and a large tree with a swing hanging from the branches.

'Looks like that's behind union lines,' Cyrus said. 'We'd better dress accordingly.'

As promised, there was a sutler at the north end of the field. A sutler turned out to be a Civil War merchant – or at least, a merchant pretending to be from the Civil War. An entire store had been set up under a large tent, where you could buy everything necessary to make yourself look like an authentic soldier: uniforms, hats, muskets, knives, boots, haversacks, canteens, spyglasses, tinware and even ship's biscuit specifically made to taste exactly as terrible as it would have in the Civil War.

A man in period merchant dress looked up from polishing a musket as we entered. He had a beard so bushy it looked as though he'd glued the tail of a squirrel to his chin. 'Greetings, good citizens,' he said. 'Can I be of some service today?'

'I hope so,' Cyrus replied. 'We're long-standing re-enactors, but unfortunately, our house burned down this year and we lost all our gear. We're in need of four full Union uniforms from caps to boots and we understand this is the place to come for the highest quality merchandise.'

A big smile blossomed beneath the merchant's moustache. 'That it is, good sir. I can get all of you fitted out in a jiffy, although . . .' he nodded toward Erica, 'I can't help but notice that one of you isn't qualified for service in this man's army.'

Erica's eyes narrowed. 'You ever heard of Sarah Emma Edmonds? She disguised herself as a man and not only fought valiantly in the war, but also served as a spy for the Union.'

'Of course I've heard of her,' the merchant said.

'Well I happen to be her great-great-great granddaughter,' Erica told him. 'And as such, I believe that gives me the right to fight as a man in whatever battle I choose.'

The merchant turned bright red. 'I'm terribly sorry to offend you, Ma'am,' he said. 'I had no idea you were the descendent of such an important figure. I'll get you fitted out right away.' He scurried off to grab some clothes for us.

I turned to Erica, surprised. 'Are you really Sarah Edmonds' descendent?'

'No,' she said. 'I only know about her from *History of American Espionage*. Although I did have quite a few ancestors who were spies for the Union.'

'Of course you did,' I said.

Half an hour later, Cyrus handed over a wad of cash that had been stashed in his utility belt and we left the sutler's dressed from head to toe in authentic Civil War gear. I quickly discovered that, in the world of Civil War battle re-enactment, 'authentic' means 'incredibly uncomfortable'. My uniform was poorly-made, itchy and ill-fitting. It was also dirty, smelly, full of holes and horribly hot. Despite the summer sun beating down, I was wearing three layers – long johns, the regular uniform and a heavy topcoat. I was also weighed down with a musket, a bandolier of ammunition and a haversack stuffed with my old clothes and a few new supplies. Before I'd got halfway across the battlefield, I was dripping with sweat. 'Did we have to be completely authentic?' I asked Erica. 'I'll die of dehydration.'

'You don't want to look like a farb out here,' Erica

told me. 'You'll draw attention to yourself and we don't need attention.'

I nodded and sighed. A 'farb', I'd learned from the merchant, was a re-enactor who didn't strive for authenticity – for example, someone who had the good sense to wear nice, comfortable cotton underwear beneath their uniform.

In this spirit, Erica had hidden any trace of the fact that she was a woman, just as Sarah Edmonds had probably done. Her hair was tucked up under her grey cap and she wore the same clothes that I did. I had originally worried that we'd stand out, given our ages, but it turned out that there were plenty of kids dressed for battle. Apparently it was common for children to participate in the Civil War, so lots of fathers had brought their sons along for a fun family weekend of simulated violence and bloodshed.

As opposed to Erica's family, who had brought her along for a weekend of *actual* violence and bloodshed.

We reached the Union camp closest to the farmhouse where we suspected SPYDER was holed up. A soldier on post pointed his musket at us. 'State your business,' he demanded.

Cyrus gave him a sharp salute. 'Cyrus Hale and family, looking to join your forces so that we may aid in ridding the Union of the Confederate scourge.'

The Union soldier relaxed his guard and smiled. 'The 34th Regiment under the Honourable General Robert Milroy appreciates your help. We took a terrible beating in this morning's battle and could use some extra hands.' He pointed towards the 'battlefield' where dozens of men still lay in the summer sun, pretending to be dead or wounded, waiting for nurses, medics and coroners to come collect them.

'Where might we be of the best service?' Cyrus asked.

'Well, we always need basic infantry,' the soldier said. 'Though I don't suppose any of you knows how to fire a cannon? One of our usual cannoneers came down with dropsy this morning.'

'Dropsy?' I asked. 'Really?'

'Well, no,' the soldier confided. 'In truth, he got a bad case of irritable bowel syndrome, but "dropsy" sounds more authentic.'

'I know how to fire a cannon,' Cyrus said with a smile.

'You do?' the soldier asked excitedly.

'You do?' Alexander echoed.

'Of course,' Cyrus told him. 'My grandfather taught me.'

The soldier quickly brought us over to the cannoneers, where the news that Cyrus knew how to fire one was met with great excitement. After a brief quiz to establish that Cyrus actually knew what he was doing, the four of us were placed in charge of an actual working cannon. Cyrus was to serve as head cannoneer while the rest of us were in charge of loading and firing. There was no real ammunition – even the re-enactors weren't that committed to authenticity – but there were gunpowder charges, so that the cannons would boom and smoke just like the real things, along with cork cannonballs that could be fired at the enemy.

Our cannon was one of ten arrayed along the western edge of the battlefield, aimed toward the Confederate forces on the east. The farmhouse SPYDER had commandeered was behind our lines, further west of us, but the union camp we'd fallen in with was a large one and we were able to case the enemy compound without much fear of being noticed. We used our brand new Civil War scopes, which actually worked quite well. They didn't have the laser-guided digital focusing of the scopes we used in Spy School, but I could still see everything in the distance quite clearly.

The battlefield sloped gently, so that we were

slightly uphill from the farmhouse. This meant I could look straight through the first floor windows into what appeared to be the master bedroom. There was a gauzy window blind, but it was flapping in the breeze, and as it did, I caught sight of someone sitting in a chair in the tell-tale ramrod position of someone whose wrists are tied behind their back. There was a blindfold wrapped around her eyes.

'I found Zoe,' I said.

'Where?' all the Hales asked at once.

'First floor, southernmost room,' I replied, and they all swung their scopes that way.

'Chip's there too,' Erica reported. 'And Jawa.'

'Looks like they've got the whole gang,' Alexander said. 'I count six hostages.'

I did too. Claire, Hank and Warren were also in the room, tied to chairs and blindfolded. They weren't alone.

'There's guards in the room with them,' I said. 'Two men, both armed.'

'Which means there's probably a dozen more we can't see,' Cyrus said. 'I'll go a bit closer, do some more invasive recon.'

'All right!' Erica exclaimed excitedly, but Cyrus held up a hand, signalling her to stay put.

'I said *I'll* go,' he said. 'You've stuck your neck out enough already today, little lady.'

'Aw, Grandpa—' Erica began to protest.

'No,' Cyrus said firmly. 'First of all, it's dangerous. Second, we need to keep a low profile here. An old coot wandering around the battlefield in uniform won't attract much attention here today. An old coot wandering around with his granddaughter will.'

'I'll be careful,' Erica said. 'They won't see us.'

'They *will*,' Cyrus told her. 'These guys aren't amateurs. So just park yourself right here until I get back.' Cyrus shifted his attention to Alexander. 'Make sure she listens.'

'You mean I'm not going either?' Alexander whined.

'No. We can't afford any screw-ups right now,' Cyrus told him.

Alexander recoiled as though his father had slapped him.

Cyrus took no notice of his son's hurt feelings. He handed Erica his haversack. 'There are two walkie-talkies in there. I've got the third,' he said, then slipped into the crowd of Union soldiers and disappeared.

Erica opened the rucksack and took out the walkie-talkies, amused by how out-of-date they were. 'Radio communication,' she said with a smile. 'I'm surprised he didn't just give us a tin can on a string.'

Alexander slumped against the cannon, looking miserable. Yes, he was a cad, a phony and an opportunist, but I got the sense that he'd spent a great deal of his life trying to impress his father and had never received so much as a smile in return.

Meanwhile, Erica seemed to be at the opposite end of the emotional spectrum. While a few hours with Cyrus had beaten Alexander down, Erica was as happy as I'd ever seen her. She had resumed her surveillance of the enemy compound, whistling happily as she peered through her scope.

'You don't seem that upset he left you here,' I said.

Erica shrugged. 'I'm not thrilled about it, but grandpa's right about needing to keep a low profile. He's always right when it comes to these things. He's the best spy the CIA ever had.'

'Ever *had*?' I repeated. 'He still looks like he's working to me.'

Erica shook her head. 'No, he's been retired for years. He still consults every once in a while, but he's never agreed to be activated again until now.'

'Really?' I asked. 'Because he certainly seems to enjoy it.'

'Oh, I know he does,' Erica said. 'But he says that

spying is a young man's game.'

'He looks fine to me,' I said. 'He held his own against those guys at Apple Valley today.'

Erica smiled. 'He didn't mean physically. He meant that the longer you stay in, the more enemies you make. And Grandpa racked up plenty of enemies over the years. Plus, you can only keep your identity a secret for so long. Eventually it becomes too dangerous for you to stay active. In fact, it's even dangerous to be inactive. Grandpa had to go underground years ago. I don't even know where he lives.'

I turned to her, stunned. 'But you're his granddaughter!'

'When you've had a career like his,' Erica said, 'there's no such thing as being too careful.'

I realized that, while I'd spent an awful lot of time thinking about life as a spy, I'd never spent any time thinking about life *after* being a spy. It suddenly seemed awfully sad and lonely. My mind flitted back to the first conversation I'd had with Murray Hill when he'd tried to recruit me to SPYDER, where he'd emphasized all the negative aspects of a life in espionage. Now there was another one. 'How often do you get to see him?' I asked.

'Oh, every month or so,' Erica said. 'He drops in

when he's sure the coast is clear. Of course, I suspect he keeps tabs on me the rest of the time, though I've never caught him at it.'

'Of course he keeps tabs on you,' Alexander said sullenly. 'You're his pride and joy. The perfect student that I never was.'

Erica turned to her father. 'That's not true,' she said.

'Yes it is,' Alexander grumbled. 'Nothing I did was ever good enough for him. I couldn't disarm an enemy in two seconds. I couldn't build a bomb out of household chemicals without blowing up the kitchen. Even now, I can't be expected to help on a simple surveillance run. You heard him: I'll just screw things up.'

Erica sighed sadly. Despite all the bad things she'd told me about her father, she seemed to feel sorry for him too.

The ensuing silence was pretty uncomfortable. I tried to distract myself by scoping out the farmhouse again. Not much had changed, though. My classmates were in the same places they'd been the last time I checked, which made sense, since they were tied to the furniture. The same two men were still on guard in the bedroom. The only difference was that I could now see a third guard. He was downstairs, in what appeared to be the kitchen, looking furtively out of the window.

I wondered where Cyrus was.

I scanned the crowd of Union soldiers, but couldn't find him. As I searched, something began to nag at me. I had a sense that something we'd just discussed was important, although I wasn't quite sure why. I felt like I was looking at a hazy picture that had barely begun to come into focus.

I lowered my scope and turned back to Erica. 'The CIA has tried to activate your grandfather before?'

'Oh sure,' she said. 'He says they come to him all the time.'

'So why did he agree this time?'

'For a chance to actually confront SPYDER,' Alexander said. 'Defeating them would pretty much cement his reputation as the greatest spy of all time.'

As Alexander said this, however, I knew it was the wrong answer. I locked eyes with Erica. She'd realized it too.

'No,' she said, growing concerned. 'He agreed because of *me*.'

'I think so,' I said. 'Like your father said, you're his pride and joy. He knew you'd gotten involved in this and he was worried about you.' The hazy picture was becoming clearer now.

A bugle blared from the Confederate lines on the far side of the battlefield. A war whoop rose from the rebels, followed by an excited cheer from the spectators.

'To arms!' yelled a bearded man on horseback. He wore a general's uniform and waved a sabre above his head. 'Johnny Reb prepares to attack! Let us make these fields run red with his blood!'

Now the Union soldiers whooped. The men around us leapt to their feet and shook their weapons in the air. After milling about in the hot sun for a few hours, everyone was excited to play war.

Erica, Alexander and I were the only ones focused the other direction. We were all staring at the farmhouse.

Erica asked her father, 'Did Grandpa know I was involved in this when the CIA approached him about activating?'

Alexander frowned. 'I'm sure he did.'

I turned to Erica, worried. Everything was beginning to make sense. Like why SPYDER had been so blatant in their intentions with me.

'This isn't about me at all,' I said. 'SPYDER never wanted me.'

'They wanted Grandpa,' Erica said. 'They knew

you'd come to me for help, and that if I got involved, he'd get involved.'

'No,' Alexander said. 'They couldn't be that far ahead of us.'

'They're always that far ahead of us,' I said. I suddenly felt hollow inside. In part, this was because, once again, SPYDER had completely fooled everyone – including me. But in part, I was also ashamed. There *hadn't* been anything special about me. I had no incredible innate skill that made me invaluable to SPYDER's plans. SPYDER had made it all up to mislead everyone involved. I was a patsy – and a fool.

All around us, the Union soldiers were rushing to form tight ranks in front of the cannons.

One of the walkie-talkies in Erica's hand suddenly crackled to life. 'There are fewer agents on hand than I expected,' Cyrus reported. 'And this battle's distracting them. I'm going for the hostages.'

'No, Grandpa!' Erica shouted into the radio. 'Don't do it!'

'I have to,' Cyrus told her. 'We're not going to get another chance like this. I'll be in and out before they even know what's hit them. Going to radio silence.'

'Wait!' Erica yelled. 'They know you're coming! They've wanted you all along!'

But there was no answer in response.

'He's turned off his radio,' Erica said. I'd seen her in danger before, but until that moment, I had never seen her look scared. 'I'm going after him.'

'Me too,' Alexander said. He appeared both determined to prove his worth to his father – and absolutely terrified about facing the enemy.

'Count me in,' I said.

'No,' Erica told me. 'You're still only a first year and these men are dangerous.' She handed me a walkie-talkie. 'Stay here. Be our eyes on the farmhouse. I'll be in touch.'

Before I could protest, she was running off the battlefield, fighting her way through the surging Union forces. Alexander was on her heels.

'Hey!' the lead cannoneer shouted at them. 'Don't desert your posts! The battle's about to begin!'

Erica and Alexander didn't even look back. They vanished into the sea of blue uniforms, leaving me alone on the battlefield.

Battle

Winchester, Virginia
June 15
1530 hours

I leaned back against the cannon, feeling useless. All the things SPYDER had said about me had turned out to be lies. I didn't have a secret, amazing talent. I wasn't more valuable to them than Erica Hale. I wasn't an incredible spy in any way, shape or form. It had all been a ruse to lure a *real* incredible spy out of hiding.

And now that Cyrus Hale was in trouble, all I could do was stand aside while his granddaughter ran to his rescue. Yes, Erica had told me to be the lookout for the operation, but in spy terms, that was basically like being asked to be the towel boy for the school football team; it was the job you assigned to the earnest kid who really wanted to help but who didn't have any actual skills to contribute. In truth, I was relieved I'd been ordered to stay behind – I didn't have a clue what to do in this situation – and so, in addition to feeling useless, I felt guilty as well.

I raised the scope, hoping that I could at least keep an eye on things without screwing up. Although I quickly proved to be rather inept at this, too. I couldn't find Erica anywhere. I scanned the SPYDER farm in vain for her, but she was too good to be seen.

I *could* find Alexander, however. He was even more useless than I was. Somehow, in the process of fighting his way through the Union troops, he'd got turned around and had ended up going the wrong way. He was currently asking for directions at a souvenir stand, proving that his father had been right not to bring him along.

I directed my attention back to the farmhouse. The SPYDER agents were going about business as usual. They appeared completely unaware that Erica was en route, or that Cyrus was already somewhere on the premises.

Most of the fake Union soldiers had filed past me

and formed ranks to meet the Confederates. Three long lines of blue uniforms stretched from one side of the battlefield to the other, whooping war cries and taunting the enemy. Around me, men were scrambling to load their cannons.

On the other hand, I was merely propped against mine, staring off in the wrong direction.

It didn't take long for the lead cannoneer to notice. He was a gangly college kid who couldn't even grow his own sideburns – he had fake ones glued to his cheeks – but he was taking his position way too seriously.

'What is going on over here?' he demanded. 'The Confederacy is about to charge us and you're lolling in the sun like an old hound dog! Do you not care a whit for your country?'

'No, I do. I care many whits for my country,' I assured him, keeping the scope trained on the enemy. 'It's just that something very important is happening.'

'The Battle of Second Winchester is happening, Private!' Lousy Sideburns shouted. 'And you're missing it!' With that, he snatched the scope from my hands.

'Hey!' I snapped. 'I need that!'

'No, you need to load this cannon. That's a direct order. Should you disobey, I'll have no choice but to find you guilty of treason and send you to jail.' Lousy Sideburns pointed toward the sidelines, where there was a small fake field prison full of traitors, dissenters and a few farbs in 'Confederates Suck' t-shirts.

On the far side of the field, the rebels had formed their attack lines as well. Commanders on horseback raced along both fronts, shouting rallying cries that probably would have been inspiring if I'd had the time to listen to them. The soldiers fell silent in preparation for battle and an eerie calm before the storm fell over the field.

'I don't have time to explain this,' I told Lousy Sideburns. 'There's something going on here that's much more important than this silly re-enactment.'

Lousy Sideburns recoiled as though I'd slapped him. Apparently I hadn't chosen my words well. 'There is nothing "silly" about re-enacting! It's a glorious way to pay homage to the heroes who made this country great!'

'Then why doesn't anyone re-enact battles from World War II?' I asked, before I could help myself. 'You never hear about folks dressing up like doughboys and Nazis and re-enacting the D-Day invasion.'

'This isn't dressing up!' Lousy Sideburns gasped. 'We are embodying the spirit of heroes!'

A bugle call rang out from the far side of the battlefield. The confederate cannons fired.

Our cannons answered. It was staggeringly loud. We were suddenly enveloped in a cloud of thick, sulphurous smoke.

My walkie-talkie buzzed. It was Erica, though she spoke in code so that anyone from SPYDER would think she was just a re-enactor using inappropriate technology. 'Commander Ripley, this is the advance party. I have failed to convene with my superior as he is already in place to engage the enemy. I intend to extract him – and the others – but it won't be easy. There are far more rebels here than originally suspected. So I need you to create a diversion for me.'

I glanced sideways at Lousy Sideburns. 'Uh, how soon do you need it?'

'Sometime in the next two minutes would be nice,' Erica replied.

'Is that a walkie-talkie?' Lousy Sideburns demanded, looking apoplectic. 'You can't use twentieth century technology in a Civil War battle!'

This, coming from a man whose sideburns had been made in China.

I did my best to ignore him. 'Exactly what kind of diversion were you thinking of?' I asked Erica.

'You have a cannon, don't you?' she asked. 'That could be handy.'

For a moment, I was overwhelmed by the request. How was I supposed to help Erica, rescue my friends and deal with Lousy Sideburns all at once? But then an idea came to me that, despite everything, actually brought a smile to my face. 'I'll see what I can do,' I told Erica.

Then I spun back to Lousy Sideburns and saluted. 'Your words of wisdom have made me see the light, commander. You're right. This isn't dressing up. This is a great way to honour the heroes of yesteryear. Rest assured, those Confederates are cannon fodder.' With that, I went to work prepping the giant gun for battle.

Lousy Sideburns was surprised, but pleased, by my sudden turn. 'Very good, soldier,' he said, and then asked, 'By the way, where's the rest of your crew?'

'Picked off by snipers,' I reported. 'Medics already took them away. But I can handle this myself.'

'Nonsense!' Lousy Sideburns said. 'You keep at this. I'll find some fresh recruits to help.' He handed my scope back to me and raced down the cannon line.

There was a final bugle call from the battlefield, this one longer than all the others. The call to attack. The air was instantly filled with the roar of a few thousand fake Confederate and Union soldiers crying out at once – and then the lines charged one another.

Even though this was happening quite close to me, I couldn't see it all that well. There was no breeze at all on the field and the cloud of smoke from the cannons hadn't drifted away. Instead, it still hovered around, cloaking the entire cannon line in smog. I only had the haziest view of my surroundings.

However, that meant everyone else, from the spectators to my fellow re-enactors to the enemy agents in the farmhouse, couldn't see *me* well either.

I'd paid close attention when Cyrus had explained how to load the cannon, so I knew how to do it. And I'd learned a thing or two about rigging explosives during my time at Spy School. Now I scrambled to create the diversion Erica needed before Lousy Sideburns sent reinforcements my way.

There was a bag full of gunpowder charges by the cannon. By themselves, they would just pop and smoke for the enjoyment of the spectators, but altogether, there was enough gunpowder in them to make a good-sized explosion. I threw two charges down the barrel of the cannon, then dug through Cyrus's haversack.

As I'd expected, there was a roll of duct tape inside.

On the battlefield, through the haze, the first wave

266

of enemy lines met each other. Three hundred fake fights broke out at once, Yanks and Rebs pretending to stab one another with dull knives and clobber one another with toy muskets. Hundreds of men dropped to the ground and died in the hammiest way possible. In real life, when someone gets killed by the enemy, they tend to do very non-heroic things like cry and soil themselves. Out at Winchester, virtually every man went down valiantly cursing the enemy and imploring his fellow soldiers to go on without him.

The spectators loved every moment of it.

A giant ramrod hung from the bottom of the cannon. It was a long metal shaft with a padded end that made it look like a cotton bud for an elephant. I used it to ram the two gunpowder charges down the barrel of the cannon, then quickly wrapped the remaining charges to the shaft with duct tape.

Three men suddenly emerged from the smoke beside me. They were all considerably older than I was, dressed as basic infantry. 'The cannon leader says you've lost the rest of your team,' one with a shaggy beard said. 'We can take it from here, son.'

I knew I couldn't give up the cannon. If I did, I'd be letting Erica, Cyrus and all my friends down. So I tried to imagine what Erica would do in the situation.

It wasn't hard to do. She'd simply assume the position of authority.

I didn't even look at the men. I simply continued working, as though this was exactly what I was supposed to do. 'You men got here just in time. I could really use some help turning this cannon around.'

Two of the men didn't even question this. They simply rushed to help me. Big Beard held back, however.

'Turn the cannon?' he asked. 'Why? It's aimed toward the battle.'

'The Confederates are planning a sneak attack behind us,' I said confidently. 'My team spotted them right before the battle began. But Johnny Reb picked them off before we could counter.'

Big Beard bought it. 'Well then let's give Johnny Reb a little taste of Union vengeance,' he said.

There were chocks under the wheels of the cannon to prevent it from rolling backwards down the hill it was perched on. All we had to do was pull the chock out from under one wheel and give a little push. The cannon rolled backwards and spun so that it now faced the farmhouse.

The haze was clearing a bit around us. I could now see the farmhouse again, which gave me the ability to sight my target well. Since it also gave the enemy the ability to see us, however, we had to work fast.

Thanks to my gifted mathematical brain, I was able to quickly calculate the proper angle to set the cannon at, given the approximate distance to the farmhouse and our position above it. (It was quite easy, given that there was no wind to account for.) Together, my new team and I set the barrel and locked it in place.

Unfortunately, Lousy Sideburns had now spotted us as well. He stormed toward us again, sputtering in rage. 'What on earth is the meaning of this disobedience?'

'We're countering a Confederate sneak attack, sir!' I said, snapping a salute. The other three men followed my lead.

Lousy Sideburns' anger dimmed. He now looked confused. 'I don't think there's a sneak attack in this battle.'

'Of course there is,' I replied. 'It's in all the history books. Jubal Early sent a squad of Confederate commandoes to circle around behind enemy lines to assault the Union forces from behind.' I struck a match, lit one of the charges in the bag taped to the ramrod, then dropped the entire makeshift missile down the barrel of the cannon.

Lousy Sideburns was squinting in the direction of the farmhouse. 'I can't see any commandoes,' he said.

'They wouldn't be very good commandoes if you could,' I replied. Then I turned to Big Beard and said, 'Light it.'

Big Beard gleefully lit the fuse on the cannon. 'This ought to show those traitors a thing or two,' he laughed, then he stepped back and stuck his fingers in his ears.

'Package is en route,' I told Erica through the walkie-talkie. Then I plugged my ears as well.

The cannon boomed. The ramrod screamed out of it and rocketed through the air towards the SPYDER farm. My calculations were almost dead on. It stabbed into the ground less than a metre from its intended target: one of SPYDER's minivans. But that was close enough.

The bag of charges taped to the ramrod exploded a second later. The blast crumpled the minivan and knocked it onto its side. After which the van exploded as well.

Even in the middle of the battlefield, which was filled with chaos and noise, this was noisy and chaotic enough to grab people's attention. A hundred tourist videocameras swung from the battle to the farmhouse. Yanks and Rebs paused in the midst of fake fighting to turn towards the explosion. Men who'd just spent a good minute dying gloriously in battle suddenly came to life again, sitting up like zombies to see what had happened.

Inside the farmhouse, the SPYDER agents came to look, too. Through my scope, I watched them race to the windows to peer outside.

Which was exactly the diversion Erica and Cyrus needed. It turned out – although it didn't surprise me – that they were already in the house. One moment, SPYDER agents were standing in the windows and the next, they'd dropped out of sight, presumably unconscious on the floor. I didn't get so much as a glimpse of Erica or Cyrus, only their handiwork.

To my side, Lousy Sideburns was going nuclear. He hadn't taken our cue to step away from the cannon, so his face was blackened from the blast. One of his fake sideburns had been torn from his cheek and was now perched on his ear like a small rodent, but he was too angry to notice. 'What have you done?' he screamed at us. 'What have you done?'

'Well it's obvious,' I said. 'We've blown up a rebel minivan.'

In the farmhouse, the SPYDER agents disappeared from the upstairs windows and never reappeared again.

Then Erica emerged. She pulled off Chip's blindfold and Chip gave her a huge thankful smile. Erica sliced through his bonds with her army knife, and once Chip was free, he started to help free the others.

'The Confederacy doesn't drive minivans!' Lousy Sideburns raged. 'They ride horses! You have destroyed the property of an innocent bystander!'

'No,' I said, keeping my eye to the scope. '*You* have.'

'Me?' Lousy Sideburns asked. 'How am *I* responsible for this?'

'I didn't want to use this cannon,' I said. 'You *ordered* me to. I'm only a kid. What kind of lunatic lets kids use a cannon?'

Lousy Sideburns gulped, suddenly very concerned.

The three men who'd helped me quickly backed away from Lousy Sideburns, pointing fingers at him. They quickly broke character, desperate to divert any blame from themselves. 'We had nothing to do with this,' Big Beard informed everyone nearby. 'We were only following orders!'

Through all this, I kept watching the farmhouse. In the bedroom, everyone was free. No one wasted any time rejoicing though. Erica herded them all out of the door. She started to follow, but then something caught her attention. She whipped around, ready to attack…

And suddenly, I saw an emotion on Erica's face I'd never seen before. Surprise.

Her eyes went wide. Her face paled.

Whatever she saw was so startling, she did the unthinkable. She dropped her guard.

It was only for an instant, but it was enough. Whoever was in the room with her had the upper hand. Something struck Erica and she dropped, unconscious.

The next thing I knew, I was running towards the house.

There was no actual decision to do it. If I'd taken the time to decide, I would have thought about all the enemy agents inside who were better armed and more competent than me. I would have worried about my own safety. But I didn't.

I simply ran across the field as fast as I could, determined to help Erica. I yelled into my walkie-talkie, 'Cyrus! Erica is down in the bedroom!' but as I'd feared, there was no response.

'Hey! Get back here!'

I looked back to see Lousy Sideburns racing after me, his fake facial hair flapping in the wind. He'd mistaken my running away as an admission of guilt.

'Back off!' I told him.

'I'm not letting you out of my sight until we get to the bottom of this!' Lousy Sideburns yelled.

We were getting dangerously close to the farmhouse.

Without even thinking about it, I suddenly stopped and wheeled around. Lousy Sideburns' momentum carried him right into me, but I braced for the impact and used his inertia against him. I grabbed him by one arm and flipped him over my shoulder. He landed flat on his back in the grass so hard that it knocked the wind out of him.

'I said "Back off,"' I told him. 'This doesn't concern you.' I wasn't faking authority any more. I could feel it.

Lousy Sideburns sensed it as well. His eyes went wide with fear and he held up his hands in surrender. 'All right,' he said. 'I'm sorry.'

I spun around and raced for the farmhouse, feeling a bit less useless.

The hostages were streaming out of the front door, racing in my direction, so thrilled to be free that none of them had noticed yet that Erica wasn't with them. I waved my arms violently at them, signalling them to stop and turn around.

Most of them misunderstood what I was doing and cheerfully waved back.

I reached the edge of the battlefield, darted across the road and leapt the white picket fence.

Zoe reached me first. She threw her arms around me and hugged me tight. 'We're free!' she shouted. 'Thank you! Thank you!'

'Erica's still in there!' I told her – and everyone else. 'They got her!'

Everyone's expression went from joy to concern in a second. They all spun round to face the house.

An engine roared. A minivan that had been hidden behind the house hurtled down the driveway. I raced after it, but didn't stand a chance. The van skidded into the road and sped away. There was nothing I could do to go after it. The only other vehicle close by was the minivan I'd just blown up.

There were several SPYDER agents inside the van that was speeding away, though not a single one looked back at us. They couldn't have cared less about me and the hostages. They'd got what they'd really come for.

It only took a cursory sweep of the house to confirm this.

Both Erica and Cyrus Hale had been captured.

Debriefing

Maynard Farm
Winchester, Virginia
June 15
1800 hours

The six hostages – Chip, Hank, Claire, Zoe, Warren and Jawa – were fine. On the other hand, Alexander Hale was a wreck.

He'd finally arrived at the farmhouse a minute after SPYDER had fled, gasping for breath after running all over the battlefield. I met him on the front porch. 'What happened?' he wheezed. 'Where's my family?'

'SPYDER has them,' I said. 'We need to commandeer a car and go after them.'

Instead of leaping into action, however, Alexander glazed over instead. He simply sat on the porch swing and stared off into space.

'Alexander?' I said, waving a hand in front of his face. 'Did you hear me?'

Alexander didn't answer. He didn't even blink. He'd apparently gone catatonic with shock.

And I'd thought I was useless.

I went back inside. My fellow students were ransacking the kitchen. SPYDER hadn't fed them since breakfast and they were starving.

'We've got to get moving,' I said. 'Now.'

'No,' Hank told me. 'First, you need to debrief us.'

'There's no time!' I protested. 'SPYDER is getting away with Erica and Cyrus. Every minute we waste is another mile between us and them!'

'They've already got too big a head start for us to catch them,' Hank said. 'So if we want to rescue them, we need to figure out where they're heading. And that's not going to happen until you tell us what on earth is going on.'

I was annoyed at Hank for saying this – every fibre of my being was telling me that we should be racing after SPYDER at that instant – but I reluctantly realized he was right. 'All right,' I said.

'Bingo!' Chip yelled. He'd found a stash of Ben & Jerry's in the freezer. Claire grabbed spoons, and while everyone dug in, I tried to bring them up to speed.

'I'm still working everything out,' I said, 'but I believe that all of this has been a plot devised by SPYDER to capture Cyrus Hale.'

'Hold on,' Zoe said. 'I thought they were trying to capture *you*.'

'No,' I said. 'That was all a ruse. They never wanted me at all. I was just a pawn. That's why they were so obvious about coming after me: Sending me notes, having Murray Hill show himself in broad daylight, delivering a contract. They had two motives. First, they wanted me to freak out. They knew I'd go to Erica for help – and they knew Erica wouldn't be able to pass up the chance to prove herself against SPYDER.'

'And the second?' Chip asked.

'I think they wanted the CIA to freak out a little too,' I said. 'The agency sent their top man, Alexander Hale, to keep an eye on me. So now Cyrus Hale's son and daughter were on the mission. And then the CIA asked Cyrus to reactivate – which he did to protect his family.'

'So, when SPYDER attacked our bus, they weren't trying to capture us?' Jawa asked. 'They were trying to catch Alexander and Erica?'

'I think so,' I said. 'The whole point was to put them – or at least Erica – in jeopardy. Because Erica is the only person Cyrus would come out of retirement to help. When Erica thwarted their attack, though, they changed their tactics. They took you all hostage, knowing that they could force her to attempt the rescue mission – and that Cyrus would come along as well.'

'So SPYDER was expecting all of you to attack just now?' Claire asked.

'Yes,' I said. 'Maybe not at that exact moment. Erica might really have got ahead of them by showing up a day early. But they were still prepared for us. They've been one step ahead of us all along. They even knew we'd go to Apple Valley to try to figure out how Murray had escaped . . .'

'How *did* he escape?' Warren asked.

'He didn't have to,' I replied. 'He never even went in. SPYDER had double agents in the CIA. They swapped the real Murray out with a fake Murray, who agreed to be placed in the facility in return for cash.'

Everyone looked pretty shocked at that. Except Claire, who looked disgusted. 'Multiple double agents?' she sneered. 'Wow, you lot have some shoddy internal affairs. MI-6 would never let something like this happen.'

Zoe wheeled on her, furious. 'Do not start down that road, Princess. From what I understand, MI-6 has more moles than the White House lawn. And for all we know, you're one of them.'

'I certainly am not!' Claire gasped.

'Really?' Warren asked, always quick to back up Zoe. 'This trouble with SPYDER didn't begin until you showed up.'

'Actually, that's not true,' I said.

'It's not?' Warren asked.

'No,' Jawa said. 'Ben got the first note from SPYDER well before the MI-6 contingent arrived at camp.'

'That still doesn't prove she's not a double agent,' Zoe said.

'She's not,' Hank told us.

'How do you know for sure?' Chip asked.

'Because I vetted her myself,' Hank said, 'when I was studying in London. So drop it. Remember what Woodchuck told us on the bus? The first step in any emergency situation is to figure out how to work together. Well, this is an emergency situation all right. So we are going to work together. No more interagency rivalry garbage, no more arguing, no more petty disagreements, got it?'

Zoe glowered at Claire a while longer, but then said, 'Got it.'

Hank looked to Claire.

'Fine,' she agreed, though she returned Zoe's glower with her own.

'OK, that's settled,' Jawa said. 'So let's face the big question here: *why* did SPYDER want Cyrus Hale so badly?'

None of us had an answer to this. So everyone looked out of the window towards the one person they figured would know.

Alexander still sat on the porch swing, staring ahead. If he'd heard any of our conversation, he didn't show it.

'What's up with Agent Hale?' Jawa asked. 'What's he doing out there?'

'He's obviously thinking,' Zoe said, before I could come up with an answer. 'Look at the concentration on his face. He's probably devising a comprehensive strategy to track down SPYDER, thwart their plans and rescue his family right now.'

Apparently, I wasn't the only person Zoe always assumed the best about.

Almost everyone else nodded, buying this. None of them knew Alexander the way I did. They just knew him by reputation.

The only person who seemed remotely suspicious was Claire, who'd never heard of Alexander until recently. 'He doesn't look like he's thinking,' she said. 'He looks more like he's zoning out.'

'That's a look of focused concentration,' Zoe snapped. 'Alexander Hale is a Zen master. And besides, the man's daughter and father just got kidnapped by the bad guys. Zoning out a bit under the circumstances is understandable.'

Claire started to protest, but a sharp look from Hank made her back down. 'OK,' she said, raising her hands. 'Sorry.'

'I hope Alexander's come up with something,' Chip said. 'Because I have no idea how to track SPYDER down.'

Everyone else nodded. 'Yeah,' Jawa said. 'Thank goodness he's here. We're definitely going to need his help on this.'

'What about the rest of the CIA?' Warren asked. 'Shouldn't we notify the agency?'

Chip thwacked him on the back of the head with an open palm. 'Haven't you been listening? The CIA's full of double agents for SPYDER. We can't trust anyone there.'

'For now, the only agent we can trust is Alexander,' Hank agreed.

'Um,' I said awkwardly. 'You know, if we really had to, I'm sure we could handle this without him.'

Everyone looked at me as if I was crazy.

'Are you kidding?' Zoe asked. 'That's Alexander Hale! The greatest agent in CIA history! We're just a bunch of kids who've never had a field assignment before. If anyone's dead weight here, it's us. Alexander can probably handle this whole mission on his own.'

'Of course, we're willing to lend whatever support we can,' Hank said. 'But Alexander certainly ought to be team leader.'

Everyone chorused agreement.

Chip looked to me. 'So can you go and find out what he's come up with?'

'Me?' I asked.

'Yes, you,' Chip said. 'You're the only one here who's worked with him. He doesn't know the rest of us from a bucket of spit.'

To my astonishment, I realized that even Chip Schacter – who barely respected anyone – was in awe of Alexander Hale.

I considered my options. I was certainly wary of letting Alexander spearhead any operation; he'd screwed up pretty much everything I'd ever known him to be a part of. And yet the others were expecting guidance from him. I could have told them the truth about Alexander – that the man was a fraud who didn't deserve a jot of their respect – but what would happen afterwards? Everyone would be even more devastated – if they even believed me. And they still wouldn't know what to do next.

So that was out. We were all mere students who'd found ourselves in way over our heads. And in that moment, everyone needed someone to look up to.

'Give me a few minutes,' I said, and walked out onto the porch.

Alexander didn't even look up.

'Alexander?' I said.

There was no response.

'Alexander,' I said again. 'We need your help.'

'No you don't,' Alexander replied sadly. 'My help is the *last* thing anyone needs right now.'

'That's not true,' I said. 'None of us has any idea why SPYDER wanted to capture your father . . .'

'Well neither do I,' Alexander sighed. 'See? I'm useless.'

'Come on,' I pleaded. 'Think. Maybe your father knows some sort of classified information that SPYDER wants.'

'My father knows *tons* of classified information that SPYDER might want,' Alexander said. 'The question is, which information? The secret entrances to the White House? The launch codes for NORAD?'

'Your father knows the nuclear launch codes?' I gasped.

'I don't know,' Alexander said. 'I was being rhetorical. But he *might* know them. It's not like he'd tell me. He never told me anything . . . except what a disappointment I am.'

'I'm sure that's not true,' I said.

'Oh, it is. And he was right. I'm a failure. A disgrace to the Hale family name.'

'So you're not going to help us rescue him?' I asked. 'Because he was tough on you?'

'No, I'm not going to help because I'm a bad spy,' Alexander replied. 'How am I supposed to pull off a rescue? I couldn't keep my family from getting captured in the first place! I should have been there to protect them. Instead, I got lost like a moron.'

I completely agreed with all of this, but I still tried to be supportive. 'Everyone makes mistakes,' I told him.

'Well, I make them constantly,' Alexander said. 'That's all I do. I'm a sham. A fake. A charlatan. My entire career has been built on lies.'

It has, I thought. But then something occurred to me. 'No,' I said. 'That can't be true. That's Erica talking. I mean, I know you've lied. I know you stole the credit from me for capturing Murray Hill . . .'

Alexander turned away, embarrassed.

'But you can't build an entire career on that,' I went on. 'You couldn't possibly have the reputation you do without *some* talents.'

Alexander considered that for a moment. A tiny smile played at the corners of his mouth. 'Perhaps,' he said.

I pointed towards the house. 'There are six students in there willing to do whatever it takes to help Erica and Cyrus. But they don't know where to begin. They need something to believe in right now, and what they believe in is *you*. If you give up right now, they're going to give up – and then your family is as good as lost. So are you going to wallow in self-pity here, or are you actually going to get off your butt and do something?'

Alexander turned towards me. There was now a flicker of determination in his eyes. 'What do you need me to do?' he asked.

'Be Alexander Hale,' I said. 'Not the *real* Alexander Hale. Just the Alexander Hale everyone *thinks* is real. The man who can take out twenty terrorists with six bullets and defuse a bomb in his sleep. The best spy in the entire CIA.'

Alexander got to his feet. He looked through the window into the house.

Everyone inside had been watching us, though they quickly turned away and pretended like they hadn't been.

Alexander patted my shoulder. 'All right,' he said. 'I'll do my best.'

He walked into the farmhouse. I followed.

Everyone stood respectfully.

Hank actually snapped to attention and saluted. 'Hank Schacter, sixth year. This is Chip Schacter, Claire Hutchins, Jawa O'Shea, Zoe Zibbell and Warren Reeves. I think I speak for all of us when I say it is an honour to have the chance to serve with you, Agent Hale.'

Faced with adoring fans, Alexander quickly morphed back into his old self. It was almost a reflex. He straightened his back. His eyes gleamed brightly. 'Oh no,' he said graciously. 'It is my honour to serve with such a fine-looking troop of students.'

'There's no need to be diplomatic,' Zoe said. 'I've read every one of your case files, Agent Hale. Or at least, the ones that haven't been classified. You're the most talented spy in the whole CIA! You once disarmed a nuclear warhead while flying a helicopter!'

Alexander flashed Zoe a grin that made her turn pink. 'Well,' he said, 'that story has been slightly blown out of proportion . . .'

'How about the time you took out an entire terrorist nest in Afghanistan with only a Swiss army knife?' Warren asked.

'Or when you prevented the assassination of the Premier of China at the very last second?' Jawa added.

Alexander chuckled. 'My goodness,' he said. 'You all know my own files better than I do.'

'Of course they do,' I told him. 'You're a legend.' Then I lowered my voice to add, 'And legends, no matter how preposterous, are usually based on fact, right?'

Alexander met my gaze and nodded agreement. 'Right.'

Hank stepped forwards. 'I'm sure we could go on flattering you all day, but right now, time is of the essence. We are willing to do whatever it takes to rescue your family from the evil clutches of SPYDER. So, what's your plan?'

Alexander's smile faltered. It was evident that, after all I'd gone through to get him to step up, he had no idea what to do next. But then, he noticed my fellow students looking at him expectantly and rallied to save face. 'Well,' he said, 'this may sound a bit unorthodox, but . . . Sometimes, the best way to figure something out is to see if someone else has already figured it out before you.'

'You mean like copying someone's homework?' Claire asked suspiciously.

'In a way,' Alexander admitted. 'Only in real life, that's not always such a bad thing. Why should we waste time trying to determine where SPYDER has taken my family if someone else has already done the legwork? Now, does anyone here know of anyone who might already know where SPYDER's hideout is?'

I couldn't believe my ears. After all I'd done to beef his ego back up, the only plan Alexander could actually devise was to get someone else to do the work for him. I was just about to express my annoyance when something astonishing occurred to me: Alexander's moronic idea could actually work. 'I think someone might,' I said.

Everyone's gaze shifted to me. 'What do you mean?' Chip asked.

'When I got the first note from SPYDER, Erica found an extremely tiny piece of grit on it,' I explained. 'She thought it might be a lead to where the letter had been written and was going to get someone to analyse it for her.'

'Who?' Hank asked.

'I don't know,' I admitted. 'She didn't tell me.'

'Probably Chester Snodgrass,' Alexander said. 'He's a forensic geologist in the Department of Evidence Assessment. He's always been a big fan of Erica's.'

Everyone turned to Alexander, impressed, as if he'd actually deduced something.

'Can you call him?' Zoe asked.

'Unfortunately, no,' Alexander sighed. 'The International Forensic Geology convention is in Orlando this week. Chester never misses it – and I lost all his contact information along with my phone in the river.'

I frowned at this, but then Hank said, 'Well, we wouldn't have to talk to Chester directly. It's standard procedure to log all evidence analysis on the CIA central computer system. We simply need to access it.'

'Can you do it remotely?' Warren asked. 'There's a computer in the house.'

'It's not that simple,' Jawa explained. 'For security

reasons, you can't access the central system with any old device. You can only use a device linked to the system. All our phones are, but SPYDER took them.'

'So we just need to call someone at the CIA and have them access the system for us,' Warren said.

Chip bopped him on the back of the head again. 'Did you forget already? The CIA is crawling with double agents. We can't trust anyone there.'

'I didn't forget,' Warren snapped. 'But you're going to tell me that, in the entire CIA, we can't trust one person?'

'Everyone is suspect,' Hank said. 'If we get someone who's a stooge for SPYDER, instead of giving us the info we want, they'll send us on a wild goose chase.'

'Not everyone is suspect,' I said. 'I know who to trust.'

Now, everyone's gaze turned to me. 'Who?' Zoe asked.

'It's simple,' I told her. 'If you want to figure out who's definitely not working for SPYDER, you simply look for someone whose career SPYDER has ruined.'

Zoe's eyes lit up with understanding. 'Tina Cuevo.'

'Exactly,' I said.

21

Forensic Geology

Maynard Farm
Winchester, Virginia
June 15
1830 hours

I made the call from the farmhouse kitchen. I never forget a phone number. It goes with the territory as a maths prodigy.

Tina answered on the fourth ring. 'Agent Cuevo.'

'Tina! It's Ben Ripley.'

'Ben! How nice of you to call.'

'How's Vancouver?'

'I've got to admit, you were right. It's not nearly as bad as I thought it'd be. The city's beautiful, the agents are cool, and my internship is actually really exciting. I've only been here two days and I already got to go on my first raid.'

'Really?'

'Some psycho American rock star was trying to have a polar bear smuggled across the border. We saved the bear and got the smugglers to give us the evidence in, like, ten minutes. It was awesome.'

'Sounds like fun, Tina.'

'It was. Plus, there's a fantastic sushi place right around the corner from our office. I think I'm really going to like it here.'

'That's great. Listen, I was wondering if you could do me a small favour . . .'

'You mean you're not just calling to wish me a happy first week on the job?'

'Well, no. Not exactly. You see, some things have happened with that whole SPYDER case I came to you with. A couple of students ended up getting kidnapped . . .'

'Oh. Er . . . Well, the thing is, as much as I'd like to help, I'm in Canada, Ben. If you have a problem, you really ought to talk to Hank.'

'He was one of the students who got kidnapped.'

'What?'

'Don't worry. We got him back. Him and everyone else. But now SPYDER has Erica Hale and her grandfather.'

'How did that happen?'

'It's a long story and, unfortunately, I don't have time to explain it all right now. The short version is, the CIA is rife with moles and you're the only person I know I can trust.'

'Aw, Ben. That's sweet of you.'

'Erica turned in some evidence a few days ago that might be a lead to where SPYDER's hideout is. Our guess is that she gave it to Chester Snodgrass in forensic geology. Can you access the central system and see if Snodgrass posted his results?'

'Sure. I'm at my computer right now. Hold on.'

I heard the distant sound of Tina's fingers typing rapidly.

My fellow spies, huddled in the living room, looked at me expectantly. 'She's working on it,' I told them.

'Tell her I said "hi,"' Warren said.

'Got it!' Tina told me.

'What's it say?' I asked.

'Give me a few moments. It's a long report. Wow. Who ever knew you could tell so much from one piece of grit? Let's see. Spectroanalysis, radio carbon dating, elemental assessment. Ah, here we go. It's a piece of coal.'

'That's it?'

'No. There's quite a bit more.' Tina hummed as she scanned through the report on the computer. 'Seems like every vein of coal is different. Slight alterations in the various elements and such. So Snodgrass ran all these tests to try to determine the exact make-up. Looks like he got two matches. The bit of coal either came from a seam in Vladivostok, Russia . . .'

'Ugh,' I said.

'Or the Junction Mine near Shepherdstown, West Virginia.'

I felt a shiver of excitement. 'How far is that from Winchester, Virginia?'

'Hold on. Let me map it. Here we go. Only about thirty miles. Looks like it's been abandoned for a few years now. And FYI, it's only an hour from downtown Washington.'

'That sounds like the place. Do you have coordinates?'

Tina rattled off the exact latitude and longitude of the mine and I committed them to memory.

'Thanks,' I told her. 'You've been a huge help.'

'Just make sure the higher-ups back there know

that. In case I ever change my mind about saving polar bears and want to come back.'

'Will do.' I hung up and turned to everyone else. 'Sounds like SPYDER's taken over an abandoned coal mine thirty miles from here.'

'Let's go get them,' Alexander said.

Everyone else cheered excitedly.

Except Warren, who gave me a cold glare. 'You didn't tell Tina I said "hi,"' he said.

22

Reconnaissance

Junction Mine

5.6 miles from Shepherdsville, West Virginia

June 15

2300 hours

In the rucksack Cyrus had left behind, there was a stash of emergency supplies. This included medication, tourniquets, flares, a Swiss army knife – and a great deal of cash. There was over five thousand dollars in US currency (as well as large wads of Canadian dollars, Euros, Russian rubles, Mexican pesos and six other currencies I didn't even recognize. Apparently, Cyrus was always prepared to leave the country at a moment's notice). Alexander took three hundred dollars and rented a minivan.

Next, we went to WalMart.

Turns out, you can actually supply an entire spy mission at your average superstore. Things that James Bond would have found incredible in his early movies, like night-vision binoculars, are now available over-the-counter. We picked up camouflage gear for everyone, walkie-talkies, backpacks, head-mounted flashlights, backpacks, greasepaint, a few laser-sighted scopes and a dozen rolls of duct tape. There were plenty of hunting rifles available too, although we couldn't buy any without identification. So we stocked up on alternative weaponry: bows and arrows, hunting knives, pepper spray and brass knuckles. We also got plenty of bottled water and energy bars. Hank, who'd been studying advanced chemical weaponry, got some cleaning supplies. Then, just to be on the safe side, we picked up a few paintball guns too. At least they looked like the real thing. The cashier didn't even blink an eye as we rang it all up. 'Looks like you folks are out to have yourselves some fun tonight,' she said.

'You have no idea how much,' Chip told her.

It was several hours into the night by the time we finished our shopping. We loaded the van and set out to find the Junction Mine.

This was a little more difficult than we'd expected. As Tina had said, the town of Shepherdsville was only a half hour north of Winchester, where the arm of West Virginia hooked over the top of Virginia. The mine was clearly marked on a roadmap we'd bought at WalMart, but when we got to the right general area, we couldn't find it. We drove up and down the nearest road three times, but there wasn't anything even closely resembling a turnoff.

'Are you sure you memorized the right coordinates?' Claire asked me pointedly.

'Yes,' I said, although truthfully, I was wondering the same thing.

'Doesn't look like you did,' Claire said.

'Now, now,' Alexander interjected from the driver's seat. 'Let's not be too tough on young Agent Ripley. The fact that we can't find the mine is actually a good sign.'

'How?' Claire asked.

'Because it means someone has tried to conceal it,' Alexander replied. 'And that means we're probably on the right track.'

Everyone looked at Alexander, impressed. He smiled broadly, proud of his deduction. With a van full of acolytes hanging on his every word, Alexander's confidence and bravado had come back in spades – and, in turn, he'd proved what I'd suggested on the porch: He had at least a little spy savvy.

He wasn't the only one rising to the occasion. The others were all shining in their own special ways. Chip was rigging and arming the weapons. Zoe was outfitting each backpack with the proper supplies. Even Warren was being helpful: as our class camouflage specialist, he was making up our faces to make sure they blended into our surroundings.

Alexander swung the van around and now motored slowly along the same stretch of road we'd taken before. 'Everyone pay close attention to the sides of the road,' he ordered. 'Don't expect to see any official signs. SPYDER has certainly removed them. Instead, look for any indication that the road has been concealed: Unusually thick foliage in one spot, for example.'

We all pressed against the windows, peering into the dark. After a few minutes, Jawa shouted triumphantly. 'There! Something's not right.'

Alexander pulled over where he pointed, angling the headlights into the trees. At first, we seemed to be staring at a completely normal swathe of forest, but then I began to notice what had grabbed Jawa's attention. The branches didn't look quite right. They were too close to the ground and too clumped together. Someone had clipped them from trees and expertly arranged them to conceal a gate.

Once I knew the gate was there, I could see the dirt road heading into the woods behind it. It was almost impossible to see in the night, a slightly darker tunnel against the general darkness of the forest, but it was there.

'This must be the place,' Zoe said. 'Let's go.'

'No,' Claire cautioned. 'If SPYDER is as clever as you say, they're probably monitoring the road. We should approach their base through the woods on foot instead. I suspect, under the cover of trees, we could do that with stealth.'

Even Zoe had to admit that Claire was right about this.

Alexander drove on to a suitable point a half mile down the road, where there was a gap in the woods big enough to pull the van into and conceal it. Zoe handed out backpacks, Chip handed out weapons and Warren applied the finishing touches to our camouflage. Then we slipped into the woods, moving as quickly and silently as possible.

We were in mountainous country once again. We'd parked high up, near a pass so we were now heading downhill, although the slope was relatively gentle and easy to negotiate, even in the dark. After twenty minutes, we caught our first glimpse of the mine. It was still a little way below us through the trees. We searched the grounds through our night vision goggles.

SPYDER was there.

After seeing way too many spy movies, I had some misguided expectations about what an evil organization's secret hideout would look like. I didn't necessarily think there would be a multi-million dollar underground facility with thousands of anonymous minions in matching uniforms and a handy self-destruct button – but I did expect something impressive. A small army of minions, at least. Or a high-tech command centre. Instead, SPYDER's control centre looked like the world's most poorly-designed caravan park.

The evil plans of the world's most secretive enemy organization were being carried out in two mobile homes and a Winnebago. All three were arranged in a small triangle in a wide, flat space near the entrance to the mine. It was hard to tell which might have been the most important, as none of them looked remotely impressive. The mobile homes were ancient, with peeling paint and cracked windows. The Winnebago looked at least ten years old.

I wasn't the only one who was unimpressed. 'That's it?' Warren groused. 'It doesn't look like much.'

'Don't be such a Fleming,' Chip shot back. 'This is a temporary hideout, not their international headquarters.'

'Besides, the *real* centre of operations is probably inside the mine,' Jawa said. 'Look.' He pointed to a large generator chugging away. Power cables snaked from it into the entrance of the mine.

'Keep it down, you guys,' Zoe hissed. 'There's enemy agents on patrol down there.'

Sure enough, there were. Although there were only three – that I could see, at least. Each had a rifle slung across his back and at least one sidearm stuffed in a holster. Like the men who'd come after us at Apple Valley, they were casually dressed in blue jeans, t-shirts and baseball caps. In fact, I was quite sure two of them had been among the men at Apple Valley. Both had black eyes and taped noses: Cyrus Hale's handiwork.

As for the mine itself, it wasn't a modern coal mine, where the top of an entire mountain had been stripped off. Instead, it was so old fashioned it was almost quaint: a tunnel dug into the mountainside and propped up with wooden beams. Rusted iron tracks ran through it, upon which wheeled coal cars had once run. Until recently, there had been a chain-link gate blocking the entrance, but SPYDER had cut through the lock and the gates now sprawled open.

'Any sign of Erica or Cyrus?' I asked.

'Not in trailer one,' Chip reported.

'Negatory on the Winnebago,' said Warren.

'No one's in trailer two either,' Hank said.

'How about Murray Hill?' I asked.

'No,' Chip said.

'Negatory on that,' Warren said.

'Would you drop the "negatory" crap?' Hank demanded. 'It makes you sound like a moron.'

'Sorry,' Warren said.

'I can't see Murray either,' Hank reported. 'Jawa's right. Everyone must be in the mine.'

'I agree,' Alexander said. 'Let's take the guards out.'

There was some brief dissent on how to do this. Hank thought we could take the guards out at long range. Claire had been the English archery champion in her age range for six years running and claimed she could knock the stem off an apple from across a football field. However, Alexander felt we had to take out all the guards at once. If you only got one, the others would notice and sound the alarm. That meant a coordinated man-to-man assault.

My man-to-man assault skills weren't exactly my strongest suit. In fact, they were my weakest: I'd got a D in hand-to-hand combat. Luckily, my fellow spies-to-be had some expertise in this area. Hank, Chip and Jawa were among the better combatants in school. And Hank had some tricks up his sleeve.

He quickly mixed up a cocktail of cleaning supplies, then tore a $5 Walmart beach towel into rags and soaked them in the solution. 'Just get behind your target and clap this over their nose and mouth,' he instructed.

'What is it?' Warren asked. He took an experimental sniff – and passed out cold a second later.

'Knock-out drops,' Hank sighed. 'And as you can see, they work fast. So everyone else, be careful around it.' He, Chip and Jawa synchronized their watches and set off for the guards.

The next few minutes passed slowly as we waited for them to do their job. To pass the time, I kept the night vision goggles to my eyes, scanning the compound for any more of the enemy. Except for the guards, I didn't see anyone – although I did notice something odd tucked behind the Winnebago: a large metal case with Russian writing on the side.

'Can anyone here read Russian?' I asked.

Everyone else raised their hand.

'Where?' asked Zoe.

'The metal case right beside the Winnebago,' I said.

'I see it,' Alexander said. 'It says "Exterior monkey monitoring organism".'

'No,' Claire corrected. 'It says "Surface missile control system".'

'SPYDER has a missile?' Zoe gasped. 'That can't be good.'

I winced, cross with myself. 'We should have known they'd have more.'

'More?' Claire asked. 'What do you mean "more"?'

'They already fired one at us,' I said. 'Two days ago.'

'And you didn't think that was worth sharing?' Claire asked.

'There's been a lot of other stuff going on . . .' I began, but then trailed off mid-thought, as something had just occurred to me. Suddenly, I had an idea what SPYDER might have been plotting. 'Alexander, earlier today your father said that the global positioning system isn't as accurate as everyone thinks. What did he mean by that?'

Alexander's face suddenly flooded with concern.

'Goodness me,' he said. 'So *that's* why they want with him.'

'What?' Zoe asked. 'What's going on here?'

'The Global Positioning System was developed by the Department of Defence in the 1970s,' Alexander explained. 'My father was the CIA liaison on the project. The original purpose of GPS had nothing to do with giving everyone directions in their cars. It was for the military.'

'Missile guidance systems,' Claire said.

'Among other things,' Alexander told her. 'My father knew all along that the military would never be able to keep GPS under tight wraps. Eventually, the public would be able to use it. Which meant *anyone* would be able to use it.'

'Like bad guys,' Zoe said.

'Correct,' Alexander agreed. 'My father felt that this would be a security risk, so he convinced Defence to build errors into the system to protect certain locations that might be targeted by terrorists. For example, the coordinates that GPS gives you for the White House aren't the actual coordinates for the White House. They're close, but not exact. So if any bad guys tried to fire a missile at it from a distance, they'd blow up a Starbucks down the street, not the president.'

'But your father knows the actual coordinates?' I asked.

'Yes,' Alexander said. 'He felt it was too dangerous to record them anywhere. So he memorized them.'

'But now, SPYDER can make him hand them over,' I said.

'I'm afraid so,' Alexander admitted. 'If they had only captured my father, he'd never give up the information. He'd kill himself before he did that. He has a cyanide capsule embedded in one of his teeth just for such occasions. But SPYDER must have known that, because they captured Erica too. She's my father's only weakness. He'd do anything to protect her.'

I shook my head, amazed by SPYDER's plan. They hadn't only been after Cyrus Hale, then. They'd been after Erica as well. And they'd used me to get to both of them.

'There's just one thing I don't understand,' Zoe said, shaking her head. 'This seems like an awful lot of trouble to go through. If SPYDER really wanted to hit the president, couldn't they just bring the missile to within sight of the target and fire it directly?'

'No.' Alexander shook his head. 'First, all missile systems operate via the same global positioning coordinate system, no matter how close you are . . .'

'But you could override it, couldn't you?' Zoe asked.

'Perhaps, if you were using a small missile,' Claire said, looking through her night vision goggles at the box for the control system again. 'But it looks like they've got a Russian Omsk-class surface-to-surface missile there. It's not exactly a pocket rocket. No one could smuggle something that big within ten miles of the president. It'd be like trying to smuggle a building into downtown Washington.'

I was already feeling gravely concerned, but now an even more worrying thought came to me. 'Exactly how big is the payload on one of those?'

'I can't recall off the top of my head,' Claire said. 'But it's quite substantial. Enough to level the entire White House.'

'So then, SPYDER's probably not going for a mere assassination here,' I said. 'They're trying to take out a lot of people at once.'

Everyone met my eyes, now looking as worried as me.

'Congress?' Zoe suggested. 'Could they take out the whole capitol building with one shot?'

'Maybe,' Alexander said. 'Although my father also knows the true coordinates for the Supreme Court and the Pentagon as well.'

'Perhaps,' Claire said. 'But SPYDER *couldn't* be targeting those places. The Omsk is an old missile. We're talking early Cold War. Despite the large payload, its range is limited. Less than thirty miles, I believe. Washington DC is too far from here.'

'Then what's the point of taking over this mine?' Zoe asked. 'What could possibly be of national interest way out here in the sticks?'

'Camp David,' I said.

Claire gasped. 'The country residence for the President of the United States? That's near here?'

'Less than thirty miles, I'd bet,' I said.

'Does anyone know if the President is there right now?' Zoe asked.

'He is,' Claire said gravely. 'He's meeting the British Prime Minister and a few other European leaders.'

'The perfect set of targets for an evil organization with a stolen missile,' Alexander said.

We solemnly nodded agreement.

'Looks like we got here just in time,' I said.

'Assuming we can actually stop them,' Claire told me.

'Yes,' I said. 'It'd be very nice if we could do that.'

23

Infiltration

Junction Mine
June 15
2345 hours

According to my watch, it was almost time for Chip, Hank and Jawa to strike. I peered through my night vision binoculars.

In the compound below, the three SPYDER guards were still standing.

And then they weren't.

The boys attacked so fast, I almost didn't see it. Each hit their target from behind, took him down and sedated him in perfect sync. The guards didn't have a chance to sound the alarm.

Then Hank gave us the OK sign.

'Step one's a success,' I reported.

'Great,' Claire said sourly. 'Now all we have to do is infiltrate an abandoned mine, find the captives, rescue them – and oh yes, prevent a missile from going off.'

'All in good time,' Alexander said. He sounded surprisingly confident and reassuring, although when I looked at him closely, I could see he was quite worried as well.

Warren was still out cold, so we left him propped against a tree with a paintball gun and hurried down the wooded slope to the compound. Hank, Chip and Jawa had bound the SPYDER agents tightly with duct tape by the time we got there.

'Nice work,' Alexander told them. The boys beamed, thrilled to have received a compliment from the great Alexander Hale.

Zoe, Claire and I quickly searched the trailers and the Winnebago while Alexander brought the others up to speed on SPYDER's plan. The trailers turned out to be merely bunkhouses, while the Winnebago was being used as a mobile kitchen. Everything of importance was apparently in the mine. The only thing of interest I found were the keys to the Winnebago, which had been hidden above the driver's sun visor. I pocketed them to make sure no bad guys drove off.

By the time we regrouped, the others were hatching a plan.

'It looks like this is the only entrance to the mine,' Alexander was saying. 'And in any case, we don't have time to search for another. That missile could go off at any moment. So we all go in this way. Now who here is most qualified to reprogram the missile control system?'

'Uh, I think *you* are,' Zoe said.

'Me?' Alexander asked.

'Yes,' Zoe replied. 'According to your files, you've reprogrammed the control system of a missile before. Twice, in fact. Once with only twenty-three seconds until firing.'

'Ah. So I have.' Alexander smiled weakly. 'Does anyone else know how to do this? As a sort of emergency back-up system, in case something should happen to me?'

Everyone shook their heads. 'Reprogramming missiles is a very advanced course,' Hank said. 'Only seniors get it. Looks like you'll have to handle it, Agent Hale. Take Ben with you. He's the maths genius, so he can help with any calculations you need to make. The rest of us will rescue Cyrus and Erica. Let's move.'

There was no time for me to protest. As Alexander had said, time was of the essence. We strapped on our headlamps, helped ourselves to the weapons of the unconscious guards and set off into the mine.

Entering an abandoned mine shaft would probably be somewhat spooky on a nice, sunny summer afternoon. Entering one filled with enemy agents plotting the simultaneous assassination of a dozen world leaders on a dark, moonless night was downright nerve-wracking. Even when I was surrounded by fellow spies-in-training. Because the fact was, no matter how talented everyone was, we were still spies-*in-training*. Only Alexander had ever been on a real-life mission – and his espionage talents were questionable at best.

The mine shaft was incredibly dark and claustrophobically narrow. If I stuck out my arms I could touch both sides. In addition, it was dank and damp. Water trickled down from the roof in spots and pooled on the floor in others. Roaches and millipedes of startling size scurried along the walls while bats darted over our heads. A thick black power cable from the generator wound along the tunnel floor; in the faint light of our headlamps, I repeatedly mistook it for a very large snake.

Alexander was at the point position at the front of

our attack. He hadn't actually chosen this position. I had no doubt that, in similar circumstances with real CIA agents, Alexander would have positioned himself towards the back of the pack, where it was safer. But my fellow students had ceded the point position to him and Alexander had taken it to save face.

I reluctantly joined him there because I needed to talk to him.

'Have you ever actually reprogrammed the control system for a missile?' I whispered.

'Uh, no,' he said, glancing behind him to make sure the others couldn't hear. 'In one case, a fellow spy named Ken Parker did the reprogramming, but then he whacked his head during the escape and got amnesia, so I took the credit.'

'And the other time?' I asked.

'The missile just sort of blew up on the launch pad,' Alexander told me. 'Probably an error in construction. It was a North Korean missile and their handiwork is generally quite shoddy. But I said I'd made it happen in my report.'

'So then, you have no idea how to stop this missile from firing?' I asked.

'No,' Alexander admitted. 'But then, I don't really have any idea how to rescue my father and daughter, either. So it's kind of a relief that someone else is handling that.'

'You have to be honest with the others,' I said. 'This isn't a game. The lives of the leaders of the free world are at stake here.'

'I don't think that's necessary,' Alexander said. 'I'm sure you and I can handle this.'

'I don't!' I said. 'The only time I've even *seen* a missile was when that one nearly blew us up. And as far as you're concerned—'

'Shhh!' Hank hissed. 'Enemy ahead. Lights off.'

We were immediately plunged into darkness, save for a faint glimmer of light in the distance, shining from around a bend. I could hear the distant sound of voices and footsteps echoing from the same direction.

We were close. We pressed forwards, closing in on SPYDER. I wanted to stop them all and explain that there was a large flaw in relying on Alexander, but there was no way to do that without making a sound – and it was so dark that I couldn't even signal anyone else manually. I had no choice but to press on and hope that Alexander was right, and that somehow, he and I would actually figure out how to handle the missile – assuming we even got the chance to do that.

Our team moved through the tunnel as silently as

possible. The dim light grew brighter as we got closer – and the noise grew louder too. Finally, we were close enough to peer around the corner.

Directly ahead of us, the mine widened into a large cavern. It appeared to be a main junction where six different tunnels came together. In the centre of it, a vertical shaft rose up through the roof, apparently heading to the top of the mountain. A makeshift launch pad had been built directly beneath it. A missile sat on this, ready to fire up through the shaft.

Even though Claire had said the missile would be big, I was still surprised by the sheer size of it. It was three storeys tall and more than two metres in diameter. The booster alone was three metres long. It reeked of rocket fuel and idled menacingly.

SPYDER's choice of location was brilliant. Inside the mineshaft, they could set up an entire missile launching system less than an hour's drive from Washington DC and yet, because it was underground, it wouldn't show up on any satellite photos.

There were three other missiles resting on their sides in one of the other tunnels. Either they were back-ups just in case something went wrong – or SPYDER had additional targets planned after Camp David.

It appeared to be close to launch time. The missile

looked ready to go. Apparently, Cyrus had coughed up the coordinates.

There weren't any SPYDER agents around however.

This surprised me at first. In every spy movie I'd ever seen, there were always hundreds of enemy agents in the bad guy's lair. But when I thought about it, the lack of employees made sense. It probably didn't take too many people to launch a missile – and being around the launch pad was dangerous. You didn't want to be too close to a rocket when it ignited, so anyone with any sense would probably keep their distance.

We, however, didn't have a choice.

We hurried into the junction. A series of cables and another thick electrical cord led from the launch pad down one of the tunnels, most likely to the controls. Hank deduced the same thing, because he pointed to Alexander and I, and then the tunnel.

I figured it was my last chance to request the help of someone who might actually know what they were doing, but before I could, the voice of Cyrus Hale rang out from another tunnel. 'This is madness!' he yelled. 'Think about what you're doing!'

There was a loud *thwack*, followed by a groan from Cyrus.

Hank, Chip, Jawa, Claire and Zoe raced towards the sound, hurrying to save Cyrus.

I looked at Alexander. His face was filled with concern. 'I'm sorry,' he whispered to me. 'He's my father. I can't leave his rescue to a bunch of kids.' And then he took off down the tunnel as well.

Leaving me to deal with the missile.

My stomach, which had been churning anxiously all night, now revved up several more notches. I wanted to yell after the others for help, but there was no way to do that without alerting SPYDER to our presence. I could only watch helplessly as the others disappeared into the dark.

I had no idea what to do. A hundred emotions tumbled through my brain. Annoyance at Alexander for abandoning me. Anger at SPYDER for putting us all in this situation. Fear. Anxiety. Panic.

I almost threw up.

I had to lean against the wall for a moment to catch my breath. My hands were trembling. I wanted nothing more than to run away.

But I couldn't. SPYDER was about to launch a missile and there was no one to stop it but me. Even though I didn't know how to do this, I still had to try. If I ran, I'd probably survive – but I wouldn't be able

319

to live with myself. As terrified as I was, dying valiantly sounded better than living seventy more years with crushing guilt.

Plus, if I ran, Erica Hale would never so much as look at me again.

My stomach settled. My hands steadied. I got my breath back and pressed on.

I followed the cables that led from the launch pad. They snaked over the old tram car rails and through a few puddles before hooking around a corner.

I rounded it to find the missile control system.

It wasn't anything impressive. Only a few ancient Russian components – the contents of the metal box we'd seen outside – set up on a crummy old desk someone must have found at a garage sale. They were all plugged into the electrical cable, along with a lamp and a large computer monitor. Lots of data streamed across the screen, but the most important bit seemed to be the timer, which indicated six minutes and twenty-nine seconds until launch. A SPYDER agent sat in a spindly folding chair, watching the numbers tick down.

Murray Hill.

My arrival completely caught him by surprise. His eyes went wide at the sight of me and, for once, he didn't quite have anything glib to say. He just stared at me blankly, as though he couldn't actually believe I was there. It didn't even occur to him to reach for the gun on the desk until it was way too late.

I already had mine pointed at his head. 'Hands up,' I ordered. 'Then stand up and back away from the desk.'

Murray lifted his hands, but he didn't do anything else I said. His old confidence quickly came back to him. He grinned at me and said, 'Holy cow. You found us. I *knew* you were good.'

'Shut down the missile, Murray.'

'I'd love to, Ben. Really. But I can't.'

'Don't lie to me. I'll shoot you if I have to.'

'Well then I'll just be dead and no help whatsoever.'

'I didn't mean I'd shoot you in the head. I meant in the arm. Or the foot. Somewhere painful.'

Murray's smile wavered a tiny bit. 'You wouldn't do that.'

'Not to most people. But for you, I'll make an exception.' I plucked Murray's gun off the desk and kept mine trained on him.

'Look, I'm being honest here,' Murray told me. 'I can't shut this thing down. There are two reasons. One: I don't know how it works. I didn't set it up, and

I'm only minding the store right now.'

'And two?' I asked.

'My boss is behind you, holding a gun to *your* head.'

I didn't even flinch. I'd been expecting Murray to try something like this. 'It's not going to work,' I told him. 'I know better than to trust anything that comes out of your mouth.'

'Usually a wise policy,' a voice behind me said, as the cold barrel of a gun was placed against the base of my skull. 'Only this time, he actually happens to be telling the truth.'

I'd never heard the voice before, but I had a pretty good idea who it belonged to.

'Joshua Hallal, I presume?'

For the second time since I showed up, Murray registered genuine surprise. 'Wow, Ripley,' he said. 'You figured that out, too?'

24

Detonation

Junction Mine

June 16

0015 hours

'Drop your weapons,' Joshua told me.

I did. It's hard to argue with a man who has a gun to your head. I dropped both the gun I had brought with me and the one I had just taken from Murray.

'All your weapons,' Joshua said.

I reached into my pockets and removed the Swiss army knife I had tucked away there. And the brass knuckles. And the can of pepper spray.

Once they were all on the ground, Joshua circled around so I could see him. He joined Murray at the desk, keeping his gun aimed at me the whole time.

I could see why he'd once been regarded as the cream of the crop at spy school. He looked like the quintessential junior spy. Although he was only eighteen, he seemed far more mature than that. He was handsome, athletic and sophisticated. He moved with confidence and had a cold, intimidating look in his eye that said he could snap my neck with his bare hands if he had to.

The monitor now indicated there were only four minutes and thirty seconds until launch.

'How *did* you know it was me?' Joshua asked.

It occurred to me that his curiosity about this might be the only reason I was still alive. So I tried to distract him with it. As I did, however, my mind was racing, trying to figure out how to take out both of my enemies and reprogram the missile's trajectory in the next four and a half minutes. 'The whole time we've been up against you,' I said, 'We've been amazed by how much SPYDER knows about spy school. Everyone assumed that SPYDER must have had another mole inside the school, like Murray. But whoever it was obviously knew far more than Murray ever did. Like how to get on and off the campus – or spy camp – without being seen by a single one of the security cameras. I'm not sure that the professors could even pull that off. The only person I could think of who knew either campus that well was Erica – and she learned a lot of that information from you.'

Joshua smiled wistfully. I got the sense it was in response to my mentioning Erica.

'And then it occurred to me,' I said, 'That no one ever saw your dead body. You supposedly got blown up. All anyone saw were remains that the crime lab *said* were yours. But if SPYDER could deliver someone who wasn't Murray here to Apple Valley without anyone noticing, how hard could it be to insert a false lab test into the computer system? Therefore, maybe you weren't dead after all, but had merely faked your own death to cover up your defection to the dark side.'

Joshua nodded appreciatively, trying not to give too much away.

Murray was far more effusive. 'You see?' he said. 'I told you Ben was smart. Everyone here razzed me for letting him defeat Operation Scorpio, like it was my fault he figured it out. And now he's figured out your genius plan, too.'

Joshua frowned, not nearly as happy about this as Murray seemed to be.

'C'mon,' Murray said. 'Admit it, he's good. If he

could just drop the whole morality thing, he'd be a great fit here.' He looked back towards me. 'What do you say, Ben? You going to sign that contract or not?'

I failed to conceal my surprise. 'That wasn't just a ruse to lure Cyrus Hale out of retirement?'

'No!' Murray laughed. 'Well, not entirely. I mean, it was designed to do both: grab your attention – and get the whole Hale family involved.'

I shifted my attention to Joshua, unsure whether to believe this or not. 'Is this for real?'

'It is,' Joshua admitted. 'Despite your thwarting of Operation Scorpio, my superiors still think you have potential. However, this is the very last time we'll be able to make you this offer.' Joshua raised his gun. 'You're either with us or against us.'

The moment should have been terrifying. After all, my life was on the line. But I felt oddly euphoric. The job offer hadn't been a complete sham. SPYDER still saw potential in me. Which meant I wasn't useless at all. If SPYDER didn't want me working against them, that was because they were afraid of what I could do.

I glanced back at the timer. There were now only ninety seconds until the missile launched. Even if I could miraculously figure out how to disarm and subdue my enemies, there was no way I'd ever be able to figure out how to reprogram the system in time.

But maybe I didn't have to.

Buoyed by my newfound confidence, I had a sudden inspiration. I'd been coming at this from the wrong angle. Reprogramming a missile to not strike its target was immensely complicated.

But preventing a missile from launching in the first place might not be.

I simply had to hold everyone's attention for a little while longer.

'I didn't finish telling you how I knew Joshua here was still alive,' I said. 'I had one more clue. In fact, it was the thing that convinced me my theory was right.'

Joshua lowered his gun, unable to control his curiosity. 'Really? And what was that?'

'I was watching Erica when you captured her,' I said. 'I didn't see you, but I saw her face. I've never seen her so surprised before. In fact, I don't know that I've ever seen *anyone* so surprised before. I thought it was just that she was seeing someone who'd come back from the dead, but I realize now that there was something more to it.'

'What?' Joshua asked.

I took a step back, planting my foot into a coil of electrical cord. 'Betrayal,' I said. 'You might have been the only student that Erica actually admired. In fact, I think she might have had a bit of a crush on you.'

For a moment, Joshua's cold features softened and there was some sadness in his eyes. He nodded slightly.

'No way!' Murray crowed. 'The Ice Queen had a thing for you? No wonder she's so devastated!'

'It's not funny,' Joshua said sharply, and in that moment, I realized he might have cared for Erica too.

There were forty-five seconds left.

'No, it's not,' I agreed. 'She believed in you, Joshua. She thought you stood for the same things she did. And now, you're planning to kill off the President and a dozen heads of state at once.'

Joshua's eyebrows raised. 'You figured that out too?'

'I had some help on that one,' I admitted. 'And the worst part is, knowing SPYDER, you're only doing it for money. Some rich jerk has an axe to grind and you're happy to cast aside any morals you ever had for him.'

'That is not true!' Joshua snarled. 'The leaders of all these nations have betrayed their own people!'

'That doesn't mean they deserve to die,' I said. 'If you really cared about anything, you'd use your power to try to effect some change. But assassination? That's the spineless way out. It's easy to pull a trigger or push

328

a launch button. Any moron can do it.'

There were ten seconds left until lift off. Down the tunnel, underneath the mine shaft, the missile's rockets began priming.

'SPYDER does not hire morons,' Joshua said. 'Do you think a moron could have concocted this plan? Or bend the CIA to their will? Or obtain and install that?' He pointed his gun down the tunnel toward the missile, taking it off me for a split second.

That was all the time I needed. I kicked backwards through the loop of electrical cord, snapping it taut and yanking the plug free from the control system.

The machines immediately shut down. The monitor flashed that it was time for lift-off and then went blank.

The booster rocket fired, filling the tunnels with light as the missile began to lift off the pad.

For a moment, I thought I'd been too late.

And then the booster shut off.

Joshua swung back towards me. 'What did you do?' he demanded.

'I think I just thwarted your plans,' I said.

The way I'd figured it, the control system of any rocket was designed to shut down the moment it detected anything wrong. And it wasn't really that hard to make something go wrong. That's why space launches were always getting delayed. Thus, if I unplugged the control system, the missile guidance would immediately assume something was defective and abort.

Murray was frantically tapping on the keyboard of the control system, unaware that I'd simply cut off the power. 'Unbelievable!' he said. 'Ben, you *have* to start working with us, rather than against us.'

Joshua pointed his gun at me, his eyes narrowed in anger. 'No,' he said. 'The contract's rescinded. You're too much like Erica. We could never trust you to do the wrong thing.'

Before he could shoot me, however, the missile crashed back down onto the launch pad. And then its fuel tank exploded.

The shock wave blasted through the tunnel, blowing us off our feet. We were tossed through the air and slammed into the rock wall.

I was briefly knocked out. When I came to, the entire mountain was trembling. A shower of coal dust rained down from the ceiling.

I staggered to my feet, aching but still happily alive. Through the haze of dust, I spotted Joshua and Murray silhouetted by the flames from the explosion. Neither one was concerned with me any more. They were running for their lives.

That seemed to be a rather good idea, given the circumstances, so I followed them.

They reached the previous site of the launch pad well ahead of me. The remnants of the missile were scattered everywhere, jagged shreds of metal embedded in the walls and the roof of the cavern. Several fires burned, though the largest was in the tunnel where the three back-up missiles were stored. The warhead of the destroyed missile lay beside them, surrounded by flames.

I figured that, if that warhead blew, it would probably trigger the other three missiles, and it made sense to be as far away as possible when that happened.

Joshua Hallal and Murray Hill certainly thought so too. They jacked up their speed a few notches and headed towards the exit.

I stopped running. My friends were still in the mine. I looked through the haze of fire and smoke towards the tunnel they'd gone down.

To my relief, I saw them coming. Hank and Chip had Cyrus Hale between them. Alexander Hale and Claire had Erica. Jawa and Zoe were racing ahead. 'They're OK!' Jawa yelled when he saw me. 'Get the bad guys!'

'The missiles are going to blow!' I yelled back to him. 'Get everyone and clear the mine now!'

Then I took off after Murray and Joshua again. My brief hesitation had given them a big head start on me, but Murray had never been that great an athlete – and he'd let himself go since spy school. Even now, running for his life, he was awfully slow, gasping for air and clutching at a cramp in his side.

Joshua Hallal, on the other hand, was in very good shape. Despite Murray's cries of 'Josh! Don't leave me!' Josh left him, blazing through the tunnel like an Olympic sprinter. He disappeared out of the tunnel well ahead of us.

I caught up with Murray near the entrance. He glanced over his shoulder and tried out a weak smile on me. 'Last chance, Ben,' he said. 'I can still get you a lucrative job at SPYDER. Let me go and I'll make it worth your while.'

'It's not gonna happen,' I said. And then tackled him.

We tumbled out of the mine into the open air . . .

And were immediately raked by gunfire. As I was on top of Murray, I got the worst of it, four shots tearing across my chest.

I gasped for air, looking down at the blooms of red

on my chest, stunned that I'd come so far only to get shot now.

And then I smelled latex.

'Warren!' I shouted angrily.

'Sorry!' A nearby bush stood up, revealing itself to be Warren, armed with a paintball gun. He'd done his usual great job of camouflaging himself. 'I thought you were one of the bad guys.'

'The bad guys don't usually tackle other bad guys,' I said. 'The good guys do that.'

'Guess I just got a little over-excited.'

'Where'd the first guy go?'

Warren pointed towards the Winnebago. 'I tried to shoot him too,' he explained. 'But I missed.'

Sure enough, the Winnebago was coated with splotches of red paint. The driver's side door suddenly flew open. Joshua Hallal scrambled back out, having discovered that I'd taken the keys. He no longer looked cool and unflappable. Instead, he looked desperate and frightened. He glanced at me briefly, then darted into the woods.

I was still on top of Murray, who wasn't even trying to fight back. He was too winded from his run.

Jawa and Zoe emerged from the mine. 'Zoe!' I called. 'Can you handle Murray for me?'

'Glad to,' Zoe replied. She promptly pounced on Murray, driving her elbow into his stomach. 'That's for betraying your friends!' she snarled.

I threw her the Winnebago keys. 'Get everyone out of here before the mine blows,' I said.

'What about you?' Zoe asked.

'I'll be OK,' I said, hoping that was true. I took off into the woods after Joshua.

Jawa fell in beside me. 'Who are we chasing?' he asked.

'Joshua Hallal,' I replied. 'Turns out, he's not dead.'

Jawa's eyes widened in surprise. 'Holy cow,' he said.

I'd heard that Joshua Hallal had been one of the best students in hand-to-hand combat spy school had ever produced, a master of karate, jiu-jitsu and Lithuanian knife-fighting. Therefore, he wasn't the kind of guy you wanted to be chasing through the woods in the dark. And yet, I was going after him anyhow. I couldn't explain why, except that I felt that I somehow owed it to Erica for what he'd done to her.

Luckily, Joshua seemed to be trying to get away, rather than lying in wait to ambush us. We could hear him crashing through the forest ahead and followed the sound.

'How's Erica?' I asked, panting with exertion. I

probably should have been saving my breath, but I had to know.

'She'll be all right,' Jawa replied. Despite the fact that we were running full-tilt, he didn't even seem winded. 'But they worked her over to make Cyrus give up the information. Apparently, she told him not to, that she could take anything they could dish out . . .'

'Thanks for rescuing her,' I said.

'Thank Alexander, ' Jawa said. 'The rest of us ran right into a trap. Luckily, Alexander saved us.'

'Alexander?!' I gasped. 'Really?'

'Why do you sound surprised? This is Alexander Hale we're talking about. The guy was unbelievable. He took out six SPYDER agents all by himself.'

I shook my head in wonder. Apparently, I'd been right: Alexander *did* have some real skills. It simply took seeing his father and daughter in jeopardy to trigger them.

I wondered how big Alexander's ego would get now that he'd actually succeeded in a real rescue mission – and done it in front of a bunch of adoring students.

From the woods ahead of us came a shrill metallic squeal, the sound of rusted metal coming to life. We raced towards it, burst through a stand of trees . . . and nearly pitched over the edge of a cliff. The ground dropped away so abruptly, we almost didn't see it in the darkness. Jawa noticed it later than I did. He skidded to the lip and wobbled on the precipice, but I yanked him back to safety right before he tumbled.

The train tracks from the mine stopped at the edge as well. From there, a long, thick wire angled downwards to a lake far below, similar to the zip-line Erica had showed me at spy camp. The miners would have loaded the coal into large metal buckets hung on pulleys and sent them down the wire. However, there was only one such bucket still in working condition – and Joshua Hallal was currently racing away from us in it. Its rusty old pulley screeched and sparked as it raced along the wire. In the dark, I could barely make out the white of Joshua's taunting grin. And the gleam of the gun in his hand.

'Take cover!' I yelled.

Jawa was already doing it. We ducked behind trees as the shots rang out.

Joshua fired until his gun clicked empty.

'There's no other buckets here,' Jawa sighed. 'He's going to get away.'

'Maybe not,' I said. 'We don't need to catch him. We just need to cut the wire.'

Jawa looked at me, surprised, and then glanced

at the wire. 'Cut it with what?' he asked. 'It's over an inch thick.'

I didn't have an answer to that. I glanced around, hoping a giant pair of wire snips might have been conveniently left nearby.

There weren't any, however. There was nothing around but sticks and leaves. There was nothing we could do except sadly watch Joshua speed away, aware he was going to escape.

And then the mountain exploded.

The blast was far bigger than I'd expected. The fire in the mine must have triggered one of the missile warheads, which triggered the others in rapid succession. The domino-reaction detonation was so enormous, it blew a hole the size of a football field out of the mountainside. A huge ball of fire erupted through it, bright enough to turn night into day. Flying chunks of rock decapitated several trees around us. The ground shook like it was made of Jell-O.

At our feet, the seismic tremors tore the cliff apart. Jawa and I leapt back as a foot of rock sheared away, tumbling into the void.

The post that held the coal bucket wire went with it. In the halo from the explosion, I could see Joshua Hallal's face as he realized he'd just been done in by his own missiles. His eyes went wide in fear – and then the bucket dropped as the wire went slack. Joshua screamed, but it was drowned out by the roar of fire and flame around us. He plummeted into the darkness of the forest far below and disappeared.

'This time, I don't think he's faking his death,' someone said behind us.

We spun around to find Erica emerging from the trees. She'd been through a lot since I'd last seen her. Both her eyes were black. Her lips were swollen. There was blood caked on her shirt – although knowing Erica, it wasn't necessarily hers. Her arms and legs were covered with bruises. And yet, perhaps because she was simply alive, she was as beautiful as I'd ever seen her.

She looked down into the darkness where Joshua Hallal had vanished, seeming unsure whether to be pleased or upset by Joshua's death. And then she damped down her emotions and became her usual, distant self. 'Nice work,' she told me.

I started to correct her, to tell her that I hadn't really done anything to take Joshua out, that we'd merely gotten lucky. But then I caught myself. I realized I'd actually learned something from Alexander Hale: If a gorgeous female agent thinks you've done something impressive, don't try to change her mind.

'Thanks,' I said. 'Shouldn't you be recuperating right now?'

'Probably,' Erica replied. 'But I couldn't exactly sit still while Joshua there was on the loose. Not after what he did to me.'

The others emerged from the woods behind her. Chip and Zoe came first, having disobeyed my orders to evacuate. 'Don't worry,' Zoe told me. 'Murray's tied up nice and tight.'

'Even Warren can't let him escape,' Chip said.

Hank and Claire were next. They were holding hands. 'Where's the bad guy?' Hank asked.

Erica pointed toward the base of the cliff. 'Down there somewhere.'

Claire whistled appreciatively. 'You people don't like to take anyone out the easy way, do you?' she asked. 'No sense in shooting someone when you can pitch them over a cliff.'

'Are you two a couple now?' I asked.

'They've been a couple ever since London,' Chip said.

Hank turned to his brother, surprised. 'How did *you* know? We were trying to keep it a secret.'

'It wasn't that hard,' Chip said. 'Every time anyone

got upset with Claire, you took her side. Obviously, you two were into each other.'

Hank laughed and gave his brother a pat on the back. It seemed he'd come to respect Chip a lot more over their ordeal.

Alexander and Cyrus were the last to emerge from the trees. Cyrus had been worked over even worse than Erica, but the man was as tough as they came. Alexander still had to help him though, taking his weight as he limped through the woods. 'What happened?' Cyrus asked. 'Don't tell me we missed the show.'

'Sorry, Gramps,' Erica said. 'Bad guy's gone. Ben and Jawa got him.'

Cyrus looked us up and down, then smiled. 'You kids have done the world a great service this evening,' he said. Then he looked to Alexander. 'And I mean *all* of you. Unfortunately, the way these things work, few people will ever hear of what actually went down tonight, let alone know the part you played in it. But I, for one, am honoured to have worked with all of you.'

Everyone beamed at this, thrilled by the praise.

Cyrus let us bask in our victory for three seconds. Then he said, 'OK, enough self-congratulation. This Joshua Hallal character couldn't possibly have been the big brains of SPYDER. The kid was far too young. Which means that whoever's running the show is still at large – and as long as they're out there, they're going to be trouble. So come on, kids. We've still got plenty of work cut out for us.'

With Alexander's help, he trudged back into the forest. Everyone obediently followed.

Except me. I turned back to the cliff and stared down into the woods where Joshua Hallal had vanished.

And Erica. She stood beside me, staring into the void as well. 'I owe you my life, Ripley,' she said.

'No,' I said. 'You owe your father.'

'Who would never have found us if it wasn't for you. And he certainly wouldn't have figured out how to stop those missiles, either.' Erica turned to me. 'In fact, I'm not sure *I* could have stopped them. How'd you do it?'

I thought about using the Alexander Hale method again, concocting a tale that would make me sound brave and smart and cool under pressure. Instead, I used the Benjamin Ripley method and told the truth. 'I just unplugged the system.'

Erica stared at me for a moment. And then she laughed. I'd never heard her do this before. It was surprisingly childlike, a sweet little titter that revealed the girl beneath her tough exterior. 'Ripley,' she said. 'You're one of a kind.'

At that moment, I didn't care if the President or anyone else never found out that I'd thwarted SPYDER's plans. I didn't care if Alexander Hale stole the credit from me again. Erica Hale knew what I'd done, and that was all that mattered. Her laughter was the greatest reward I could have ever asked for.

'By the way,' Erica said, 'Happy birthday.'

I glanced at my watch, startled to see it was well after midnight. With all the excitement, I'd actually lost track of what time it was. I wasn't sure which was more startling to me: the fact that I'd forgotten it was my own birthday – or that Erica had remembered.

'Thanks,' I said.

'I didn't exactly have time to shop, given the kidnapping and all, so I got you this.' Erica pressed something into my hand.

To my surprise, it was a human tooth. There was a tiny bit of blood at the end, as though it had just been forcibly removed from someone's mouth.

'Is this Murray's?' I asked.

Erica smiled. 'I told him that if SPYDER ever messes with you again, he's going to lose a lot more than that.'

It was certainly the most disgusting present I'd ever received. And yet, I couldn't help being touched by the sentiment behind it. 'Thanks,' I said.

'Could you give me a little help getting back?' Erica asked.

'Of course,' I told her. Then I wrapped my arm around her waist to take her weight and we started through the woods together.